Praise for Beth Dranoff and *Mark of the Moon*

"*Mark of the Moon* is a one-of-a-kind paranormal erotic story. The plot is original, and Dranoff introduces truly authentic creatures.... Dana is a very complex, unpredictable character."
—*RT Book Reviews*

"With lots of action, steamy sex scenes, twist and turns, and great secondary characters, *Mark of the Moon* makes for a fun paranormal read that has me anticipating the next installment."
—*Night Owl Romance*

"Dranoff does a good job of building a world in which supernaturals exist, but not everyone knows it, or they choose not to believe. This first book in the Mark of the Moon series is a good start to what could be a great paranormal romance/urban fantasy."
—*Library Journal*

"Beth Dranoff does a great job with her storytelling.... I look forward to reading more from her."
—*Alpha Book Club* on *Mark of the Moon*

"The author has a talent for creating rich descriptions and crafting an intriguing plot with lots of action."
—*The Novel Lady* on *Mark of the Moon*

**Also available from Beth Dranoff
and Carina Press**

Mark of the Moon

**And watch for the next book
in the Mark of the Moon series**

Shifting Loyalties

coming soon!

BETH DRANOFF

BETRAYED
BY
BLOOD

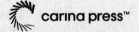

carina press™

ISBN-13: 978-1-335-58007-8

Recycling programs
for this product may
not exist in your area.

Betrayed by Blood

www.CarinaPress.com

Printed in U.S.A.

Author's Note

While this story is set in Toronto, Canada, it's a work of fiction. If anything reminds you of someone or someplace you know (or you think I know), that's great! But I promise—I've made it all up.

For Opher and Zak. All the love.

BETRAYED
BY
BLOOD

Chapter One

I heard the knock at my apartment door before I smelled him. *Them.* It was late enough that I checked the peephole, just to be sure.

I opened the door and saw Sam first. Smiled. Then I saw Jon and my smile widened before wavering, hesitant. Both of them? Here? At the same time?

So many ways this could go, so few of them good.

"Sandor's in trouble," Jon said. So much for foreplay.

"Again?" Sandor had only recently recovered from being attacked by frost demons, exact species unknown. OK, four months ago. Still, it felt like only last week I'd gone to visit my boss in that supe hospital I hadn't realized existed until I needed it. You know, because I was shifting. After Jon's *not-as-ex-as-I'd-thought* boyfriend had scratched me. Good times. I could still see Sandor lying in that bed, gnarled fingers twitching as fluids mixed with twinkling crystalline aquamarine blue bits dripped into his veins.

Things had been awkward between us since the Great Revelation—that the assassin hired to kill me was Sandor's half brother, Gus (a.k.a. Gustav, a.k.a. Gus Lazzuri), a fact he'd neglected to enlighten me on when shit went down four months ago. We'd been getting past it by stepping around it. Like all primed minefields, sometimes the best approach was avoidance.

At least that's the theory I've been working with.

Last time, the attack had gone down at the Swan Song, the bar-slash-restaurant where norms and supes can hang out without killing each other. At least not on the premises. I work there; Sandor owns it. And seriously, hadn't he been through enough for a six-foot-five demon whose neon-orange-pylon-colored tusks were worse than his actual bite? I glanced over at Sam. "What happened? I talked to him, like, five hours ago."

"Not sure." Sam crossed his arms and leaned a single shoulder against the doorframe of my new place. New to me anyway—I suspected the building itself was more turn of the century by way of abandoned sweatshop.

"Let's do this inside," I said. A sideways invitation, but it *was* after 10 PM and the hallway was more tropical jungle in July than my interior space of tepid air-conditioned relief. Toronto in June, no matter how your blood flowed, was not for the faint of sweat.

Sam and I had met about four months ago, right after I'd been scratched and started this whole crazy ride I had no choice but to call My Life. Somewhere between fighting and a semi-successful attempt at banishing bad guys, some skin-on-skin contact of the non-violent variety had started up.

Interestingly, Jon—who I'd already been seeing, and the one I'd considered my Mr. Right Now until all the shit went down—hadn't been upset with me for taking Sam on bed-wise. Not that Sam and I always ended up in bed, but you get the point.

Maybe because Jon hadn't turned out to be a *one-lover-at-a-time* vampire himself.

At least it was warmer now than when it all started.

"Weren't you supposed to be working tonight?" *Whoops.* I was supposed to let someone from the Pack know my whereabouts at all times.

"Sorry." I shrugged. "Needed a mental health day. Sandor hired a new drinks guy, Derek, which means I can now officially, occasionally, get sick." I fake coughed for effect before the *sick*.

"Why?"

"Someone delivered this to the Pack house on Roxborough for you." Sam pulled a folded sheet of fluorescent-pink eight-and-a-half-by-eleven paper from his shirt pocket and passed it over before settling into the armchair closest to me. Jon raised an eyebrow at the other man's familiarity before shrugging and folding himself, all fluid grace and bone and muscle, into the other solo-use seat adjacent to Sam. Nowhere for me to go but my couch, so there I settled in. "I said I'd drop it off after I called the Swan and was told you were home sick." Ironic emphasis on *sick*. "Ran into this guy on the way in."

"What is it?"

"Take a look," Sam said. Well then. Guess he wanted me to do the big reveal.

Fine. Indigo ink bled at the edges of the scrawled message, and I caught a whiff of what might have been pickled herring.

Requesting assistance from Dana Markovitz. Your demon has been procured as collateral. Terms to be

discussed at 11:30 PM meeting. See location provided
on map, below.

Underneath was a Google Street View printout stuck
to the original sheet with something gummy and still
moving. *Yuck*. Also…huh?

"Anshell wants us to check it out. Find out why
they're asking for you specifically, and how they knew
that delivering it to his home would get the message
to you."

That would be Anshell Williams, Alpha to Sam's
second-in-command spot in the Moon with Seven Faces
Pack. Capital *P* Pack. I kind of belonged, even though
my full-status voting membership was still pending ma-
jority approval. At least Anshell recognized me—that
helped. We also happened to share a bit of a psychic
connection; if Anshell intuited I was involved somehow, he was probably right.

Not that I wanted to admit it.

"Funny how almost everything that happens in the
Toronto supe community lately has something to do
with me." I kept my voice light. Truth was, plenty of
recent weird *could* be traced back to that frigid night
on Cherry Beach when Alina—She Who Should Not
Be Named Aloud—opened up a portal and allowed an
assortment of Scary, Snotty and Clawed Fangy creatures through. All my fault.

OK, not exactly—it had more to do with something
my father and possibly my former mentor Ezra had done
to me as a baby—but it *did* hinge on my existence. Plus
I'm Jewish. Any residual guilt was over-determined.

"Still," Jon said, using his best *placate-the-human*
tone—there might have been both a tongue and some

cheek involved. "They know enough about you to know where you might be. And the threat does involve someone of importance to you. Might be prudent to at least investigate further, yes?"

"Yeah, I guess." My words were casual despite the rock of worry that had suddenly taken up residence in my gut. Even after everything, Sandor was my friend. And I couldn't let bad things happen to good demons—not if I could help it.

"Where's your phone?" Sam glanced around at all the usual spots—coffee table, end table, kitchen counter. Except it had died and was charging beside the bed instead.

Unanswered texts from Sam, Anshell and Jon, plus two missed calls. Another text from sender unknown that I suspected was mobile provider spam-sourced.

Nothing from Sandor.

I glanced over at the guys and shook my head. Still, it didn't mean Sandor was in danger, right? Could just be an early night hookup, and whoever had sent the note was capitalizing on his prior engagement to get me to take their bait.

One way to check. I grabbed my phone and dialed Sandor's cell; five rings then straight to voicemail. Tried the Swan Song next. Ten rings before I got the canned message. Still, the place could be busy—we didn't always answer the phone because, seriously, it was a bar. One more try. This time I reached Janey, one of the other servers; she'd been there almost as long as I had.

"Hey girl," she said. My shoulders started easing down from just below my earlobes at her voice. "I thought you were sick?"

"Sick," I said, lowering my voice into the octave of

hoarse. "Yeah. Listen, is Sandor around? He's not answering his phone."

"Nah," Janey replied. "Boss Man ain't rolled in yet. You need me to get him a message?"

"Are you expecting him?"

I could almost hear Janey's shrug.

"Boss Man does what he wants, right? As long as we get paid, and those wards hold so we got no trouble, I keep my expectations right out there where I can see 'em. So no, I'm not expecting him. But I'm not *not* expecting him neither."

I tried again. "So you haven't heard from Sandor tonight?"

"Nah."

"Did he say anything about not coming in?"

"Nah," Janey repeated. "We ain't buds like you two." *Huh.* I hadn't noticed that edge before. Still, ignoring was easier than confronting for now. "Didn't he say nothing to you earlier when you called in…*sick*…?"

"Nothing," I said. "Yeah, so, let me know if you hear anything. I'm going back to bed now." Another fake *one-two* cough for effect. I was imagining her smirk, right?

"You get better soon, girl," she said. Yeah, even she didn't believe it.

Both Jon and Sam were studying my face as I disconnected, waiting for me to say something they could work with. Or maybe they were just thinking about the bed part. I shook my head.

"Nothing," I said. "Janey didn't seem too worried though."

"She doesn't strike me as someone who concerns

herself much with those who aren't her." Jon's voice was dry. He wasn't wrong; I *was* surprised he'd noticed.

"Sandor pays us. She'd notice if he was gone at the end of the night."

My phone pinged with an incoming text: unknown name, unknown number. Yeah, that always turned out well. I swiped to see more.

Freeze-frame on Sandor, wrapped in a massive purple tentacle, his eyes bulging and his mouth gaping open.

Chapter Two

"Sandor?"

Except this wasn't a video chat. *Shit.* Another ping, another text; I hoped Sandor's plan was unlimited. It was another image: Sandor holding up a white Bristol board with the time in the note (one hour from now), confirmation of the meeting place (somewhere dark and murky near the Swan), and under what I assumed were additional instructions were the words "no cops." I snorted back a laugh at that. *Right.* Because I'd call in law enforcement. Like, ever.

"You guys got that?" Sam already had his phone out and was talking while pacing, voice low, to Anshell. Would we get backup? Jon, by contrast, hadn't moved. That, combined with him being breathing-optional, made the whole scene more remote. "Jon? Coming?"

Jon gave a long blink, then started taking in air again. His skin less waxy with each inhalation even though I knew it was an illusion. The only thing to give Jon extra warmth these days was blood, regardless of how much I might want the situation to be something that was else.

"Yes." Focusing in on me, back from wherever he'd been moments earlier, his eyes sweeping up to my tousled curls then down again to my strappy pink Cool Kat tank to the matching pussycat boy shorts painted over my curves. Eyes twinkling now. "I like your rescue outfit."

I glanced down, cheeks going red. *Whoops.* So much for tough, black-on-black fashion-statement girl Dana. I did mention my earlier plan had involved staying in, right? Sam glanced over, not really seeing me, then went back to pacing again as he and Anshell worked out whatever they were planning.

I found a pair of modified baggy black cotton boxer shorts that fell to just above my knees, and paired it with a comparably loose vee-necked black t-shirt that hugged me in only the best places. Slouch socks and my Doc Martens. I really wanted to be wearing flip-flops in this heat, with the option of bare feet, but I needed to be able to run. Without tripping, that is.

"Anshell is sending over a backup team, just in case," said Sam. "Are you comfortable going in alone—or at least pretending to be? Gives us the element of surprise. Plus, it'll be fun to see what they do with a cute and harmless little lady."

I snorted. The dimple that jumped in Sam's cheek said he was teasing, trying to get a rise out of me. Because I might be cute, but I was far from harmless all on my own.

"Don't worry," Sam continued, in case maybe I was feeling it. "We'll have your back. Right?" He glanced over at Jon, who chin-bobbed his confirmation.

"Whoever texted me said no cops," I pointed out.

"Do I look like a cop to you?" Sam's mouth stretched into that itching-for-a-fight grin I knew far too well.

Remembered how it tasted, after; glanced away before anyone noticed.

I grabbed my backpack and slung it over my shoulder, grand-waving the guys towards the door.

So much for a relaxing night at home.

"You sure this is the place?" Even though we'd followed the directions, I had to ask.

The smell was familiar; a pungent reminder of the brine-soaked fish and acrid diesel fuel run-off smudged on the edges of the mysterious sheet of paper that brought us here.

It was an unremarkable spot along the recovering-from-industrialization southeast section of the Don River that ran parallel to Lake Shore Boulevard under the flaking concrete chunks of the Gardiner Expressway. Used to be an outdoor market for the First Nations communities who lived here before entitled white settlers drove them out. Now, the polluted waterway was an urban symbol of what factories and road salt and overflowing sewage lines could do to a valuable freshwater resource if left unprotected. It could have been beautiful. Instead, the place stank—despite recent efforts to reclaim it—and the shimmering waves of Toronto heat weren't helping.

"There," I said. We'd parked over the bridge leading to Cherry Beach, not far from the sludge-side patio bar, and hiked back alongside shadows flickering in the intermittent oncoming traffic headlights. If I squinted, I could make out the outline of a dock with some kind of white-painted structure—a boathouse maybe? I knew they'd started building soundstages and studios around here, but this close to the rattling grates of the lift bridge where concrete mixers still thundered by? It seemed unlikely.

The ground beneath me thrummed, vibrating the flesh of my inner thighs; from inside the building I heard tree-trunk-heavy thuds, erratic beats against wooden walls, and I wondered whether the entire thing would splinter as we watched. Would certainly save us time.

I didn't know where our Pack-backup was, or whether it had even shown up. If it was just me I wouldn't be counting on it at all, but Sam was in a different loyalty category. As Anshell's shadow, the one who flanked the Pack Alpha at all necessary times, Sam carried almost as much executional authority as Anshell. The Alpha's trust in him was that strong.

Still wasn't sure whether my sleeping with Sam made things better or worse for me with the Moon with Seven Faces clan.

"I'll be back," said Jon, melting into the night from one eye blink to the next.

Uh, OK.

"I'm still here." Sam breathed the words into my ear; for a moment, I forgot we were on a late-night mission to rescue Sandor. All I could feel was Sam. But then there was another *thud* and I shook my head to clear it, balling my fingers into fists and digging my nails into my palms until I was back in the now again.

There was a barn-door-type entryway, painted in red. No windows, I realized as we got closer—so much for getting a visual on what we were walking into ahead of time. I wasn't a big fan of surprises. Too bad the universe had determined this was to be one of my life's challenges to overcome. Attached to the doorframe was a triple-fist-sized cowbell dangling from a cast iron hook with a string.

I yanked.

The sound was louder than I'd expected, and I jumped back and glanced around in case. In case of what I wasn't sure, but if I was surprised there was a good chance someone other than me was too. Unless that last part was wishful thinking.

I was babbling in my own head now. Some kind of plan would be great other than hey, let's get there and see what happens.

Too bad that's all we had to go with.

A shadow flickered against the light peeking out the underside of the door before a portion I hadn't noticed earlier swung back to bang against something hard. I knew Sam was there without me checking. Because he wouldn't leave me. Not like that.

Couldn't see anything from this distance. I stepped inside.

The first thing that hit me was the smell. Rotting fish, briny water, roasted garlic mixed with newly decayed compost. I gagged. Smell had always been my weak spot, but it'd gotten so much worse since I was infected with the ability to shift. Even though my inner cat kind of liked the piscine part of the scent bouquet. A flickering from the neon panels overhead was doing nothing for my ability to control my urge to gag and I looked away, swallowing in convulsive gulps, before the room stopped spinning and I could make out shapes.

One of those shapes was Sandor and he was breathing. I checked. My shoulders unclenched, taking some of the tightness in my jaw with it, and I scanned the room to see what else was going on.

Other than the big pile of tentacles wrapped around my boss, and what I assumed was a head to go with it even though I couldn't see the damned thing, there wasn't much.

"Hey!" Everyone who was interested already knew I was here, so I figured calling out to get the attention of whatever it was wouldn't do too much damage. I hoped. "You texted, and here I am." At Sam's growl behind me, I corrected myself. "Here *we* are."

All around me were voices, echoing syllables along the wired twang of a guitar string. One source amplified. I tried to make out individual words but couldn't. Sam was growling again, and more; fear skittled down my spine as I tossed out a silent prayer for things not to hit exponential badness before we could figure out what was at stake and how to turn things around.

I touched Sam's arm, startled at the fur I felt already covering his forearm in a silken plush. Hadn't even occurred to me to shift. He'd been a were longer than I had—was this loss of control normal?

And if not, what was going on here?

First Sandor, then Sam. That I appeared to be as yet unaffected was reassuring and concern-inducing at the same time.

"Sandor?" I had to try again. "Can you give us a hint? What's going on here and how can we help?"

"Dana *grrrlll*," Sandor slurred. His eyes were glassy; I wasn't sure whether it was from shock or whether he'd been drugged. "I have such a craving for grilled octopus…" One of Sandor's eyes flicked to the right, then winked at me before going unfocussed again. *Oh.* So it was just an act. I could work with that.

Sandor was giving me a hint. We were dealing with

something big and octo-tentacled, while suspending our disbelief that such an entity could cope on dry land. Or could it? I wasn't sure how deep the Channel went, or whether the municipal cleanup efforts had made it any more inhabitable than it used to be, but maybe proximity to water was why we were all here. Sort of? I was still waiting for someone to tell me why Sandor was being restrained and plopped in front of me as some kind of warted, tusked bait.

"Now that I have your attention." The voice was deep enough to rattle the windows I hadn't noticed before. "We have been hired to locate a certain Gustav Lazzuri on behalf of our clients." Was that a British accent? It sounded almost there but with a weird twist at the end. Definitely not Scottish or Irish—those I'd recognize. Welsh maybe? And who was this "we"?

"Huh?" I could fake it till I make it, but then I'd have no idea what was going on.

"We wish you to locate this Gustav Lazzuri."

"Oh." *Oh.* "So why are you playing squeaky toy with my boss over there?"

"We had hoped," the thunderous voice intoned, "that he would share this Gustav's location with us. However, he proved less than helpful."

I could only imagine what that meant in Sandor terms.

"Why her?" Sam spoke up finally. "What makes you think she can help?"

"Well," the voice boomed. "This beast did try to kill her."

I checked my feelings. Gus was an asshole, and had pretty much vanished since Alina had ripped open a hole between dimensions to try and pull some of her more terrifying buddies through. That he'd switched sides at the last possible second, thank you Anshell, didn't mean I trusted him. But he was still Sandor's brother. And Sandor was my friend, even if he also happened to be my boss.

The good news was that I had no idea where Gus was, nor did I particularly care as long as he wasn't gunning for me. The bad news was that I doubted Sandor would give up his (half) brother anytime soon—even if Sandor *did* know where the prick was hiding out.

"So why am I going to help you exactly? Lazzuri and I aren't what you'd call friends."

"Yes," the voice replied. "However, you and this demon here do seem to share some kind of relationship, the nature of which matters exceedingly little to me at this time."

"My boss." See? I could be helpful. I was a helper. OK, maybe that was an exaggeration given the current context. "He pays me, and I like being paid. Is that what you mean?"

"We found your number in his contacts list. You were the only one to respond to our call."

Seriously? That pic had been sent to more than just me, and I was the only one who cared enough to do something? I thought about it—maybe I hadn't seen Sandor hanging out with buddies so much at the Swan. But I'd always assumed he had a life outside of the bar. Even if I'd never seen it for myself. Could I have been wrong?

"Oh." Because I had to say something, and I had no idea what else to say. Where were the words for *geez, I'm sorry you're so lonely that nobody else was willing to come to your rescue*? "Um."

Coolness at my back; I shivered at the sudden temperature shift.

"Let us discuss terms," Jon said. "In exchange for this human's assistance with your assignment, please confirm what you are prepared to offer."

"We won't kill this beast."

"Is there a reason you would have killed him had we not shown up?" Jon's voice gave nothing away, as cool with reason as his body temperature on a vegetarian diet. As long as he didn't drain the vegetarian.

"Well," said the voice I was at this point assuming was attached or at least related to the tentacles in some way. "No, not exactly. Not our style. But it did seem a reasonable way to motivate the female to help us."

"Next time, try calling," I said. "Also, I have no idea where the big blue ass is. So how about you let Sandor go and we call it a night."

"Certainly," it replied. Barely a hesitation. "However, while you're here…" Another tentacle appeared, coiled in the corner; I hadn't noticed that we weren't exactly alone in the warehouse. It loosened enough that I could make out the head, the shape of a mouth gaping open and closed as eyes stared out; blind, wild. As familiar as the ones I saw in the mirror every morning.

The fuckers had my mother.

Chapter Three

"You've got to be kidding me."

Sure, I could panic. There was a definite sense of *how-do-I-breathe-again* about the whole situation. And maybe I was counting to ten in my head as I clenched my nails into the inner flesh of my palmed fists, visualizing each and every one of my weapons and which one I was going to reach for first. Didn't know how to neutralize this kind of tentacle—did you cut it off or just hack at it until it unfurled?—but for once my inner *what-the-fuck*ness was overtaking any residual *frozen-in-place-thank-you-past-trauma*. You mess with my mother, you get to deal with me.

That buzzing. I thought it was my blood pressure rising with my intense need to kill something. Until Sam gave me a nudge, pointing to my pocket. *Oh*. My phone.

I gave him my best let-it-go-to-voicemail look, but he shook his head. Maybe he thought it was important. *Fuck*. Fine.

My eyes going wider when I saw who it was on the call display.

"Uh…hello?"

"Hi honey! I'm so glad I caught you." *My mother?* I eyed what looked like the woman who birthed me as

I followed the sound of her voice, my phone sliding hot against my ear. "We're still on for brunch tomorrow, right?"

I nodded; realized she couldn't see me. "Yeah," I said. Because sure, why not.

"And don't forget to bring that beaded purse I loaned you for Rachel and Matthew's wedding last year. I have a thing coming up and it's the perfect piece to go with my outfit."

"Sure." It was definitely my mother on the phone. So who, or what, was I looking at right now? "See you tomorrow."

Disconnecting didn't help—much. I walked over to where my other mother was supposedly tentacle-imprisoned. Leaned in and took a breath that filled my lungs with humid air and my nostrils with sea-weed and dinner and residual compost mixed with sludge water. Nothing that smelled of norm. Nothing that was like me.

I glanced over at Jon, then at Sam, before looking straight ahead again. Held out my index and forefinger, stiff, and reached up to what I could touch—my mother's calf as it dangled, helpless, from below the rows of suctioning cups embedded in purplish-black flesh. No longer doubting that this was a trap. The question was what would trigger it.

Goose bumps skittering across my forearm; I shivered. Crumbling roses and vanilla and earth. *Jon.*

"Let me," he said. I took a step back, grateful.

Jon's arm was a blur as he reached out to grasp my "mother's" ankle and yank it down. I couldn't help it—I yelped, as though it really was her and what Jon was doing would cause pain. Sam's hand was hot against my shoulder and he squeezed once, reminding me to be strong, biting back against the screaming in my head.

There should have been flesh. The caterwauling I'd thought was coming from me pounded against my ears, and I had to raise my palms to flatten them against the noise I couldn't bear to hear. Whatever it was, there was pain. And, as Jon squeezed harder, an explosion of ashen dust.

The suction cups detached, the flesh they were supposedly attached to becoming fluid and more gelatinous. I had a sudden image of an oversized Jell-O mold filled with the purple crystals mix, not quite enough to make it solid, not quite enough time for it to cool and take shape. Yet somehow it had convinced me that my mother was here.

I turned. Sandor was still wrapped in a similar tentacle; I wondered if it was part of the same whole that had pretended to have my mother, or whether it was somehow more solid. Only one way to find out.

This time I slid my favorite dagger out from the sheath tucked inside my boot and balanced the hilt against my palm. Dangling, not gripping, though that could change in a heartbeat. Thank you new and improved shifter reflexes. Even though I'd been no slouch of a norm before either—my years with the Agency had underwritten the motion of my muscle memory.

"Let. Sandor. Go." Each word, enunciated with precision.

"Will you help us?" The voice was everywhere at once now.

"No," I said. "You're seriously pissing me off here. You want my help? Next time ask nicely."

"Niceness is a human construct. We need you to

do something for us, and retaining possession of your overlord is how we ensure you do as we've asked. Next time we will be less polite with our offer."

There was an offer?

"I'm getting a very *do it or else* with a vague but threatening *else* vibe here. So I'm going to decline your polite ultimatum and bid you a good evening while my friends and I—all four of us—take our leave. Got it?"

"Money." A second voice, belonging to a creature more squid than oversized land-loping octopus, with feet and arms in addition to the requisite suction-cup-covered streamers. Somewhere to my left. Was that a black straw fedora he was wearing? "Name your price."

I stared at him. This was a job offer? Sure, why not—my life wasn't weird enough already.

"Thank you. No." There was nothing to think about. Even if I could use a little extra bank now and again, this entire situation was too damned weird. "Will you release my friend?"

"So sorry, luv," said the sharp-dressed demon. "No can do."

My blade barely caught the light before it was winging its way towards Fedora Squid Guy's head. I should have known; with eight tentacles, it was nothing to swat the weapon out of the way before it had a chance to get close to its target. But it *was* enough to distract him, giving Jon time to streak behind the demon and whip its head around. There was a loud cracking sound as the vampire snapped the cephalopod's neck. Did it even have a neck? It certainly crumpled fast enough.

The larger of the beasts seemed unamused by our assault, and another tentacle as thick as a century-old oak tree and probably as long snaked out to swipe us off our feet. Almost nailed us too. Except for the part where Jon was now crouched and balancing on a rafter crossbeam with me in his arms, while Sam had shifted into a lynx-sized orange-and-white-striped feline with claws out and tail twitching.

"Let me down," I whispered.

Jon shook his head. Sure, I was outmatched by this giant octopod creature. And? The last time that stopped me was…?

"Seriously."

He shook his head again, peering over me to check on Sam's progress. What was he doing down there anyway?

I followed the sound of growling; realized Sam had attached himself to the massive ropey mass holding Sandor down, wrapping himself around it and digging in first with his claws and then his teeth. My boss wasn't sitting around and being all Rapunzel about waiting to be rescued either, and I saw one of his massive fists finally work its way out of the vise that had loosened in the distraction of Sam's attack. Those curved talons could do serious damage. A fact I'd never realized before I saw them shredding ribbons in the surface flesh of Sandor's should-really-be water-based captor(s).

"So, what, this is a spectator sport?" I wriggled in the steel bands of Jon's arms. This was ridiculous— since when did he get to use that preternatural vampire strength on me, especially without my permission? "We have to help."

"They seem to be doing fine." There was a *thud* as Sam was whacked against a nearby wall. "Choosing their own battles." A roar as Sandor's head was lifted to *thwack* against the beam nearest us. His three eyes full of fury on the way up, with the bottom two shifting to unfocused on the way down. "Doing as well as might be expected."

"Come *on.*" I did my best to rotate my head to look up at Jon. As though maybe that could impart the urgency of my need for action. "If you don't want me involved, how about *you* do something."

Jon gave a pointed look at our current location, inclining his head to underscore the part where he'd removed me from danger and therefore already contributed greatly to making the situation better. I stared right back. Seriously? At this point, Jon was being purposely obtuse in a childish attempt to let Sam get a little beat up. And here I'd thought we were all good with sharing our toys. As long as nobody called me Doll. "Jon? Are you going to help like you promised or what?"

Jon managed a sigh of elegant acquiescence. "As you wish," he said, settling me onto the beam and releasing his grip before dropping into the fray.

Priorities: Jon launched himself at whatever was about to smash my boss and friend into yet another hard surface, with one hand wrapping around the suctioning limb while the other snaked back and found the *Wakizashi* I'd loaned him—a shorter version of the better-known curved Japanese *Katana* sword—strapped across his back. What can I say—I'm almost Boy Scoutesque these days with the always being prepared.

While Jon slashed at a portion of the animated flesh still gripping Sandor, Sam was doing the same with his claws. One down, seven possible more limbs available with time to do...do what? I was guessing nothing good.

Bobbing my heel in time with a beat only I could hear. Damn, I hated being on the sidelines of a fight. Any fight. Because, what, I was too dainty and ladylike to pitch in? This all felt a bit too archaic for my tastes, especially with all three of the guys down there fraying it up being actually important to me. Sure, Anshell had drilled it into my head that I was something special, the exact nature of which was still to be determined. Not to take any unnecessary risks until we figured out why I was such a recurring theme in most things supe and ritual-like. But Bubble Wrap Girl wasn't one of my nicknames. What if something bad happened down there and I could have prevented it?

Beyond the ruckus, highlighted by the moon hanging low in the inky-black sky, I saw something pale and mottled rising up to the window directly ahead of me. I would have thought it was the moon itself if it didn't have two eyes the size of my ass, an even larger beak, and was staring directly at me.

What the...?

An involuntary response; I twitched and glanced down and away from the Big Scary Head. Wait, hadn't there been a fedora-wearing squid guy there a few moments ago? Could have sworn I'd heard its neck snap. But was that even a thing with squids, come to think of it? That sound could also have come from a rotted board breaking, or even an auditory fake-out from source or sources unknown. Either way, there was suddenly another player on the confined space field and the guys didn't know it.

A fedora-shaped shadow fell across Sam's back, and there was no more time to debate my *princess-on-a-mattress-covered-pea* status, no thought about what I had to do. I took a deep breath, relaxed all of me as much as I could, and then dropped onto the creeping cephalopod before he could do anything to my man in fur.

Squid Guy swatted me off and I flew directly at Sam. At least my landing was soft. He saw me coming and, faster than I would have thought possible, managed to detach himself from Sandor's source of ongoing captivity to duck under my body in motion. If Sam wasn't such a solid and substantial beast, I might have felt guilt at our collision. But he was, and instead I shivered at the energy sparked by our propulsion-intensified contact as he wrapped himself around me.

I allowed myself a few precious seconds to inhale Sam's scent, cinnamon and sunlight tickling my nose. Then I gave a nod and we rolled away, him renewing his efforts to free Sandor and me to spin around and face the not-as-dead-as-planned Squid Guy, sliding my Indian *Talwar* sword curving out from the scabbard strapped against my back and pointing it into my personal dance space.

The convenient thing about a *Talwar* is that it works great on both flesh and bone. A theory I was able to test by feinting towards Squid Guy, backing him up further and away from Sandor, before spinning and slicing down into the limb still pinning my boss in place.

It worked. Well, partially—the thing gushed turquoise, coating my arms up past my elbows and spattering Sandor's face as it gaped and dangled, half on and half off. But it was enough of a start for Jon to finish it off, his sword back in its scabbard before he ripped the remaining attached portion of limb down with a single yank. Yes. That would be Jon and his bare hands.

The crazy part was that the limb did not stop fighting. It kept smacking at us with an autonomous intelli-

gence that had me looking for a second head and maybe
a set of eyeballs. Also there was that blue stuff. Like
I'd rolled in a vat of paint that coated breath, sweat and
things that trickled down the back of my neck. Insula-
tion. Because I needed to seal in that Toronto-in-June
body heat right about now.

"Snorfling smeg of a limbermeister guzzle-gaffling
florg!" A finally free Sandor lifted one of his size fourteen feet and slammed down the heel on a wriggling
bit. "Dana, your sword."

It was kind of like handing a toothpick to an elephant, but what the hell. I could get behind Sandor taking out some of his overflow aggression on his captors
if it meant we all got out of here faster.

Plus, the limb would regenerate. Assuming the
demon octopi form came with any of the same nifty
features the ocean-dwelling ones did.

While Sandor made sushi for a hundred from the
flesh of our temporarily vanquished enemy, Sam
shifted back to human again. Jon stayed closer to the
door, watching Sandor while tracking whatever else
might be ready to join in on the fun and even out any
odds currently in our favor. I blinked and the Fedora
Squid Guy was sliding up behind me, shielded from
the hack-n-fray by my torso. He slid a black card with
purple ink into my hand.

"Call me when you change your mind," the squid
said. The card read *Squid D'Lee, Esquire* and included
both a cell number and an email address.

"No hard feelings?"

"My feelings are hard," Squid D'Lee replied. "But
this is business."

Chapter Four

There were still some patrons hanging around by the time we got back to the Swan Song. Nobody had called the cops when Sandor vanished, and nobody seemed too surprised to see us drag our sorry asses back through the door either.

Nice supe community. See no evil, hear no evil, report no evil to the authorities. Should be on a sign somewhere.

It's not like it was usually too busy by this time; logical, given that most of our clientele had to get undercover by the time morning sun clawed its way up the horizon. Plus we were into the month-long lead-up to Toronto Pride celebrations, a.k.a. even more parties and late-night fun than usual. Jon had bailed once we safely cleared the waterways with Sandor, and even Sam had left to report back to Anshell. I had no idea why Sandor was bothering with his newly extended hours, but I wasn't going to complain—much—if it got me more shifts.

Still, he'd never worried about the brunch crowd before. Before all the fun. Before the gaping maw of lakeside portal was opened. Sandor had never even attempted to blend in and be like the norms.

That he was a six-foot-five-inch-tall demon with mottled tree-frog-green skin, curving tusks of pylon orange curving up from under his cheekbones, a drunken pyramid of three eyes over two rows, and a long tail of palm-sized plated scales skewering out might have had something to do with it.

Sandor waved to the guy covering for me in my time of faked-illness need, the bartender-alternate Derek, and put in a drink order for us on his way to the back kitchen to fix us some snacks. Hey, it was 5 PM somewhere right?

We'd gone on a mini-hiring binge after Alina opened that inter-dimensional gateway, however briefly, four months ago. Hazard pay was up, but without it Sandor might have had to go out of business already—word was out, and nobody was willing to work server minimum wage for the hassle. Sandor may not have been grabbed before, but it wasn't the first time the Swan Song had been targeted in the last few months. Too much to hope that it would be the last for a while too.

Damn, Sandor was a good cook. I munched on my fries with a side of something breaded and deep-fried—could have been a carrot but was more likely in the tastes-like-chicken/don't-ask-what-it-really-is category of the food pyramid. He'd made himself a basket of sweet and sour breaded Surimese Flamigal newt eyeballs—still twitching, which was pretty impressive what with the hot oil and all. Guess we all have a desire to live past the point of reason.

I tried not to wince as Sandor crunched away. Grateful that if they were screaming, it was on a wavelength I couldn't hear even with my heightened shifter senses.

"So," I said, taking a sip of my own virgin blue lemonade. "Gus, eh?"

"What can I say?" Sandor sighed, his corkscrew nostril hairs quivering on the exhale. "He's an asshole, but he's also my brother. Can't pick family."

I lowered my voice so the stragglers closest to us couldn't—hopefully—hear us.

"And you have no way of reaching him? Really?"

Sandor narrowed two of his three eyes at me. Suspicion, thou livest in the multiple visual orifices of my demonic overlord. The third eye, the one on top, fluttered its boredom and rolled itself a lot. It was almost like looking at a human teenager. Almost.

"Who's asking," he said, lowering his voice to a bare rumble. "You or your pack master?"

I almost snorted out blue liquid mixed with fry-related chunks at that. Grabbed a napkin and blew my nose to dislodge anything already on its way out while tears of laughter threatened to undermine my tough-girl look, sending streaks of liquefied liner dribbling down my cheeks.

"Sandor," I said finally, when I could talk again without choking or horking. "In the entire time you've known me, have I ever come close to calling *anyone* Master? In public?"

Maybe I laid it on a bit thick. Truth was, I had way too many rules to follow now that I was affiliated with the Moon with Seven Faces Pack. Sure I got the logic, sort of. But there were reasons I'd left my super-secret government job for the rewarding career path of bartending.

Rule number one of the new order? Don't do anything to undermine the safety of the Pack or its Alpha, Anshell Williams. There were a bunch of regulatory subsets to that, like keeping one's nails filed between shifts and swearing a blood oath and something about avoiding green hats in combination with pink and purple ribbons, but Safety First was the big one.

I waited for Sandor to say something cuttingly sarcastic to undermine my position and bolster the rationale for his suspicious stance.

"OK, fine," he said instead, finally. "You're right. You are a lady who doesn't follow anyone. Not even me." Sandor muttered the last part under his breath, *sotto voce*, but of course I heard.

I pretended I hadn't.

"Listen," I said, to fill up the silence. "I might not mind a bit of plausible deniability on the Gus front, but apparently I'm not the only one wondering where he is. Also I'd kind of like to get out of the way before he tries to kill me again."

"Said he wouldn't. Said he was done with all that."

"And you believe him?" Try to kill me once, shame on you. Try to kill me twice, shame on me for being anywhere close enough to you to give you that chance.

"Maybe," Sandor said. "I wouldn't go turning your back on the guy though. Just in case. I may not always be around to watch it for you."

The guy at the bar I'd thought was passed out raised his head. Swiveled it around—maybe he was looking for a refill? When nobody poured for him, he waved a thick hand at us, turquoise-blue scales shimmering with edges of orange and hot pink and deep jewel-toned purple, scrabbling its reverse-French manicured nails against the wood paneling. He looked vaguely familiar. I glanced at the general eye-ish area of its face, then away again.

"What?" I channeled bright assed and bushy toed automatically, even though I wasn't officially working tonight. Big mistake.

A large eyeball—approximately pool-ball sized—occupied the entire top-third portion of what could loosely be called its skull. Especially once you factored in the lid and various optic-related musculature. The central orb, black in the middle, was surrounded by an octagonal iris with intersecting, overlapping triangles of color that mirrored the paint palette of the scales on its hand. Each facet winked at me, reflecting my own surprise and demonstrating more clearly than I was comfortable with just how much of a poker face I *don't* have.

Where the hell had Derek gone now?

"Oi! Barkeep!" The sound came from an orifice with nesting rows inside rows of teeth encircled by raw-liver-toned lips. "Another drink if you please?" His eyes like tendrils of rolling *ick* from my head down to parts lower and more covered. "Make it something sweet, like you." *Double ick.*

"Sandor?"

"Sure," he said, distracted by something on his phone. "Why not."

Maybe Derek had gone for a smoke. Perhaps Sandor wanted to get a good online review even after last call. Either way, apparently I was going to make an exception for something liquid and double-digit proof.

I scanned the arrayed bottles. I was thinking something sweet, blue and of the still-wriggling worm with candied cherries variety. *There.* Back row on the left: a 1978 *Chablis de Cafard Caramel Sacrebleu.* Loosely translated: *Chablis of Damned Caramel Cockroaches*. Perfect.

I held up the bottle to Sandor and he nodded his approval. Then turned back to flip over a fresh glass and mix up the drink.

From one eye-blink to the next, Teeth Boy reached over the bar to snag one claw into my belt hook and yank me back. I yelped my surprise and tried to hit out as he dragged me away from the bottles and my potential sources of immediate defense. The backs of my knees hit the edge of the bar as he pulled me down towards him into an off-balance, backwards hug, and I felt tendrils curling down from his ears to interlace themselves with the dark, shoulder-length curls on my head. Almost outside my body for a moment as I noted the streaking trails of red I had painted, woven through my otherwise espresso-brown hair, reflected in the mirror beyond the bottles.

I tasted blood. Had I bitten the inside of my cheek by accident? I needed to regain control of my limbs and kick this slime ball's ass.

"And just where do you think you're going with my employee?" Sandor's voice boomed through my numbed ears. "She is not for sale, and she most certainly is not a gift with purchase. I advise you to release her. Now."

When our Patron of Aggressive Unwanted Advances growled without moving, he was lifted by the skull and shaken by gnarled green troll hands until I was suddenly released. There was grunting and possibly some blood spurting from off to my left while I slumped against the wood paneling of the bar and waited for the room to stop spinning.

"Sorry," said Derek, extending a hand and pulling

me up again. "Was taking out the garbage." He peered
down at the pile of twisted limbs under the bar. "What
is that?"

"Dunno," I replied. "Never seen one before."

There was something satisfying about seeing my
would-be attacker in a motionless puddle. Anyone who'd
been sitting close to him (or her?) seemed unamused
though, drifting back and taking their drinks and snacks
to elsewhere in the room, putting distance between them
and the twitching limbs on the floor.

I plopped down into the chair across from Sandor
again and took a sip of my own drink. Yeah, that helped
with the heart pounding and head spinning. A bit. I offered the other seat to Derek—it was the least I could
do after he'd saved my ass—but he drifted back to the
bar with a polite headshake, giving the groaning heap
a wide berth on his way there.

"So what do you think those guys want with Gus?"
I watched as the recently prostrate patron dragged himself up and out.

"Who knows?" Sandor flicked one of his curved orange cheek tusks with matching thumb and forefinger
talon. An unconscious tic as his eyes flicked between
me and the front door where Janey was trying to get
the latest patron's attention as what could have been a
she drifted in and out of the shadows. "My brother is a
master at pissing people off."

"Ma'am? Could you please close the door behind
you?" Janey raised her voice. "You're letting all the
fog in."

Fog?

Sandor and I didn't even need to look at each other,

pushing our chairs back and reaching for our weapons once more. Good thing I'd cleaned mine on the way over.

The mist was already at mid-thigh and I could no longer see the front door. Sandor slid through the smoke, roaring and swinging his double-bladed battle-axe in an arc of troll-like fury.

How was any threat able to get past the bar's entrance? And even if it did, shouldn't the unsheathing of weaponry have tripped the Swan's wards?

"Janey?" My voice muffled by the mist. "You alright over there?"

"I'm good, sugar." Janey's voice was firm with a side of *I'm-gonna-kick-the-ass-of-badness*. "Got Princess here with me." I caught a glimpse of the wicked-looking mid-sixteenth-century Asian blade with rope-bound handle she liked to refer to by its pet name. Hell, Janey could call it anything she wanted as long as she knew how to work it—and didn't use it against me.

"Derek?" Because we needed all the help we could get. "How 'bout you?"

Derek grunted. At least I hoped it was him or else we were outmatched before we'd even gotten this fight going. He wasn't much of a talker, but then I might have been distracted by the way his long, thick hair fell in gold and blue streaks that matched the shifting palette of his eyes. Maybe.

In my defense, he'd only been with the Swan Song for a few weeks. Our conversations had been largely limited to liquor stock levels, ongoing bar tabs and shift-change hand-offs. The smooth tense and flex of his muscles now said potential warrior in a way his drink-pouring skills had not.

"You didn't think I paid you all so much above mar-

ket rates for your good looks, did you?" Sandor's words
hung in the misted air, as much a joking bravado in the
face of danger as they were a warning to our frosted in-
truders. Then again, maybe the frost demons had come
in for refreshments. Something warm and salty. That
could totally be a thing, right?

"I did wonder." Keeping up the banter while watching the room. "But I figured if you were kind enough
to share the wealth, I sure as hell wasn't going to turn
you down. How about you, Janey?"

"If Boss Man wants to pay me good money," Janey
replied, strapping a sickle-shaped blade to her back, a
quiver of arrows over her shoulder, a shorter dagger by
each ankle and a crossbow in her fist, "I ain't gonna
say no neither."

"Derek?" I projected my voice to bounce off the
upper mirrors ringing the back of the bar area. Those
mirrors meant I could see his face, and also the pressing together of his lips in a zippered line. "You good
with what Sandor pays?"

Derek grunted again, but maybe he could be forgiven
for that since he was also lining up a series of bottle-
based liquid concoctions in the empty stubbies previously crated under the counter for recycling. Muttering
a series of words that sounded more like incantations
than English as he mixed and poured.

The situation clearly *had* gotten more tense. Because
it was normal to mount a collective, well-armed defense against fog.

Right.

Chapter Five

Clicking. Dripping. Possibly some flipper-slapping but I couldn't be sure—the sound-deadening foam rolls we'd installed under the floors and behind the ceiling tiles were doing what they were supposed to do. Keeping your noise pollution to yourself was one part neighborly politeness and two parts self-preservation in this largely industrial strip of Toronto's East Bayfront.

Somehow the Harbor uniforms always seemed to miss out on this section just east of Toronto's downtown core but in full view of its fluorescent-lit skyline of towering offices and condos. Blaming police neglect was too easy. The truth was that it probably had more to do with a *coppers-don't-look-here* spell than anything else.

Supes took care of their business themselves. *Ourselves.* Four months later and I still kept forgetting. I may look, talk and possibly even quack like a duck-mimicking human, but I was definitely swimming with the fishies of the beyond-norm gene pool these days.

Besides, what exactly would the non-magically skilled men and women of Toronto's finest be able to do against sentient fog that could (and did) change both shape and solidity?

"Hey girl." Janey was somewhere to my right, the

barest outline in a foggy gloom already crowding out the mood-dimmed lighting. "You gonna suit up and help out or what?"

Off to my left, Sandor was smashing brick after brick of screaming ice crystals. He'd managed to make a dent in the wall by spearing at it with his favorite Persian *Katar*, a steel version of our modern-day brass knuckles. Behind me I could hear Derek's chanting interspersed with potato-sack thuds followed by splintering crashes of glass.

I risked a single glance over my shoulder at the ice blocking any front door escape plans. But maybe there was another way to do this.

Right before the first brick separated itself from its frozen brethren (sisteren? Were there genders?) and flung itself at my head.

I ducked.

The thing *screed* past me and onto the bar counter's surface where, with a clicking clatter of stacking parts, what I'd thought was a block suddenly sprouted limbs as all four corner edges shot out and to the side. A synchronized move. Wait, were those fingers? With opposable thumbs?

No time to focus on the weirdness as a second frozen missile lobbed itself at my head, landing on the bar surface next to its mate after I dodged it. So many legs. Or maybe they were arms, what with the fingers—six on each stick-like appendage with an additional thumb—scrabbling at the slick countertop surface. There would be scratches to sand down later.

Had to assume there would be a later.

Derek and I shared a look, a cross between *what the frick?* and *let's get this done.* Then he gave me the nod, flipping his spiked baseball bat in one hand so that I could grasp the taped end without injuring myself. *Considerate.*

I took the opening and did a sliding hydroplane through the rising puddled water to land at the bar, my hands slapping against the edge to slow my trajectory. I grabbed the weapon offered with a chin-bobbed thanks, then set about smashing the bricklets with the spiked end of things.

The screams that accompanied the blue-black blood splatters flying across my face and the bar beneath left no doubts as to the sentience of whatever these things were.

They were pissed. They were also crazy fast.

I was good with a bat but it didn't matter; these things had a built-in lubricant that melted liquid from their underbellies as contact was made with the warmer counter surface. Sure, we had air-conditioning. But it was still Toronto in June; there was only so much any kind of cooling unit could do.

It wasn't enough.

Not all of those bricks were deconstructing the same way. Sure, some were melting and some were being smashed. But there was a core contingent, spread out in some kind of stacked pattern, separating itself from the icy herd. Growing arms and legs without a face I could recognize as a face.

Surely there were eyes in there somewhere. Because they were now in a vee-shaped formation and advancing directly towards me.

Shit.

It was like watching a circus trapeze performance. One brick would come flying out of the wall, dropping to the ground about four or five feet away. Then another would fling itself free from the stacked pack, bounce once or twice against the watery ground, before skidding up onto the brick stack that came before it.

Those buggers were *fast.*

And still I didn't know *why.* Why they were here, and what it all had to do with me.

Too bad Celandra, my favorite street-prowling woman who just so happened to be a dragon, wasn't making one of her random raiding-of-the-kitchen visits today. Her non-human side was handy in a fight, even if she had a disconcerting tendency to pick at her teeth with the bones of her vanquished foes afterwards.

"Dana!" Sandor's voice boomed basso, deep enough to ripple the water of our too-slow-to-melt attackers in its wake. "You good, girl?"

I waited until two out of three of his eyes were fixed on me before angling my head with a pointed stare in the direction of the hallway. Hoping Sandor would either figure out what I was doing or at least get out of my way if he didn't.

He finally nodded. I couldn't tell whether it was comprehension or trust, but as long as he backed me up I guess it didn't matter.

"Cover her," Sandor barked.

I risked one last glance over my shoulder before ducking into the darkened Employees Only hallway. Flashback to the demon on shifter action that went down back here when it was still *baby it's cold* outside. When Cybele—*Alina*—chloroformed and abducted me. My chest suddenly pressing in on me, too hard to breathe; I slapped my palms flat on the condensation-beaded surface of the wall. Some memories may be misty and water colored, but this one—with the pain and the bod-ies and the blood—was less pastel and more the stuff of nightmares. *My* nightmares, to be specific.

Because I hadn't watched enough terrors from the in-sides of my eyelids before everything went down. *Right.*

I closed my eyes and counted to ten. Although I only lasted until two—adrenaline plus closed eyes plus panic attack apparently equals a wobbly Dana of no use to anyone.

Get it together. People and demons relying on you.

Right. I could do this.

I breathed in again through my nose, counting to a measured ten, then exhaled through my mouth. And again. By that third exhale I could feel my lips; I could have held up that wall as easily as it was holding me. I pushed off with slickened palms to test that theory.

I could do this.

The noises of battle just steps away rushed back, bouncing off the concrete floors of my pathway into darkness. Sandor's office and, past that, the storeroom of all things consumable.

I was looking for that special bucket of used grease. The one reeking of kimchee and old socks and gorgon-zola cheese from last week's deep fryer. We'd usually put it out back to let it ferment; given enough time, it worked great as a base for filo pastries stuffed with jalapeños, charbroiled snake skin and Gor-Fak dung. You couldn't pay *me* to eat it, but it was big with a cer-tain fringy clientele. Just don't let them breathe on you afterwards.

My next target was a jug of 100-proof Six-Toed Grandma Vodka. Actual name. Made from some of the moldiest potatoes the Six-Toed Grandma Clan of Matron

Demons could find in Belarus and mixed with some kind of glowing sludge, the stuff was toxic to humans if ingested. It was also combustible as hell. Chances are, if you drank it by choice, you probably weren't a smoker; and if you were, you probably wouldn't continue to be for long.

I hesitated at the garden hose Sandor kept on a hook behind the door. Sure, why not. No idea why it was there, but I slung it over my shoulder anyway.

One last thing. I reached behind the jumbo tin of brine-soaked squeeball testicles until I found Janey's pack of smokes with the lighter on top. Hesitated—an old teenage habit resurfacing like acid reflux—before I slid both into my back pocket.

Hello MacGyver, meet your smart-ass (and much younger) twin Dana.

The trip back to the main area of the bar was quicker than the one out. Amazing what can be accomplished when the inside of your head takes a break from giving you an emotional beat-down.

Based on the grunts, crashes and popping sounds of Derek's combustible mini-missiles, the defense had been maintained in my temporary absence.

It hadn't been as effective as I'd hoped.

Janey and Sandor had retreated to maybe three or four feet in front of the bar stools—hadn't they been on the other side of the room before? And hadn't there been some patrons in here earlier too? I looked closer at what I'd thought were piles of desiccated ice chips, closer to the stage area. *Oh.* Not ice chips. Instead, there were crystalline sculptures of twinkling chips in the shapes of several of our afternoon-imbibing regulars, some with their mouths still open. Frozen into immobility even as they'd screamed.

Funny how I'd missed that.

I hoisted the grease bucket, vodka jug and rubber tubing onto the bar counter before clambering up after them. Next I poured the vodka into the grease. The ice bricks continued to fling themselves at us—I'd swatted away five with my bare hands already—but they were hardly trying at this point. They knew they had us cornered, the mists so thick the front door was more smudged thumbprint than any kind of clear exit strategy.

Derek had run out of empties to throw, and had gone back to muttering curses along with what I hoped was some good pro-Swan Song mojo magic. No additional help there. Nothing to lose with me over here.

I started with the hose. Only to realize that I had no way to get any of this crap in one end and out the other without spilling and therefore wasting it. I also needed some kind of forward projectile propulsion that didn't involve me swallowing anything noxious. *Damn it.*

OK. One problem at a time. Transferring a substance from a larger receptacle to a smaller one required a funnel. Something we kept behind the counter.

"Derek!" Forced stage whisper—I didn't want to yell, but I needed him to hear me. "Pass me the large funnel, would you please?"

His eyes widened. Maybe he hadn't noticed me there? Either way, after no more than a second or two of startle, Derek's eyes re-focused and he grabbed the plastic funnel we used to refill some of our bottles. Only for those too drunk to tell the difference though. Really.

Now I just had to figure out how to make it fly once I poured it in. Unless—

I took one end of the garden hose and tossed it towards the thickest clump of ice bricklets. Stuck the narrow tip of the funnel in the other, at which point I realized I was at least one hand short of the number I needed to pull this off. *Crap.* Glanced back and down at Derek again, about to ask for his help; he surprised me by grabbing the tube with the hand he wasn't currently using for defense.

Let's do this.

I picked up the bucket, lined it up with the funnel opening, and poured. The sludge moved slower than I wanted, and I raised the hose up before lowering it again to add more of the noxious mixture. Jiggled both hose and bucket to try and speed up that process as the mists kept getting thicker. At this point the front door was a memory of freedom rather than a stairway to anywhere I could get to, especially with the ice grasping at my ankles.

I leaned in towards Derek, hoping he wasn't too magic-tranced out to hear me.

"Hey, Derek," I said, over my shoulder, "I may need some flame in a minute. Can you back me up with heat if I need it?" He nodded.

"Guys?" I made sure Sandor and Janey heard me too. "I'd be getting behind the bar now."

Sandor and Janey took the hint, diving behind the barrier and pulling Derek down with them. The bricks paused their assault. Confused?

I climbed back on top of the bar and pulled out Janey's pack of smokes, grabbing one between my teeth and dangling it off my lips.

Stared at the mist as it stared back at me.

"Hey, assholes!" I stomped my feet a couple of times to divert their attention. "Anyone got a light?"

I puffed up the burn to orange. Then flicked the cigarette straight into the widespread puddle of grease.

Nothing happened.

I lit up another smoke and tried again. There was a bit of a popping sound but that was about it.

Damn it.

"Hey, Derek?" His head easing up, cautious, from behind the bar. "You got anything back there I could burn and throw?"

The bartender hesitated, then grabbed a couple of half-empty bottles of the better stuff—Jamaican rum and some kind of gin—before shoving in some rags and passing one over to me. Pulled his own lighter from his pocket as we got our flaming vessels lit and loaded.

"Here goes nothing," I muttered, nodding my thanks to Derek before he ducked back down again.

This time I tossed the lit liquor bombs directly at the grease, relaxing only slightly as I heard the glass shatter. *Success.* Flames shooting up and spreading.

Of course, now the room was on fire. Drops of liquid springing to life and dancing over the screams of the burning and melting as solids liquefied and the water level rose once more.

I almost heard it too late. The rush of water turning on overhead. This was a bar, and all bars by law have a sprinkler system.

"Duck!" I yelled, diving over the bar and under the counter lip.

As the flame boomed out and scattered.

Chapter Six

Silence. Followed by dripping. Some crackling at the edges where fires still burned. But at least there were no more frost demons, and I could almost smell Lake Ontario again through the dissipating smoke.

Sandor surveyed the damage.

"This is coming out of your pay," he said.

"What's with your wards?" We both knew Sandor would be covering his own deductible. Plus there was no proof this latest attack had anything to do with me.

"I've been wondering that myself," he replied, picking at something black and gummy from his inner ear flap. "Bad for business." He reached behind the counter for a square napkin from a stack remarkably unharmed in the downpour—dry even—and smeared the goop onto it before folding the paper and sticking it in his shirt-front pocket. "Evidence."

Maybe Sandor wouldn't be the one paying his deductible after all.

There was a splash by the front door, and I held up my hand to block my squint as the late-afternoon sun lit up our newcomer in hazy relief.

"We're closed," Janey called out. "Pipe burst. Sorry to inconvenience."

"A snicker snacker came skitter scatter. Tasty toasty fleshsicles with crumbs blowing here and there and making me hungry hungry more."

Celandra. Of course. Sandor had put the dragon lady on retainer to show up whenever the smoke alarm was tripped.

She was looking particularly mismatched today with a turquoise-blue dollar-store special foam flip-flop on one foot and an almost identical magenta purple one on the other. The black of her feet, dirt worked into grooves and ridges of skin, contrasted with her outfit: a brown Lycra-stretch t-shirt about three sizes too small and rolling up into her stomach folds, under which she'd layered a mossy green tank top that over-stretched down to her knees and out way past the circumference of her hips. The mossy green part was a guess. At this point, it was more mud brown with cracks of what could have been baked ivy.

I was relieved Celandra wore pants. Or something resembling lower-body wear coverage, despite alternating between orange and blue and yellow fluorescence that hung low in the crotch before going tighter around and below the knees.

Too bad there was no way to hide her pungent *it's-June-and-hot* smell. Didn't dragons love the water? Then again, what with the fire and all, maybe not as much as I'd thought.

Celandra opened her mouth and tasted the air around us.

"Mmm." She smacked her lips together, bouncing up and down on the balls of her feet. "Demon dandy short and randy. Alina pepina macka Macarena." Celandra did a pirouette while wrinkling her nose and flapping her hands like a person who thinks they're a bird. "Frost demons too trickly now for Mistress so fickley."

Wait, what? Who was the fickle(y) mistress in this scenario. And did she just say *Alina*?

"Greasy fix from rancid mix!" Celandra was clapping her hands now and kicking at the water with her toes. Glad someone was enjoying it. My skin was starting to itch from the ash and who knows what else I'd blown up with that frost-melting fire.

"Would you like a straw?" I thought Sandor was joking until I saw Celandra's eyes widen and her mouth pucker into a smiling O.

"*Yesssssss* a straw to suck a straw to blow lookie lookie what's below!" She bobbed up and down some more, somehow managing to skitter over the water while the rest of us got wet. Classic.

Maybe Celandra would be able to suck back all the melted demon char in here using that candy-floss-pink curled straw she was squatting with over the murk. So far she'd been doing a lot of poking, slurping and belching. It was possible she'd be able to do it. But just in case, I'd better grab the ShopVac and a broom.

I followed the sound of Janey's raised voice towards the back. Maybe she was talking to Derek?

"Don't tell me you haven't noticed what's been going on around here." I heard a muffled grunt from Derek. "I know she and Boss Man are tight, but come *on.* Wherever she goes, there's trouble." Another grunt.

"Sandor's decision. Not ours," Derek said.

Janey huffed.

"And what the hell," she continued, her voice rising. "Who took my smokes?"

I dipped into the doorway, fishing both cigarettes and lighter from my front pocket.

"Sorry," I said, handing them over. "It was for a good cause." At least Janey had the decency to look away. But then she met my eyes after all and I wished she hadn't; polite if not exactly warm, her tough scowl warred with fear—of me, and of the baggage that could show up with me at any time.

I was surprised, but not as much as I probably should have been. People are who they are. Janey couldn't say what had changed about me in the last few months— that information was on a need to know only—but she knew on a gut level I was different.

"Thanks for the smokes," I said, grabbing one of the wide-bottomed, black-bristled brooms from beside the door and the ShopVac. "See you back out there."

Janey gave me a long look and nodded. Derek did the chin bob, acknowledging but not engaging.

So much for the lasting bonds of work friendships.

I smelled the acrid char of a match being struck, fol- lowed by the prickle in my nose and the way my chest clenched from the smoke of Janey's cigarette. Sandor wasn't one to let anyone light up inside, but given that the air was filled with burned and flaking demon bits, really, what was a bit more to choke on?

Celandra let out a loud burp that lasted a full forty- five seconds (I counted) as I walked back into the main bar area. Clearing space for more? Since the water lev- els hadn't gotten noticeably lower in the time it'd taken me to get the broom, I used that broom to start pushing the sludge out the front door. Swish and push, swish and push. Still slow going, but at least I was doing something to help. My mind churning with each rush of water I shoved out the door.

Another attack averted. And for what? We didn't even know what they were after, and desiccated piles of mush tell no tales. Janey wasn't wrong though. Chaos did seem to have me on speed dial these days.

The air over my shoulder moved, prickling along my spine and the back of my neck; Anshell. My nose twitched as my fingers started to lengthen and sharpen in response. *No.* This wasn't the time for show-and-tell; I shoved my hands into the pockets of my pants to make sure.

Anshell filled the space with his energy without needing to say a word. He simply *was.*

My chest clenched then, followed by heat that craved something, some*one* else. *Sam.* He shadowed Anshell in surveying the bar's damage, before scenting closer to me, checking for any injuries. As though I was his mate? And yet—

"I'm fine," I caught Sam's hand in my hair as he lifted it up, making sure my head was still attached to my neck. Even though I reeked of smoke and grease and the char of melted demon bits. My breath catching as we made contact. Even now. Even still. Even though Jon. "I'm fine," I repeated, covering for the shakiness. "You should see the other guys." I pasted on a grin, cockier than I felt.

Sam let me have my pride.

"I can see that." Sam grinned as he made a show of brushing grey soot flakes off my shoulders and into the puddled floor below. There was a scar on the back of his right hand from the time he'd been skewered with a trident prong; another one on his left forearm where he'd been sliced open by a Jangmuth demon's poison-tipped claws. Sam had almost died. Fingers that knew how to touch that part of me, down deep, when we were just us and clothes were scarce.

My breath caught and I had to look away. It was either that or find somewhere private—now.

Raised my eyes to find Anshell watching me. I realized, as his energy spiked, that equine might be only a fraction of what my Alpha was capable of given the right motivational nudge. Something with sinew and scales and something that was else.

I filled Sam and Anshell in on the attack at the Swan. Broad strokes only. I skipped the part where I had a panic attack. Who would that nugget of psychological turd-stacking knowledge benefit? Not me, not now. But the projectile sentient ice bricklets, our collective defense and Celandra's claim that Alina had been behind it—that was shareable.

"Do you find it at all curious that you are still alive?" Anshell's voice was mild. I knew what he was doing. Suggestion that led you to the conclusion he could see even if you weren't there yet. That's OK. He knew you'd show up once you followed his trail of mental breadcrumbs. "Why do you think the Swan was attacked?"

"I have no idea." Sharper than intended. Until I realized. "Oh. Shit." *Understatement.*

"Alina? What if it was a test?"

Chapter Seven

"See you at the meet later?" Sam's voice was casual, but I'm pretty sure there was an element of *I-don't-want-you-out-of-my-sight-for-long-so-I-can-keep-you-safe* to it.

"Uh huh," I replied. Brain elsewhere as I replayed the details of today, thinking through the implications. Alina sending minions for me again, and said minions testing the Swan Song's defenses. Defenses which had fallen short and had gotten dangerously close to the edge of not quite enough.

"We'll have eyes on the Swan," Anshell said, quiet. "You're not alone."

"Uh huh," I said again. Would Pack reinforcements have helped? I wanted to say yes but who knows. And what if it happened again? Would the Pack come if I needed it, what with my not being full status yet? I hoped I wouldn't have to bet my life on that.

"Want me to wait?" Sam. Being sweet. I squeezed and flexed my fists behind my back. Chafing from Pack life, its expectations and my place with the greater whole. Maybe a run wasn't such a bad idea after all. If danger wanted to have words with me, danger would have to catch me first.

I released my hands and reached up, pulling Sam towards me. His lips met mine before breaking contact, only to touch down again and feather their way along my neck. *Oh.* I could feel him everywhere, exposed, even the hairs on my arms standing up and reaching for him. Kissing again.

I shivered.

No. Space. I needed to breathe.

"It's OK," I said, pulling away. Harder than I'd anticipated. "I'm good."

Sam stepped back and crossed his arms, my skittish self nothing new to him by now. Don't spook the commitment-phobic female, especially with all that post-fight adrenaline in her system. Let her approach you.

"Eleven-thirty at the Leslie Street Spit," he said. "You know the spot?"

I nodded, grateful. Most guys would have taken my *come-hither-go-away* personally by now.

"Maybe," I said. I needed… I didn't know *what* I needed. Nothing. Something. What?

A flash behind Sam's eyes before the smile, now familiar, was back. All good. No reason for Sam to worry about me, wonder where I'd be or who I'd be up with later. Right?

Sandor called in reinforcements, who swore they could fix up the Swan in time for the bar's afternoon re-opening. One of the benefits of having *an all-acts-of-mystical-attack* rider in your insurance policy. I should probably get one of those.

With the emergency repair crew sent by the adjuster already on site, there was nothing for me to do but leave. Without pay, of course—Sandor and I might be friends, but I was still considered "casual contract" even after almost four years. I got payment for services rendered, plus tips. Period.

I thought about heading over to the Pack house. Anshell had space for me if I needed my own room, and Sam had yet to kick me out of his bed if I wanted to be there. Not that we always made it to his bed, but maybe after...

The glimmer of impending dawn stretched ahead and around me as I made my way through the heat-bleached yellow grasses whispering on the breeze. The city's concrete and glass towers, with its murmurations of office workers pouring in and out during office hours, stood in abrupt contrast to the reclaimed nature of this area with its weeds, wildflowers and urban wildlife. As though peace and cubicle living were mutually incompatible existences.

Kind of like *normal* reality and the one last winter's bleed and feed ritual had pushed me into; the normality I'd left behind after Claude, Jon's other lover, scratched me.

Dana...

My name whispered on the wind.

Danyankeleh...

My heart in my throat.

I hesitated, slowing my steps but not stopping. Not yet.

I heard laughter in snatched cadences drifting past. Could be partiers on their way into the brush, or maybe a beachside drum circle fire pit. I looked back over my shoulder but saw nothing.

Dana...

I whipped around this time, trying to catch whoever

or whatever was there in my ear. Breath hot and lips dry. I tasted lemon and fish and sweet grass as my tongue curled in on itself. And I knew.

You have something I want.

"Get in line," I muttered. To myself? Crazypants Dana, talking to herself and hearing voices. How many hours had it been since I slept again? My truck now twenty feet in front of me.

Danyankeleh.

A different voice. Layers and threads weaving together. So familiar.

Run!

My keys were out and jiggling in the lock, too long until the door opened; diving in, smashing down on the latch after me. Next time around I was getting remote keyless entry. Seriously. The new battery and replacement starter purred the engine to life and I reversed, spinning my rear tires and spitting gravel bits at whatever was behind me before slamming the gearshift into drive. A *splat*, and then a *thud*. Another *splat*, another *thud*.

I glanced into my rearview mirror.

Dark shapes, two that I could see, had attached themselves to my back window. I swerved, trying to throw them off.

More thuds. I'd driven into a hailstorm of sticky, gelatinous crap. How many had stuck to my truck and how many had I managed to shake loose? I couldn't tell.

Boom. My entire truck shuddered and I skidded to a stop, spinning gravel. All I could see was translucent pink-grey flesh, veined threads of ashen blue and blackish-purple tentacles like dreadlocks trailing down from the amorphous mass blocking my view. Then stars, as one of those limbs smacked me in the face through my open window.

I hissed, and the thing that shouldn't be able to survive on water-free land paused, the follow-up to its appendage one-two counterpunch hesitating instead of knocking me out. My face burned and tickled as my adrenaline fight response shoved fur through my pores and whiskers from my cheeks. The shift coming on too fast. I'd gotten better with my control but not good enough. Oh *shit*. Shifting while driving would get me nowhere good—and fast.

Forced myself to slow my breathing. I didn't have to change. It was a choice. My fingers lengthened and my nails became claws with points that curved to press into my steering wheel. There would be marks later. My feet were still my feet—small mercies—so at least I could drive, foot to gas pedal, even as my steering ability was questionable. Got to try, right?

From the corner of my increasingly night-vision-improved eyes, I caught the tentacled limb winding back for a follow-up smack, light-bulb-flash quick, to what I assumed would be my head.

It was fast; claws out, I was faster.

No thought—the arm closest to the open window ended in a paw, and that paw wasn't taking the sea creature's shit anymore.

Whoa. Where did that come from?

The limb pulled back, oozing greyish-green slime from its fresh wounds. I rolled up my driver-side window using both paws at once, clumsy and slower than I'd like; no choice, given that I temporarily lacked prehensile thumbs. But I was motivated. And stronger in my alternate form, even if I managed to keep the shift partial. I steered with the wheel wedged between my elbows, the skin of my inner arm tacky with sweat against the skin covering my rib cage, and wished I had air-conditioning that worked.

I wondered what Sandor had been thinking when this thing came for him.

I pushed the gas pedal to the floor again, or tried, even though I couldn't see a damned thing. I didn't care. *Away* was as good a destination as any, and I was betting that *there* was better than *here*.

Funny. The last time I'd pressed on the gas it was more satisfying. And locomotive.

I might as well be stuck in a snowbank. Wheels spinning, digging a hole of slick that only embedded me further into place; I could either keep on forcing the engine and burn it out, or I could take a break. Grey goo spread across my windshield. I tried to use my wipers to clean it off; the sharp resulting *crack* suggested something expensive. Especially with that burning smell. Did I just fry both my wiper motor *and* my truck engine?

No. Happy thoughts. Or at least productive ones, as I shifted into Park and turned off the engine. It's not like I was going anywhere, not with those tree-trunk-sized limbs draped across my truck. I know why the caged cat yowls when trapped behind mutant sea-creature flesh. Frustration, baby.

As good as my claws felt, flexing and retracting, there's no way those nails would be more than a short-term annoyance for the thing sitting on my hood. What

I needed was one of those blades I'd used earlier. If only I could get a good grasp on it.

Not going to happen unless I shifted back to the shape where I had hands with four fingers and a thumb.

Fur stroked against the inside of my skin, a purr in my still-human throat. Even in the confined area of my truck's cab, staring deep-sea mortality in the suctioning cups, I wanted to slide back the seat and wrap myself around myself, naked skin to soft downy fur. All mine. I could let go and *be*. The yowled beginnings of a cat under a hot and confined reinforced steel roof.

No.

I tried to remember why I couldn't give in to the back-arching, toe-curling, deep-down itch that could be scratched so easily if I just let self-control go. Fidgeting in my seat as my nerve endings sang a rousing discordant chorus of need and want versus should and could. A flash of Sam on my mind, the touch of his lips a sense memory on the side of my neck. Fur sprouting in the wake of his phantom kiss.

Not helpful.

Jon. I fixated on my undead other lover. The coolness of his fingertips, the dusky rose-cinnamon taste of him; the goose bumps his touch left behind, the ache of cool loss deep inside when he was gone. Always gone, until he wasn't; wanting more but getting as much as he could give. Ashes to dirt.

The pull of Jon's chill cooled the heat calling to heat of Sam. Both extremes catching my breath in my throat. Fur tucking back into pores; curved claws softening and rounding to fingers; paws becoming palms.

We seemed to be at a temporary impasse, the gelatinous on-land sea creature and I. The only proof I had that it was still alive was its pulsing flesh puffing up and contracting; I watched the fluid in its veins mirror the rhythm. What was it waiting for? Someone? Something? If so, I was pretty sure I didn't want to meet whoever or whatever that was.

What can I say? Call me anti-social.

But maybe I had it all wrong. Even though I'd been party to it losing a limb earlier this evening, whatever this was just wanted to talk. The head-thwacking by tentacle was all a misunderstanding.

Sure.

Still, better to gamble on my safety over a short-lived future of regret. I tilted my seat back, rolled the rubber mat behind me further to the back, and found the edges of my thumbprint-activated lockbox. A carryover from my days when this kind of situation was normal.

Guess everything old really *is* new again.

I leaned across and grabbed a couple of hand-to-tentacle combat-friendly weapons. A walnut wood-handled *Kukri* knife I'd gotten on a mission in Nepal, its arced blade glinting light from overhead. And a machete. Because sometimes you just have to go with the machete.

With my free hand, I hit the speaker on my phone and called it in.

"Hey, it's me," I said. "So about that backup…"

The sound of my voice through the glass woke it up.

I cracked my window. Enough to get some air in and sound out; not enough to get whacked in the head again. My forehead was clammy with something other than summer sweat, as my heartbeat rushed past my ears. Forcing myself to be brave. I clenched the steering wheel with fingers unable to hold their form, my own fur absorbing the sweat of my fear. Focusing on my breath, recalling the sounds of my last yoga teacher; the timbre and tone and texture of her voice. Until my fingers and breath and mind were my own once more.

"Hey," I said. Did these things even have ears? Then, louder: "Hey! Mind moving a bit so I can get by?" No response. Not even a twitch. Was I really expecting one? Squid D'Lee was chatty, but maybe the larger the octo-beastie, the fewer words it had to share?

One last try. I rolled down the window a few finger-widths more. Oh wow, a breeze. Nifty.

"Excuse me," I said. This time all the appendages moved at once, the metal creaking and groaning above my head followed by a slithering, then a suctioning. *Pop on, pop off.* A giant head of a creature that shouldn't exist on dry land bobbed, upside-down, in front of me. And blinked.

What the hell was it?

"Human." The multi-limbed creature's accent was a vague British, as though it was born in the island's north but had lived here long enough to take the edge off. Weird hearing it coming from that pointy-tooth-filled head on the other side of my windshield. "What do you want?"

"Uh…" I lost my words for a moment, putting the pieces that could fit together in my head. "To leave?" If that was an option, I was *so* taking it.

"Not yet," it said. I wondered whether a single one of those teeth would be enough to death-impale me on its own. "We have unfinished business to discuss first. We were interrupted with great rudeness earlier."

"Oh?" I resisted adding the word "yeah" to the end of that. I got the impression that this creature only responded to being politely addressed, seeing as my "excuse me" approach had worked where the "hey!" opener had failed. *Interesting.* I inclined my head to convey my curiosity. *Poker face poker face poker face.*

"We wish to discuss further the mercenary by the name Gustav, or Gus. Blue fellow. Rather nasty." I think it was watching my face for any reaction. Could it tell if I was lying from its upside-down vantage point?

"Oh?" Like I didn't have vivid nightmare precision-vision 2 AM sweaty recall on a regular basis of the diamond-and-blue demon who'd almost ended me. Four months was not enough time to forget. Believe me— I'd tried. "How can I help you?" Besides telling Sandor so he could warn his MIA brother, assuming he knew how to reach him.

"Would you be willing to help us?"

"That depends," I said. "What do you want with Gus?"

"We're not at liberty to discuss this." I was starting to wonder if this was a royal "we" situation.

"Could you at least tell me your name? I'm Dana— but you already knew that. And you are—?"

"Oh my," the giant octopus said. "My manners. I do apologize." It was hard to tell whether he was being serious. "I am…" I wasn't sure if he'd said *zicorapheto rezmantilus* or whether I was language-anthropomorphizing the clicks and squishes and squeaks I was hearing into something my brain could process. "But you can call me Frank."

"Nice to meet you, Frank. So, could you possibly tell me a bit more about why I should help you?"

"At first we needed the help, and we were willing to compensate you monetarily for your trouble," he said. "Now, however, you owe us a debt of pain and inconvenience."

"Pardon?"

"You, and those associated with you, severed one of our limbs. For no good reason. It also hurt."

"I'm…sorry?" I wasn't really, seeing as he was holding Sandor as leverage against me at the time, but it seemed like the expected thing to say.

"It will regenerate with time," Frank said, ignoring my apology along with its insincerity. "Be that as it may, you now have a duty to us that did not previously exist. We expect you to honor our wishes in order to restore balance."

"And if I don't? Or can't?"

"Do your best," he replied. "Otherwise we might be motivated to conduct comparable limb-regeneration experiments on you next time." *Fuck.*

"We expect you to contact us should this Gustav reappear. I believe we now have an understanding of the mutual benefits of cooperation?"

"How do I reach you?" Because clearly I had no choice. Even if I didn't formally acquiesce to the terms.

I'm not sure how Frank did it, but suddenly there was a business card stuck to the bottom left-hand corner of my windshield, followed by a targeted stream of blue ink to make sure the card stayed in place. I guess it was moisture-repellant somehow?

"I look forward to hearing from you, Ms. Dana,"

he said. "Good day." He hesitated until I nodded back, awkward with the pause.

"Good day."

I watched as the tentacles released my truck, before the oversized cephalopod named Frank lumbered past the brush, headed in the direction of the lake.

And here the Toronto harbor folks thought their biggest issues were Japanese carp and pollution.

Chapter Eight

I turned the key in the ignition again. Hallelujah—not only did it start, but the engine thermostat was back down and out of the red.

I floored it, spraying gravel and weeds and nothing I wanted to pause and examine closely in my wake. The hell with potholes on Lake Shore Boulevard and the damage they were doing to my shocks. Even though I flinched with each rubber-on-asphalt groan as the frame of my truck complained at its treatment. *Suck it up sunshine*. It was time to be somewhere very much in the *else* category.

My lead foot on the gas pedal didn't start to ease off until I was heading north along sleepy city streets, the people inside just starting to straggle out of bed and reach for that newspaper and morning cup of coffee. There was time before rush hour jammed the streets, lego blocks on wheels clouding the air with exhaust fumes as those stubbornly resisting public transportation idled in stop-and-go traffic. The sun still tucked below the horizon, leaving only the setting moon to offset the overhead street lamplights that flickered at regular intervals on my face and arms as I passed.

At least once I jammed on the brakes, swerving to

avoid a dark streak of nothing that darted out in front of me on the road. Unless it wasn't there. Unless I was so tired I was seeing things. Adrenaline could only carry me so far.

Home was a bit further west than it used to be. Better this way. Apparently my old neighbors hadn't been big on living next to—in a row house with fully attached walls kind of way—someone whose kitchen mysteriously blew up that one time. My former landlady, a woman with under-eye smudges that matched the grey streaking her harsh blue-black hair dye, had given me the broken English version of the *it's-not-you-it's-me* speech. Even though it clearly *was* me.

My new building squatted on the corner of Ossington and Dupont with the train tracks at its back, a cheap gas station to its left, a storage facility to its right and the lake way too far away to see or hear. A former factory, with windows that opened onto the street, it housed artists and students and those like me who lived on the edges of what other people considered normality. My neighbors didn't care what I did or who I did it with, as long as I returned the favor. *Judge not lest ye be judged.* Or something like that.

The fact that I'd taken a place even further from the Swan Song was no accident. I'd needed more distance between work and the rest of my life.

Yeah. That was working out *so* well.

I woke up thinking about what had happened with Frank. Putting aside the threat—because hello, must be Tuesday—I realized I'd been getting cocky, shifting with the Pack. Overlooking the part where shared energy made the change come on faster, easier. Forgetting that, on my own, I wasn't quite the control-my-own-physical-form superhero I liked to pretend I was.

I recreated each stage of my earlier intermittent transformation in my head as I ran through my morning Sun Salutation yoga routine. Tried to call up the muscle memory of my claws digging into the steering wheel even as I struggled to regulate my breathing. Stomach crunches didn't help. Neither did knuckle push-ups. If this was my old place, I might have segued into skipping rope or punching at something; here, the walls were thinner and I couldn't be sure that repeated pounding on the rotting floor wouldn't result in me falling through. I flirted with the idea of a jog; rejected it again when the thermostat outside my grime-smeared window informed me it was already 32°C in the shade.

I settled for thirty minutes of kicks, punches and blocks in front of a mirror, monitoring myself for form. Emptying my mind of everything but the flowing sequence of moves, familiar with repetition. *This* was how I needed my shifts to be.

If my involuntary response to Frank proved anything, I wasn't there yet.

My phone buzzed. *Anshell.* He was so retro—what, he couldn't text?

"Hey," I said, patting down the sweat with my towel before answering. "What's up?"

"I wanted to confirm that you still plan to train this afternoon. Or do we need to reschedule?" The word Anshell left off was *again.* A valid question seeing as I'd canceled and re-booked three times already. I mentally slapped myself on the wrist. *Bad Dana. Selfish Dana.*

At least Ashell wasn't giving me guilt. No, he instead was being patient with my ambivalence over becoming a shifter. He hadn't yelled, given me the silent treatment, or even tossed a disapproving lip-pursing my way. Not over this. So of course I felt even more of a need-to-run urge.

Just because Anshell wasn't dishing it out didn't mean I wasn't feeling it.

"It's good," I said instead. "See you in an hour."

Funny how the less I knew about something, the more confident I could be in my own abilities. Ignorance and bliss really did make for great drinking buddies.

"Again," Anshell said, as Sam watched. We were in the backyard of the Roxborough Road house. A mansion by Toronto standards, where a semi-detached in not the best of neighbourhoods had already priced most first-time home buyers out of the city's real estate market. And this was *not* a lousy neighbourhood. You could tell by the century-old trees overhanging the grass-and-flagstone mix, blocking what we were up to from anyone who might be curious enough to look over.

Just as well. Did I really need norms with telescopic lenses taking pictures of me as I arched my back and twitched both tail and whiskers that hadn't been there moments before, wouldn't be there in a handful of minutes? I was getting faster with my transitions, but not that fast.

The sun dappling my fur through the leaves warmed my now-fully-tufted haunches, and I leaned back to lick my pads and groom the bits of dirt that tickled my chin. Rough pads with sharpened tips scraping along all the right spots. *There.* Catching my own scent of chai and lavender and vanilla in the pod; underneath it all an underbelly of acrid coffee-bean char.

"Again," said Anshell.

Pushing down the instinct to yowl my protest, inhaling the fur and feline until it tickled my surfaces from the inside, until I was smooth and pink and blinking up at my Alpha and Sam again. Covered in a thin layer of something viscous that I'd swear was lube if I didn't know better. Panting from the effort.

Sam crouched down to face level and passed me a Mason jar of water, its beaded moisture sliding through my fingers and onto the concrete slab below. Almost. Sam's reflexes were faster than mine, with one palm under the bottle to cushion its fall even as his other hand, still dry, held the mouth upright. Of course, to do this Sam had rolled onto his side and was now at eye level with me. He flashed me a grin and waggled his eyebrows. I was covered in some kind of bodily fluid and Sam still found me at least sort of attractive.

Normal in relation to my life had come and gone and left the For Sale by Owner sign behind.

At least he could deal with the Dana I was now.

Sam curled up to sitting—*someone* was diligent with his stomach crunches—and reached over to bring the jar's rim to my lips, tipping liquid towards me. I touched his wrist, gentle, steadying myself and helping to regulate the flow of my thirst relief.

"Small sips," Sam said. "Don't drink too much. Remember the shape of your stomach changes as you transition. Last thing you want is a stomach ache."

I nodded to let him know I'd heard, but didn't stop drinking. My tongue was sandpaper and my muscles were syrup. Surely it was time for a break.

"Again," said Anshell.

Sam held the glass, a gentle separation of liquid and

human-shaped lips, then edged back several inches. Not as far as before, but giving me enough space to do what needed to be done. Lending me his energy by proximity.

"Anshell," he said, watching the fatigue drip off me as I panted and tried to find the strength for one more shift. "I think she's had enough."

"She can't control her shift unless the muscles have the routine so ingrained she can do it in her sleep." If Anshell was surprised that Sam was pushing back on my behalf, he didn't show it. "You know this."

"Look at her," Sam said again as I struggled to push the fur back through the flesh, catching the yowl of frustration in my still-too-human (for the moment) throat. "You're pushing her too hard."

"Dana missed the last three sessions, then lost control under pressure." Anshell stared Sam down, as cool as I'd ever seen the Alpha. "You know what happens if she can't hold it together. There are rules. Dana is new to this, so we can overlook last night's lapse—for now—but we can't protect her indefinitely. She's going to have to stand on her own four legs."

"Funny," Sam said, not smiling. "But does it have to happen in the next twenty minutes?"

Anshell didn't answer, watching me on all fours, my mouth slack and drool pooling at the edges before trickling down my chin. I wasn't sure I could go through it one more time even if he told me to do it. And then:

"Again," said Anshell. His voice a steel-tipped whip that burned past my shoulder blades; I arched and yowled and breathed in Sam's scent and then I was silken fur and pointed teeth and belly rubs and claws digging beneath the surface of anything I wanted. Bumping heads with Sam, gliding along and through and around Anshell's legs before finding a patch of sunlit heat to stretch across. Purring, my exhaustion released at the sound of the Alpha's command.

Sam cupped one hand and poured water into it with the other, holding it towards me. When I didn't respond, or even really notice, he flicked a few drops at my nose. I growled; he held his hand out again. This time I slunk forward, because I recognized his scent, knew him to be safe. *Trust.* The liquid smelled of him, even as it mixed with traces of what had been in that jar before it became a vessel of drink; briny pickled green tomatoes with dill and garlic. I wrinkled my nose, but drank, thirst overriding my suddenly delicate nasal sensitivities.

"Again," Anshell said as my tongue ran rough against the flesh of Sam's palm, the last droplets of liquid gone. And again his voice was a physical command every cell of my body responded to, pushing my fur-lined id into the superego of human existence. Until it was me, and there was dirt, and the weeds that poked up between the cracks in the stones tickled the small of my back.

I opened my eyes to see Anshell looking down at me. Couldn't tell if I'd passed whatever his test was, if he was going to force me to change once more. Then he gave me a nod, and said, "Good job," before turning around to go back into the house.

Guess we were done for now.

I realized, after a bit, that Sam was still here with me. Waiting until I could form words again, until my breathing steadied and my heart stopped pounding so hard. Considerate. Finally I pushed myself up on my elbows and looked over at him.

"Thanks for before," I said. "Water good."

"Still thirsty?"

I nodded, saving my voice for the really important words. So tired. Sam passed over the Mason jar from before, miraculously refilled without me noticing. No limits now on how much I could have, and I downed half of it in fewer gulps than I could have imagined even six months ago. Before I became so far from the norm I wished I could go back to being.

"What time do you start at the Swan today?"

Oh. Right. I had to work.

"Uh," I said, trying to remember, channeling human thought along my still-cat-like synapses. "Five? What time is it now?"

"Two," said Sam. He angled his head to the side as he took in my sticky, gritty self in all its naked glory. *Ha.*

"You're going to want to shower first."

"Ya think?" I pushed myself up to sitting and the ground swayed beneath me. Waited until the tilt normalized to something on the non-Escher scale of skewed before I allowed Sam to pull me the rest of the way to standing. *Whoa.* Was it always this hard?

"C'mon," he said, holding my hand and leading me back to the house. "Let's get you cleaned up."

Showering was good. Climbing into Sam's bed, wearing one of his t-shirts and wrapping myself in the scent of him as I pulled the sheet over my shoulders, was better. Sam was talking, about what I had no idea, and the sound of his voice lulled me to sleep.

"It's 3:30," said Sam, his hand hot against my shoulder. "Are you going to work?"

I groaned. "Five more minutes." Famous last words.

It was never just five minutes for anything involving me and bed. "Really."

Sam put the chai latte with whipped almond milk foam and cinnamon sprinkles on the table doily beside me. I slitted open my eyes, tracking the smell of bliss. Sam had actually left the house to get me my second-favorite caffeinated beverage, after coffee, and without me even asking?

"Wow," I said, pushing myself up to sitting and reaching for the cardboard cup with the name *Sayme* scrawled on the side. "Thanks."

"No worries." Sam had a cup of something sweet and hot himself balancing on the arm of the chair he'd settled into. The pile of jeans and shirts didn't seem to bother him. "You sure you're up to it?"

"I'd like to pay my rent and eat this month so yeah," I said. The concept of full-time work with paid benefits and sick-day entitlements seemed very far away. Agency-employed kind of distance. "I'll be fine." Was I trying to convince Sam or myself?

"Sore?"

"Yeah," I grunted. As though every muscle I didn't realize I had was busy seizing the moment.

"How's this?" His hands slid under the covers and up along my legs. Better than any deep-heat lotion. Kneading, rolling the muscles beneath his fingers, worrying at a knot until it released before edging higher. Even now my cat reached out to his; a lazy purr trilling in my throat before I could swallow it back. Sam chuckled. "Roll over," he said. "And take that off." Nudging the hem of the shirt up, in case I wasn't sure what "that" referred to.

His thumbs worked their way over my ass, then in

towards my tailbone. I wondered whether they would keep going or whether they'd be taking a dip first. Wanting more even as my muscles suggested otherwise. Sam hesitated, fluttering his fingertips against the fleshy rounds of my hips, before continuing his ministrations up and along my spine. Yeah, that worked too.

By the time his fingers had loosened my soreness into a puddle on the bed, I was halfway to snoring again. Instead I forced myself to roll onto my side, surprising Sam, and pulled him towards me with my palm flat against the back of his neck. His lips brushing against mine.

"Feeling better, I see."

"Mmmm," I replied. My limbs like Jell-O, and yet… that smile, the one that reminded me what else we could be doing right now.

Sam leaned over and hooked a curl that had fallen onto my cheek to tuck it back behind my ear. And then kept going, pulling goose bumps from my skin, nerves sparking to his touch as he trailed along my curves.

We kissed again, and this time it was filled with the promise of what could be with less clothing and more time. Or at least firmer intent and—*oh*—OK, the firm part was already there. Well then.

I hooked my leg over his hip and pulled him closer; he didn't resist. Instead his arm snaked up along my spine to cradle the base of my skull as it rested against the pillow, pulling me in for a kiss that wandered. Higher, to my eyelids fluttering shut; lower to my neck, and then lower still. I gasped. Pulled him back up to me, but not right away. Track pants were a good thing, no buckles or zippers or buttons to block my path, and I slid my hand down around the curve of his ass.

Sam kicked off his pants, then reached up to pull his shirt off. Mine was next. Had I been wearing underwear before? I wasn't now. His finger confirming that hypothesis.

I arched as his mouth found the breast closest to him, but not before my hand found his hardness and did a little theory testing of my own.

"Now?"

Sam nodded, reaching over to the side table to grab a condom from the pile before opening the wrapper with his teeth. I stroked the thin sheath of rubber along the length of him. And then I was on my back, my hands over my head and my fingers interlaced with his, and he was inside me and there was no more thinking for a while.

Chapter Nine

The banging of hammers and whirring of electric saws weren't too nails-on-chalkboard annoying. Really.

I kept my self-directed drink order simple—vodka (the human, Polish potato-based kind, not the demon one I'd used earlier to set fire to the frost tribbles) with orange juice. Yeah. It was one of those nights. Apparently Sandor was in a similar need-for-alcohol mood—he'd asked for a Steaming Gorzak Screamer. Blue Curaçao, two squirts of Libertina umbilical juice, a pinch of paprika, cherry schnapps, Tabasco sauce, three cubes of ice along with a handful of undead Zorgot eyeballs served in a bowl-shaped glass goblet. Sandor had assured me that the Zorgots were dead before their eyeballs were harvested. My choice to believe him.

I brought over the two drinks, his steaming as though filled with dry ice. The eyeballs were already starting to mutter amongst themselves; when I put the glasses down on the table, the sound intensified. Couldn't make out actual words, thankfully, but I found myself starting to feel guilty being the purveyor. Because maybe Sandor wasn't telling me the truth.

Right. No trust issues between us whatsoever.

"They're like raw oysters," Sandor said, taking his

first sip as the contents of the glass started screaming. "Or cooking a lobster by dropping it in a pot of boiling water while it's still alive to feel it."

"I don't do seafood." Those shrieks and moans would haunt my dreams tonight. "Seriously, Sandor, can we *not* do Steaming Screamers anymore?"

"Fine," he said, pushing the drink away with two smooth-sanded clawed orange nails. The cries receded to a murmured babble. "What did that giant octopus want?"

"Gus," I said. "Again." All three of Sandor's eyes did a long blink. "Frank—that's giant octopus guy's name—said he was going to hire me to find your brother, but then we went and hacked off one of his limbs. So now I owe him, and I'm supposed to help for free."

"Or else? Where's the stick?"

"My kneecaps, apparently," I said. "I help find Gus, or we find out whether regenerative limbs is one of my spiffy new superpowers."

"Charming." Sandor, King of the Understatement. "Still no hint about who hired these guys? Why they were hired?" He was right. If we could figure that part out, maybe I could get out of this indentured-servant deal before I had to hand over anybody big, blue and demony.

"Nope," I replied. "Your brother doesn't have a lot of good karma going for him though." I punctuated my words with a gulp of citrus vodka bitterness. "What're you thinking? Dissatisfied customer? Or did he do a cephalopod hit himself maybe?"

"Hard to say." Sandor scratched the side of his left nostril, absent in thought. "So many possibilities." He took a sip from his Steaming Screamer again without thinking. "Sorry," he muttered, pushing the goblet further from easy reach than it had been before.

"What do you want me to do?"

"Do I want you to hunt down my only brother and turn him over to some group of should-be-water-dwelling creatures because they asked you politely? What do *you* think?"

"So that's a no then." Couldn't blame a girl for asking. Especially since said only brother had tried to kill me. The part where he later helped out the Pack didn't change his attempts to end me.

Sandor didn't bother answering. He'd started toying with his phone, twirling the unit between fingers so large I was surprised he could hold it. It was so disproportionate that I felt like I was watching sushi maki roll acrobatics in motion. Did demons do Freudian? If so, I suspected Sandor's phone held the information needed to reach Gustav, a.k.a. Demon Blue.

I pretended not to notice what was right beside me by checking my own phone for messages. Because if I officially saw it, I might have to do something with the information.

"I'll be back." Sandor's subject change was abrupt. I had a pretty good idea what he was planning to do. "Keep my drink…" He faltered, as his thoughts of Gus collided with his recent recall of my distaste for the Screaming Steamer. "Keep an eye on my drink, would ya?"

I nodded but wasn't happy about it. I'd swear those eyeballs were watching *me* now, dead or undead or whatever state they were actually in. A few more sips of my vodka orange didn't help. Were those de-socketed orbs following the path of liquid from my glass to my lips?

Enough of this. I just wanted to enjoy my drink in peace, and without being watched by eyeballs that were seriously creeping me out.

I scooped up Sandor's drink and carried it to the bar counter across the room, sipping at mine on the way.

Turned back as a shadow crossed the entrance.

"We're not open yet," I called over to whoever was there. No reply but the trick of light wavered and I wondered whether I'd seen anything at all.

Danyankeleh.

My father's voice in my ear; my shoulders clenching as I scanned the room for someone who shouldn't—*couldn't*—be there.

Chapter Ten

The shadow solidified as it stepped forward into the light, and my heart dropped to somewhere around my knees. In that moment I forgot how to breathe.

Not my father.

Years. It had been years since I'd seen Owain Mc-Cready. Fought beside him. Felt his touch on my skin, lips that brushed softness against the insides of my wrists before trailing higher until his breath blew hot in my ear. Whispering words like *love* and *forever* that tangled my heart and made me believe.

I'd thought it was real.

"Dana," Owain said, settling into the chair across from me. He'd traded in the t-shirt and jeans I was used to for a custom-fitted navy blue suit with deep purple pinstripes, highlighted by the shimmering indigo of his dress shirt. Helped emphasize his eyes, so blue they bordered on purple, above the crease of his tie.

Guess Owain had moved up in the Agency since our split.

"What?" I tried not to snap out my response. He'd broken my heart before he walked away, hardening it to glass and then grinding the fragments under his boot heel.

Irish bastard.

Owain watched me as I glared. I tried not to remember the coolness of my fingers winding through the carrot-red curls of his hair, now cropped short, or the prickly curry-ginger-cardamom scent of his skin behind his ear when I inhaled deeply.

"Seriously, Owain." I dropped into the chair opposite him. "What do you want?"

He reached into his suit pocket and pulled out a thin, palm-sized electronic tablet. Grey edged, grey screen, powered down. Nothing to highlight my surprise, nothing to reflect back my thoughts. Theoretically.

"The Agency could use your help. Freelance. I've been instructed to make you an offer." Owain slid the device across the table to me.

"I see," I said without touching it. Four years of freedom, now this. Wasn't sure which trigger was responsible for the sudden ice pick of pain stabbing at my temples—the message or the messenger. Maybe both.

"It's all there," Owain said, pushing the tablet closer to me with the tips of his manicured fingers. He amped up the Irish brogue with a smile designed to charm. "Don't worry," he said. "It won't bite."

"Right," I replied, not entirely sure about the tablet's lack of teeth—figurative or otherwise.

"I'm told it's keyed to your old coordinates," he said. "Your service numbers, and whatever your last password was. You'll be wanting to change that, by the way."

"Mmm." Non-committal. Didn't want to find myself accidentally (at least on my part) bound to the terms of a contract I hadn't read purely because I touched the case that housed it and accidentally clicked *OK*.

"I'm still not feeling the trust," Owain said with an exaggerated sigh. "You pain me."

"You'll get over it. So if there's nothing else—? I'm at *work* here." Ignoring the part where we didn't actually open for another twenty minutes. "I know it's not important to you, but it means something to me. Food. Rent. You remember what that's like, right?"

"Come on, Dana," he said. "You don't really take this gig seriously, do you?"

I raised an eyebrow.

"I don't?"

Owain reached into his pocket and pulled out a business card. White, heavy-threaded linen card stock; navy, square lettering in as non-descript a serif font as possible. I half expected it to say "Mr. O" or maybe just "O" like in a *Men in Black* movie. Except that he still had his fingerprints—I could see the lines smudged on the table's surface where the pad of his fingertips had overlapped with the edge of the card. Sloppy. Not like him.

"Run them," he said, picking up the offer tablet and tucking it into the breast pocket of his jacket. "I'm still me. And if you're about knowing more, I'll be reachable."

"That would be a first." Nope, I wasn't bitter. Not me.

"See you soon." Owain stood up, confident that he'd hooked my interest whether I liked the taste of fresh worms or not, and leaned in to give me a kiss on the cheek.

I froze. By the flash of surprise widening Owain's eyes, he seemed affected too. But the moment passed and then the mask came down, smoothing his features to unreadable once more.

He tried, again, taking it slower this time. Casual.

"Think about the offer, Dana," he said. "I promise—

you won't be locked into anything just from the reading of it."

I pulled back and looked into his eyes, trying to gauge for emotion that wasn't there.

"For real? No back-door clauses or magical spring locks?"

"I can't promise that." He smiled, and I found myself remembering his black satin sheets and how I'd never slept on anything like them before. Worried every time I rolled over that I'd slide off the bed in my sleep. "Don't sign anything without reading it first. You know how that goes. And call me—from a secure line please—if you have any questions at all. Good seeing you again, Dana, my girl." Owain turned to leave.

"I wish I could say the same." Not sure if he heard that last part as he passed through the door and into the brutally moist night.

You'd think, after all these years, my ex wouldn't affect me. Of course, if that's what you were thinking, apparently you'd be wrong.

My mind jumped from idea to memory to my latest To Do list and back again; an infinity loop that solved nothing. My phone vibrated its calendar notification, reminding me that the Pack meet was starting in a few hours. The moon had only begun its arc, though; I still had time to go home. Maybe shower.

As if water could cleanse me of what time had not.

Instead I found myself on Jon's doorstep. The gallery was open, but it was between showings so patrons were sparse. His eyes flicked over as I entered, and he murmured some kind of pleasantries to the well-groomed couple he was chatting with even as he tracked my path through the room. Hunting me with his gaze. Jon still had a business to run, and he was doing it, but a canary had entered the room and suddenly birdseed—whether in a three-piece suit or a sleek red dress paired with precariously high heels—wasn't enough to satisfy his craving.

I wasn't much for diets myself.

It was only a handful of minutes before Jon was ushering his potential business out the door with postcard invitations for the next show opening and a wink coupled with a casual hand on the woman's back. Even with me in the room, watching, Jon could get his flirt on with someone else.

Or maybe that was part of his game.

"Dana." Jon's whisper bounced off the exposed brick walls as his front door clicked shut, the deadbolt turning into place. My vampire lover, my Mr. Right Now who was also Mr. Still Here Even Though. I could have told him about his role in my new debt—my original plan in coming here—or about the return of my ex, or asked questions about his not-so-ex Claude, or about where he'd been before he was here now.

Instead I went to him, dropping my bags and shedding layers of damp until my flesh pressed against his exposed coolness. One of the bonuses of being with a vampire during the summer that nobody tells you. The contrast of his chill against my heat; goose bumps rising to touch ice while still burning.

It wasn't long before Jon was fully naked, his outline glowing in the reflective light of the half moon pouring in through the curtainless window. I wasn't, not yet, still wearing my sheer purple boy short-style underwear and matching purple sateen plunge bra with spaghetti straps. What can I say—heat brings out the color drama in me.

I flashed back to Sam's whispered confession. My chest ached and I inhaled a shaky breath; it would never be just us between Jon and me. Not as long as there was Claude, or someone like him—or Sam. So instead I stood there, silent, and kissed away the words Jon would never think to say.

He broke away first, lips trailing from the side of my mouth, down, along my jaw; down again along the side of my neck to that sensitive spot where my neck sloped down to meet my shoulder. I shivered and traced my hands up along the back of his neck and into his hair.

Friends with benefits. Not the same as I had with Sam, but I also wasn't ready for Sam. Not committed. Jon was my exit strategy, and a tasty one at that. As long as sometimes he was here and sometimes Sam was here I didn't have to confront my certainty that one day Sam would leave. Me. *Us.* Even if what I feared most was something I would bring into being by being here, doing this. With my *other* lover.

Jon's mouth drifted lower and I gripped harder.

"We can't keep doing this," I said, nuzzling into Jon's neck where we'd ended up, against the wall and with my leg slung over his.

"Sure we can," Jon replied. "If it's what you want, I'm happy to oblige."

Yep. That was Jon—a giver.

"Listen," I said. Because I'd forgotten earlier. About

Frank, and my new debt, and the *or else* portion of my imposed arrangement.

"Huh." Jon kissed the top of my head, his arms wrapped around me as I leaned back against him. "Wasn't it me who actually cut it off? Why isn't that crew after me?"

"Low-hanging fruit?" I shrugged, my shoulder coming closer to Jon's mouth, and he nipped at it. *Mmmmm.* "What could they threaten you with? Plus you have no real connection to Gus—unlike me, what with Sandor and the thing where Gus tried to kill me."

"True." Jon had found a softer spot, closer to my neck, and was kissing his way along it again. "I'll help." He found my earlobe, used his teeth a bit. I groaned and squirmed, but I couldn't escape with his arms hugging me in place. Did I have somewhere to be? His palms glided up until they found my breasts, his fingers ghosting over the nubs until they hardened up to meet him. Oh yeah, he was a giver all right. Then, going lower again until I needed more. We spun around, and then I was straddling him; sliding over and into and under until there was no more thought.

Chapter Eleven

I spaced out during Anshell's ceremonial introduction to the event. Nothing new there; the man sure did like to make a production of things. I entertained myself by practicing my micro-shifts. A form of meditation Anshell had taught me. Nails sharpening, then blunting, fur sprouting from the tops of my feet and then back again. Beauty and Beast in one Dana-sized package. I shook off the sand that had gotten in my hairs as they fell to my skin, ticklish scattering grains; a splatter of tiny dry crystals that twinkled in the moonlight.

Sam's lips twitched as he stood slightly behind Anshell and off to one side. Those eyes, watching me.

I wondered if he smelled Jon on my skin, even after I'd showered. What Sam would think of Owain. I thought maybe I wasn't ready to share that gaping, sucking chest wound just yet. Or, you know, at all really. Which was why I was here. The meet was optional; my need for a run was not.

Would Anshell ever stop talking? What was he even saying at this point? I tried to focus. Something about the upcoming Summer Solstice. Our responsibility as Pack members to contribute through our deeds to the community around us in a positive way. I wondered if that included the norms. I wondered when Anshell would be done.

Sam was shaking his head. At me? *Pfft.*

Finally the raising of the arms and the answering howls and growls around me. *Yes.*

"Run well, and may all your moons face at least seven ways."

An answering wave of animal noises as those who'd come out drifted towards the shadows to get their shift on. Where was Sam? His scent, cinnamon and cream and fur warmed by sunlight, was suddenly behind me. I turned to look over my shoulder, and my reward was the lazy answering smile that stretched wide across Sam's face, deepening the creases of skin at the outer edges of his eyes.

"Let's run," he said.

The breeze made windy as it rushed past my ears. Seagulls by the shore. I slunk past, tail twitching, my head down and my butt swaying high as I prepared to pounce. Another feline shot over and past me, scaring my prey into a flurry of feathers and sand displaced. *Sam.* Teasing me with a flick of his tail before circling back to touch noses when I didn't respond.

I looked up at the unnaturally bare trees, stripped by the cormorants flocking north, lured by the warmer temperatures and seasonal shifts. Without natural predators, the birds were breeding faster than the native environment could support and branches that should have been part of a lush super growth of June-in-Toronto green were instead these bleak grey spikes of delayed death.

But climate change wasn't real. *Right.*

There was white, and feathers, and the unguarded moment. Fish and brackish water and rust and sweet smoke hanging in the air that clung tacky against my skin, a contrast with the grains of sand rubbing at the softer bits between the pads of my paws. The rhythmic pounding from a drum circle across the water echoed its driving beat in my chest.

I spotted my prey and tracked it with whiskers that twitched in the breeze. My ears flicked forward and back, angling, a live satellite dish on a search and capture mission. A splash down the beach; stones displaced with an after-tow of water bunching and smoothing. *Hungry.* Yes, I hungered. Satisfaction was *there.* I wanted it.

The string, invisible, drawing me towards the potential. Craving. Satiety. I could have both. Closer. Almost...

I pounced, and the bird was in my mouth, its neck snapped, blood and feathers dribbling down my chin. My human self wanted to puke. But the me that was *me* in this moment sucked and chewed and swallowed. Whole again inside where nobody could see.

The water was cool on my tongue as it washed away the taste of bird and grit and feathers. My reflection startled; even after so many months it was only my expression, familiar in its dispassionate wariness, that I recognized. Too bad water alone wasn't enough to cleanse the palate of my human experiences.

I turned around again, quenched but not sated. Ready to share my spoils.

I was alone.

Here kitty kitty kitty.

Buzzing, followed by a popping as though the atmospheric pressure had dropped and I needed to be chewing gum. A whispering that stroked down my back and between my ears. My answering growl, raising the fur into a Mohawk peak along my spine, ending in a purr I could not control. The unguarded moment seized.

Exactly how many times was I going to be threatened in a single twenty-four-hour period?

And where was the Pack?

I couldn't hear anything over the buzzing in my head, the chirping roll from my throat. But there were other senses to access—sight, scent—and neither of those were telling me anything other than *you're on your own again, girl.*

Suddenly wishing I truly was.

The smell is what hit me first: flesh stripped and left to ripen in the sun, decaying fish carcasses, milk curdled and souring beyond fermentation and well into the inedible mold stage. And yet I felt that hand running fingers through my softness, blocking out the stench and honing in my attention on where he or she touched. The yowl of a cat in heat.

I burned.

Some infinitesimal part of my awareness beat its metaphorical fists against the inside of my head. Demanding my attention. This feeling, this need, was familiar in a way that did not automatically breed contempt. *Remember.* Something I had to remember. But what?

It had happened before.

This happened *then.*

Oh. Oh *shit.*

Alina.

Danyankeleh.

My father's voice in my ear, in my head, hanging on the wind.

Remember who you are. Where you are.

RUN.

I ran.

Not fast enough; I could feel the ooze against my skin of She-Whose-Name-Must-Not-Be-Uttered-Aloud, even as the single word echoed in my mind: *Alina.*

I knew enough now to be scared. Flight winning over fight. Had to get her touch away from me.

But how?

There was water, but no amount of residual humanity was convincing my cat self that liquid immersion was an appealing option. I could shift back, but I couldn't tell whether anyone was close enough to see. Not ready—*safe*—for me to come out of the *not-quite-as-normal-as-you-think* closet yet.

I realized the bird had been a way to Pied Piper me away from the safety of the group. Stalking my hunger, turning me from predator to prey. Would anyone in the Pack even notice me gone? I'd already proven beast brain was more driven by craving than by deductive, dispassionate logic.

This was my own stupidity, so it was up to me to get myself out of this too.

Mental breath. I made a conscious decision to empty my mind. Nothing and no one to interrupt the expansive fluffy goose-down comforter of white I wrapped around and up and along the walls of me. My core. Remembering I existed in this form but also as something else. Two legs, not four; words and not sounds.

Two as one under the slivering moon.

I could do this.

I dipped my paw in the water. Hissed at my own reflection, the chill that dripped beneath and between my pads; I snatched it back and started licking. Alina's laughter in my ear. Cats have hackles apparently, and mine were sticking straight up. Hey Dana, why don't you show the crazy lady who wants to skin human you just how much her presence is freaking you out? Yeah, that'd be super helpful.

Kitty kitty kitty. You have a secret to share.

I glanced over my shoulder. Alina had materialized a few feet back to stand between me and freedom. Theoretically at least—the beach was pretty big and there was only one of her. At least I hoped she was on her own. And what the hell kind of secret did she think I wanted to share with her? What, we were going to be hair-braiding buddies now? After she'd tortured me for information and left me lying pooled-river-of-blood-adjacent to die? Seriously?

She must have taken my silence as agreement, or at least an opportunity for her to keep going.

"Do you know who I am?" What, she didn't recognize me? I angled my head to one quizzical side, playing at a game whose rules I was still waiting to make sense of. Pretending she was the stranger she was not.

Alina invaded my personal space again, holding out the back of her hand. Touching my nose to her skin, I sniffed; an involuntary response. I fought against the urge to rub my head against her, marking my territory. *No.* Couldn't let that happen or she might realize my scent was familiar.

I waited. Tried not to flinch as she reached out

and scratched behind my ears, even though I couldn't control the growl vibrating in my throat. Alina was a demon, and powerful, but it was only the two of us here and I was a big cat with claws.

She backed away. But didn't go far.

Instead she reached into a pocket and pulled out a piece of something that smelled like salmon sashimi rolled in fresh milk and garnished in some kind of nip that made my head spin. Dancing and twirling, arms outstretched; a Dionysian band with Pan and flutes and pointy shoes with poufy dresses. I held my breath while music that couldn't be there even so pounded in my ears. Or maybe that was my heart. I was panting while standing still, weighted with that Sisyphean boulder at the bottom of a hill without end. Alina held out her hand with her offering hanging on the damp air, pulling against the remaining shards of my self-control to a place I still had to resist.

It was getting hard to remember why.

Human Dana was yelling, trying to get the cat brain to see, go back to the place where trust was bad. Alina was a demon. Alina the demon equaled pain. Equaled fear. Equaled *bad*.

The screams, the blood; the head of Ezra rolling to the ground at the replica of a facility I used to know. Human Dana remembered and wished she didn't. *No.* Human and feline, we were one. Feeding the other. Left brain and right brain integrated into a single whole.

Neither of them trusted the green-horned, dark-haired Alina.

"I would ask a favor," she said. Wait, what? Alina raised her hand and waved it through the air, slowly; as it passed, my skin hummed and a yowl—pure alley cat in heat—burst from my throat. No way to contain it. Losing the thread that suggested I shut up and play dumb. "I could take what I want from you." Musing. "But I want *you* to want it. To give it freely." She chuckled, rotating her hand; the pleasure I'd been feeling turned suddenly into the stabbing of a thousand needles everywhere and all at once. Yowling now, only this time with pain.

Alina dropped her hand and I crumpled along with it. Prostrate in the sand, no longer caring that I was belly-deep in water as long as its coolness meant relief.

"There is someone new in your midst," she said, watching me pant; a scientist observing the outcome of a specific set of applied criteria. Knowing what would happen yet conducting the test again and again because why not. "Dana Markovitz. She has a relationship with your Alpha. I want you to watch her, profile her, and report back. Understand that you will represent *my* interests in your world now, and you will tell me what I want to know. Or," her eyes holding mine in their infinite black abyss, "your pack will be slaughtered and I will kill you last after making you watch. Do we have a deal?"

Oh yeah. The Pack was totally going to stand behind me after this.

My paws were crossed under my chin, negating my promise, but I nodded. Sure, let's pretend to make a deal. We both knew this was a proposition I couldn't decline and walk away from.

She was there and then in a single blink she was not.

Wind rushed past my ears and echoed with the pounding of the drum circle again. I licked at my paws—a compulsion—and then at my hindquarters. Grooming the scent of Alina from my skin.

But I had a new piece of information: once I'd shifted, Alina couldn't tell it was me.

Chapter Twelve

The tree was still thick with green and yellow foliage. If you were to ask me what I was doing, rational me, I'd probably have said surveillance. I *was* watching the entire beach, taking in the partiers and the slackers, but that wasn't all I was looking for. Or how I found myself thirty feet from the ground. Or why I couldn't stop shaking.

The beating drums tapered off and campfires were tamped down. Distant sounds of metal on grease as cars started up, their headlights piercing the gloom as the evidence of their paths receded.

Relative silence was no better. Every twig that snapped and each splash of a fish or a bird hunting that fish had me tasting blood. My blood. I bit the side of my check, licked the pads of my paws and washed behind my ears. *Again.* Compulsion. Repetition. The cat in me at odds with the human.

So I stayed where I was.

More cars, more headlights. The pack was thinning, heading home to shower and get some sleep before work.

My tail twitched and cracked a branch as it thwacked. I jumped, not recognizing the sound as my own.

More darkness, even fewer cars. Had they forgotten about me?

Maybe it was for the best.

Forget I existed. Then maybe I would never fall under Alina's control again.

I heard the *clip clip cloppitty clip* of hooves as the hard edges met with soft sand, spraying water and displacing serenity in its wake. I smelled familiarity, and home, and I forced myself to look towards its source. Down. Beneath where I still hid.

Only shadow. But a shadow that got closer, claws cracking bark as it climbed. I backed away, deeper into the gloom, hoping it wouldn't find me. But it knew my scent—*he* knew my scent, in any form—and then he was there, on the branch beside me. Edging forward so I could see him, remember that I knew how he smelled. Tasted. He watched me, then blinked and looked away. I yawned. No threat here, nothing to see.

He came closer, making himself more vulnerable so I could feel less threatened. I could have swiped at his face with my claws.

My hackles released a bit as he edged in, nearer, just enough to reach over and touch noses.

He purred; I answered with one of my own. Bumping his head with mine. He licked my cheek and I rubbed it along the scruff of his neck.

Pinks and blues smudged at the far edge of the water, the light reflecting against the streaks of grey and black and brown in his coat. Different than I remembered. Still familiar.

He looked at me, at the tree trunk and then down. Repeated the sequence again, waiting for me to understand. I retreated a few steps and the branch I was on groaned. A warning growl, deep in his throat; an answering whinny from below. Also familiar and yet I could not lay name to it.

Trust. I remembered trust.

"Dana." Yes, I knew that voice. "Come down, girl."

I couldn't claim that name. Not safe. I growled warning; the other cat echoed my concerns.

"You're safe," the man down below was saying. Human? Was he human before? I edged further away, the tree limb I was on bending even more precariously under my weight. "No," he said. "Stop. That branch you're on will break if you go any further. Come down."

I whined. I did not want to see the scary *not*-cat again, have her figure out who I was when I wasn't *this*. The me who was me on two legs and not four paws.

And in that moment I remembered who I was. That the human on the ground could not climb up to me in his other form, and that he was Anshell. And of course the one with me in this tree was also known because he was Sam.

Sam angled his chin again, indicating the way I needed to go. Rubbed his head up against me; bumping at me, gentle, when I didn't immediately respond.

I wanted to feel the safety of their proximity. Getting closer, close enough to taste their scent. Both men waited until I was more them than me, wrapping their shared presence around my shoulders, willing myself to believe in that. No room for doubt, the flicker of it held a moment in my head and then like a candle released and snuffed.

I jumped. A moment later, Sam landed beside me. We touched noses, and he gave my forehead a couple of quick licks before padding off into the underbrush to shift back. I realized that I, too, could hide. There was a reason to run away, a reason to stay in this form and not the other. Safer somehow.

But it was getting lighter, and I was feeling skin—human flesh—pushing its way up and over my surfaces. My consciousness shifting as my external form did the same. Until I was on all fours, naked, watching the sun peek up over the bare-treed horizon.

Anshell was as naked as I was, and parts of him were at eye level; I had no choice but to see what was in front of me. I tried to pretend otherwise by looking down, along his muscular legs and down to his feet partially buried in the sand.

Anshell extended a hand to help pull me back up to standing. His smirk told me I'd hidden nothing and that me and books were in a wide-open kind of relationship. No, I really didn't do poker face well. Or, you know, at all.

Sam was there as I steadied myself on two bare feet. Both men waited for words I didn't yet have. Finally, Sam:

"What happened?"

It took me a couple of tries, a few more thick swallows to force those words past my throat. As though by shaping specific sounds the source of my panic would materialize, all-knowing; my cover blown and my Pack decimated.

"Alina," I said.

The Cherry Beach house was closest so that's where we went, in a caravan of vehicles hugging the last bits of shadow as dawn made its presence known. Parking in the pebbled public area stained with oil and littered with broken beer bottles and decomposing cigarette butts, hoping the early morning windsurfers had decided to sleep in just this once. It *was* mid-week so we might get lucky. I didn't want to have to explain three naked people streaking across the beach who vanished as soon as they got close to what appeared to be a decrepit lifeguard shack.

Sure, we all had extra clothes in our vehicles. Plus whatever we'd been wearing earlier. But the sun's rising warmth was licking at my post-shift nakedness, and my toes curled with an answering warmth somewhere more personal.

I lost my nerve at the last moment, reaching into the gym bag I kept on the floor behind me for a pair of clean boy-short underwear with matching cotton bra, deep magenta with black stretch lace trim, and my flip-flops. Also black. Getting the undergarments actually on was a challenge but hey—what female hasn't gotten dressed while pretending she isn't already naked before? I felt around in the bag again until I found that black cotton maxi-tank that doubled as a dress and pulled it on over my head.

Good thing I bothered. No windsurfers on the water yet, but there were a couple of kayakers pulling their crafts towards the shore. Two lifeguards were setting up at the station closest to us, but lucky for us it was Anika (a.k.a. Tattoo Vine Girl) and Murtaz. Turned out they were both university students, albeit at different schools. Anika was at the Ontario College of Art and Design, and Murtaz was studying to be a chef at George Brown. Lifeguarding this particular Toronto beachfront was lucrative—they got one paycheck from the City for

services rendered, and a second from Pack coffers for
security and surveillance.

Anshell's vehicle was there but I couldn't spot him,
which meant he'd probably already gone inside. Sam
hadn't though; I caught his scent before I spotted him
leaning against the railing, elbows on the weathered
wood as he pretended to watch the water. He wasn't
fooling me. Sam's eyelids narrowed as he scanned the
horizon, watching for any potential threats; making
sure we were all safe.

Even nearly naked, he was far from vulnerable.

I came up beside him and mirrored his position. Sam
passed me the coffee he was holding—an Americano
with almond milk and enough sweetener to know it was
there. *Yesss.* The world coming into clearer focus. I took
another couple of sips before passing it back.

"What happened earlier?"

I shook my head. Sam waited as I stared at the water,
willing my breath to calm in time with the rippling lines
smoothing and bunching, a lattice-patterned fabric of
brown and green.

He bumped against me, shoulder to shoulder. Flashed
me a grin. Like we were buddies. I knew he was trying
to snap me out of it, that dark place where my nightmares lived and I woke up sweating with my voice
hoarse. Forcing my scream through vocal cords dulled
by sleep. Waking myself. Shaking.

Sam knew because he'd been there, with me. He
couldn't see what I saw, but he'd helped me change the
sheets after I'd soaked them through.

He reached out and stroked the back of my hand with
gentle fingers, sending electric heat along the surface

of my arm to the tips of my ears. I shuddered; this time fear had nothing to do with it.

"I love that expression you get when I touch you," Sam whispered in my ear. His fingertips trailed higher, drifting across the underside of my wrist. All of my attention cradled in his palm as it hovered over my bare flesh. Moving energy. I wondered at his side job as a contractor; if he was like this with anyone but me, Sam had missed his calling in bodywork.

"Dana."

I jumped at the sound of Anshell's voice. Sam's hand was back on the railing again, so smooth it could have been there all along.

Anshell handed me a coffee of my own.

"Thanks," I said. Grateful. Was I so addicted that everyone in my life had figured out a caffeinated Dana was a coherent Dana?

As long as it meant I had coffee in the morning, did I care?

"Let's go inside," Anshell said. "You can tell us about last night away from any prying ears."

I nodded and followed him through the screened-in porch doors, up the winding staircase to the third-floor solarium, Sam flanking from behind. They weren't taking any chances with me this time.

Light filtered in through the skylight above, adding to the sunlight pouring in through the floor-to-ceiling windows wrapping around us. I was floating somewhere above my body, looking down, even as I knew intellectually I was anchored to the floor. Not quite real. I tripped on the edge of the area rug and spilled about a third of my coffee onto it, the heat splattering against my feet and thrusting my consciousness back to where it needed to be. *Whoops.* Good thing the overgrown forest pattern meant it wouldn't show. Much.

I put my mug down on the ring-stained oak table, knee level, sinking into the corner of the couch closest to it. Both Sam and Anshell chose the padded armchairs opposite me, their mugs following mine onto the table. Coffee for Sam, fresh-sprigged peppermint tea for Anshell.

The silence stretched as I tried to find the words. It was hard to recognize myself—the person who kicked ass and took only the prisoners I chose to take—paralyzed with the fear of memory proven real once more.

I'd been hiding this for months. Managing. I'd gotten better at pretending too; the reassuring lie so convincing I'd been just about able to think maybe what happened wasn't real. The bricks of blank in my memory helped.

But then she'd been there, and I remembered. If I could find the words.

"Alina," I finally said. "She was on the beach. By herself. She wasn't afraid—why would she be?—but she also didn't recognize me. Thought I was just some random big cat she'd managed to separate from the herd." I paused. The next words even more difficult. "She wanted me to spy on *me*. Threatened to wipe out the Pack if the cat she thought I was didn't find out the connection between Anshell and the newcomer. You know, me. It means someone else in the Pack—or more than one someone—will betray us." I amended that. "No, not us. *Me*."

Sam started pacing; if I squinted hard enough, I could almost see the agitated twitching of his phantom tail.

"It's not a done deal," said Anshell. Did anything

surprise him? "We don't know that she approached any-one else for certain. Nobody has spoken of it with me."

"And your Pack mates tell you everything?" I touched Sam's wrist with two fingers as he stalked past me for the fifth time. "Sam, please. You're mak-ing me dizzy."

"Sorry," he said, leaning his sweatpants-clad ass against the arm of the far side of the sofa. Coiled ten-sion, strategically placed. If someone came up those stairs with harmful intent, Sam could be in front of me or Anshell in seconds. Not that we couldn't defend our-selves. Or that there was any danger to be had in this split-second moment.

Still. He cared.

"I would expect to be apprised if a threat of this magnitude was leveled against us, yes," Anshell said. "But what of your other most recent adventures? Alina was not your first threat of the last twenty-four hours, or even the second."

"Those don't impact the Pack," I said, considering. "I think."

"And what of the siege on the Swan?"

"When we were attacked by… I want to say frost tribbles, although now I'm not positive. It was kind of like a few months ago, with the frost and the ice, but not quite. I couldn't tell for sure whether the bar was the target or whether I was, but it seemed like maybe they wanted me?" I described how the frozen bricklets had sprouted arms and legs before hurling themselves at me. Plus the screaming when Sandor smashed them. "Even that was weird. Like they weren't trying to end me so much as wall me in with their frosty brick selves. Celandra smelled Alina behind it."

"So our theory of the attack being a test makes sense," Sam said.

"Of what? My patience?"

"Of the Swan's defenses," Anshell said. "If one were planning a more extensive offensive, perhaps one might consider it prudent to assess the target's vulnerabilities in advance."

"They did plenty of damage already," I said. Not wanting to validate the uncomfortable hypothesis. But it could be true, and begged the question: why *had* Sandor's wards failed? He'd splurged on the gold standard security package this time. Nothing was perfect, but those chilled tribblets should not have been able to get past the front entranceway with their murderous plans. After all, the new system included a scan for intent.

Which meant slaughter hadn't been the goal—this time. Either that, or any intent happened outside the boundaries of the Swan itself, and the frost hadn't been as independently sentient as we'd been assuming.

"I have to tell Sandor," I said, reaching for my phone.

"Wait," Sam said. "Did anything else unusual happen today?"

"Let me see. Well, my ex showed up and offered me a job."

That got their attention.

"Explain," said Anshell.

"Seems the Agency wants to hire me for some kind of freelance gig. I haven't read the offer yet." My turn to jump up and start pacing. "I left for a reason. Also they don't know I'm a shifter now. Have I mentioned the part where they don't like supes and have a tendency to experiment on them using tests said supes tend not to recover from? So I'm thinking no."

"You said it was your ex who approached you with the offer?" Sure, trust Sam to touch on the competition angle. "Is that normal?"

"I have no idea. It's been years." Anshell touched my arm and I stilled again, sinking back down into the couch and grabbing my mug. "I don't want to talk about that. My ex, I mean."

Anshell nodded, willing to drop the subject—for now. I suspected Sam wouldn't let me off the hook as easily when he got me alone.

"Anything else we should know about?" Anshell kept his voice level; let's not spook the skittish cat. "You mentioned three things that happened. There was the attack on the Swan, the reappearance of your former lover along with a job offer from your similarly former employer, and what else?"

"Oh, you mean the surreal conversation I had with that giant octopus creature who grabbed Sandor yesterday and who we also chopped a limb from? That guy? Yeah, so this time he caged *me* in my truck with its tentacles. On dry land. While sitting on the hood of my truck with his head upside-down. Does that count?"

"Yesterday?" Anshell gave me the look. You know, the one that said *why didn't you tell me this earlier when we saw each other.* Sam looked like he wanted to dive out the window with something sharp and do some defensive attacking. "What did it want?"

Was I wrong to expect more of a response from Anshell?

"Apparently it *had* wanted to offer me a freelance gig where I'd catch Gus for them and they'd pay me for my efforts. Of course, that was before we chopped off one of his limbs. Now, apparently, I owe him a debt—even though the damned thing will regenerate in a few weeks on its own—and I'm supposed to do Gus for free."

"Popular guy." Sam started stalking an invisible dust mote around the room again. "Why is the debt on you though? Wasn't it Jon who actually severed it?"

"Probably because I was there, and putting the debt on me means you guys and Jon will help me discharge it by bringing in the big blue bastard."

"And nobody has told you *why* they want Gustav?" Anshell's voice was surprisingly level for someone who'd just found out his Pack might be on the hook for another thank-you-Dana mission.

I shook my head.

"And if you ignore the request?" Sam's question was a valid one. "What are they going to do?"

"An eye for an eye, a limb for a limb," I replied.

Chapter Thirteen

Sam followed me home. He took his own vehicle, pulling in two spots over from me at the side of the building. Too early for anyone to be in the main floor offices yet, too late to avoid the lineup of cabs that wrapped their serpentine tails of exhaust fumes around the pavement-kissed tires. Engines idling as they waited their turn at a fossil-fueled gas pump, one of the cheapest in the area.

Sam got out first and came over to join me. Scanning. "It's too busy here." He shoved his hands into the front pockets of the jeans he'd changed into. "Are you sure you don't want to stay with me at the house?"

I shook my head.

"We don't know who Alina got to," I said. "I don't want to chance it until we do."

"You're not wrong," Sam said, crossing his arms over his chest. Leaning one shoulder against the side of my truck bed, casual, but I didn't believe it. "Let me go make sure your place is safe."

"My safety. *That's* why you want to come up." I flashed him a half grin over my shoulder as I held the door open. The *locked* door that never seemed to stay that way for long with all the bike couriers, residents and commercial space workers that passed through.

Teasing aside, I knew my building's security sucked. But I appreciated the *don't-ask-don't-tell* attitude of my neighbors, and my landlord being of the slum variety didn't hurt when it came to staying out of my business.

Easier that way.

At least one of the bonuses of my recent transformation: Sam wasn't the only one able to move silently down a hallway of creaky wooden floors anymore, never mind avoid the saggy bits without looking. Should I be surprised the building hadn't been condemned yet? The fact that it was still standing gave me hope it wasn't as structurally unsound as it felt.

Yeah, I should really look at moving again.

Caught a whiff of something other than the familiar mildewing carpet as we neared the sliding barn door that separated what was mine from what belonged to everyone else. A quick glance at Sam confirmed he'd smelled it too.

Plus the door was open, which was definitely *not* how I'd left it.

Too many threads to pick out that one I recognized, tickling my nose with clover and shells and hoary dew.

Instead I stepped inside with Sam a breath behind me.

"What are you doing here?"

A knife, blade glittering with aquamarine frost, cerulean diamonds in the hilt, embedded itself in the wooden beam beside my ear. Close enough that I felt the wind tickle.

A blur of man-beast as Sam streaked past me to grab the blue-skinned, diamond-twinkling threat by the throat, one-handed and up against the far wall. Too fast for the demon to go for any other weapons of up-close destruction.

"Just getting...her...attention." Demon Blue, a.k.a. Gus, was gasping under Sam's grip; I'd known Sam was strong but *damn.* He'd clearly earned his place as Anshell's second.

"How's that working out for you?" I stood a few feet back so the assassin could see me, even though Gus's eyes were daggers at my question. "Sam, let him down. Can't find out what he wants if he's dead." I thought about it a moment. "We can't, right?"

"Jury's out," said Sam, lowering his arm and loosening his grip on Gus's throat. Not completely, but enough for the blue demon to do that breathing thing again.

"Listen, girlie," Gus said, reaching up to rub his throat; changing his mind at the look Sam gave him. At least I think that's what it was since I couldn't see Sam's face. "We've shared this dance before. If I wanted you dead, you'd already be dead."

"So what do you call this?" I pulled his blade from my wall and held it up where he could see it.

"Conversation," he said.

"Translate then," I replied. "Or, better still, try calling first. Texting? Email? You can even tweet it. But throwing a knife at my head?" Gus opened his mouth to correct me. "Fine, *beside* my head? Not cool."

Gus angled his head to one side, measuring. Was I really worth the trouble?

Did I care?

"Tell me what you want or get out," I said, crossing the floor to slide my door closed. Whatever was going on, I didn't need my neighbors deciding to get involved.

Sam yanked the scruff of Gus's Hawaiian shirt, using

the bunched fabric to maneuver the demon into one of
the two chairs opposite my couch, where I was now sitting. Sam sank into the other chair. A strategic choice—
this way he could watch both of us, while being able
to reach Gus if conversation came suddenly off our
shared To Do list.

"We're conversing," I said. "What are you doing
here?"

"Testing the theory that what you've lost will always
be in the last place you look." Gus chuckled. "Did you
see what I did there?"

"Idiot." I was muttering but given the look both
males flashed me, I guess I could have been more under
my breath about it. Then, louder: "What do you want?"

Gus sank back into the chair, his shoulders slumping
and his third eye—the one above the bridge of his nose
and a little to the left—fluttered and rolled. Adolescent
defiance paired with adult maturity-level resignation.

Sam and I shared a look. Gus *really* didn't want to
be here. So why was he?

"My brother," Gus said. "The tables have flipped,
yes? I'm being hunted now?"

By a giant cephalopod that can render pickup trucks
useless, an octopod squid named D'Lee and who knows
how many others? Karma coming around to tentacle
his blue ass?

"Yeah," I said. "Still waiting on why you're *here*
though."

"You're gonna help me," Gus said.

I started laughing. Tears streaming down my face.
Too bad I was the only one in the room who got the joke.

"No. I'm not." Swiping at the tears with the back of
my hand. The irony sitting around my coffee table was

a spiced cinnamon candy on my tongue that burned. "Go fuck yourself."

"Sandor told me to come here." Gus ignored my insult. "Yours is literally the last place anyone would look for me."

"There's a reason for that," I muttered. Then, louder: "So what?" I leaned forward, met his gaze. Scary, ice-cold; my spine stiffened and I felt my fingertips tingle with claws shifting under the skin. I grabbed a throw pillow, turquoise with threads of pinks and orange, and wrapped my arms around it, hiding my anxiety spike with restless motion. *No.* We were two to one in here.

Still, I may have snagged one of those bright strands by accident.

"You break into this woman's home," said Sam, leaning forward to break Gustav's fixation on scaring the crap out of me. "A woman you were trying to kill quite persistently until recently. You tell her you're here because you're being hunted and you're, what, surprised she's disinclined to help you?"

"No," said Gus, the moment broken. "But she's still going to do some things for me."

"Oh? Why's that?" Smart-ass Dana was back, or at least pretending to be. It helped that Sam was there.

"Because," Gus said, turning his head so I could see the fathomless certainty of his stare; alien, in that moment, from anything I'd seen before. "Me owing you a favor is worth it."

I stared him down. My heart may have been pounding but fuck it—this fear of everything, of him, was making me crazy. Maybe I was chicken or egging it. Crazy therefore fear. Did it change my irritation at yet another somebody trying to push me around?

"No guarantee you'll stay alive long enough for me to collect," I said.

"Odds are better if you help me," Gus countered. "Even more so if pretty boy here gets that Pack of his behind it."

"Pack sanctuary?" Sam shook his head, arms crossing over that chest I had a distracting urge to touch. And taste. And this was *so* not the time. "Why would we give you that?"

"I could pay," said Gus, opening his six-fingered hands and scattering a glitter of azure diamonds across my table. "Enough here to buy weapons, pay some property taxes," swiveling to look around my space, "get yourself out of this shit hole and into someplace less shitty."

"Hey," I said. "Not a shit hole."

"I'll take your offer to my Alpha," Sam said at the same time.

I stared at him. Gus chuckled at my surprise.

"What, girlie, you thought you were special? There's the kind of loyalty that comes from blood, like my brother, and then there's everything else. Everyone can be bought. Even your precious Pack."

"Sam?"

"It's Anshell's call," he said. Not a straight answer, not meeting my eyes. Oh this was just great. What happened to loyalty for each and every one of us? "We'll be in touch with our answer."

"How do you plan to do that?" I wasn't letting this go. "More importantly, *where* do you plan to do it?"

Gus watched me. None of his eyes blinked. Mine started to water, trying to outstare him and failing. I brushed the moisture away with the back of my hand. Annoyed.

"No," I said. "You're not staying here."

"Then where?" Gus spread his hands again, scattering more diamonds onto the table.

"Not my problem," I said. "And put those toys back in the Cracker Jack box they came out of."

Gus narrowed his eyes. Yeah, that's right. You go right on serving your bullshit. I'm on a crap-free reality diet right now, thanks.

"Consider it payback for Sandor covering your ass since you showed up in his bar looking for a job. Helping me would be a drop in the very deep bucket of things you owe him." Gus smiled; he thought he had me. But my debt was to Sandor, not his brother, and it's not like Sandor was calling in his chits.

"Don't owe you anything," I said. "Sandor wants a favor? He can ask me himself."

"Dana." My phone was vibrating. Call display said *The Dude*. Sam used two fingers to nudge it towards me without taking his eyes from Gus for more than a second. "Maybe you should answer."

I glared at him. Long enough for the call to go to voicemail before it started buzzing against the hard wood surface again. *The Dude*. Stopping, restarting. *Fine*. Third time was apparently the charm I needed to push me past my situational passive-aggressiveness.

"Please don't be calling for the reason I think you're calling," I said, skipping the *hi-how-are-you* formalities.

There was a hum on the other end of the line as Sandor hesitated. But he'd called for a reason, and it was important—to him.

"I need your help," he said. "You've got to hide my

brother until I can either get him to safety or get that price off his head."

I grabbed the phone and went out into the hallway. Not much more private, but I needed that illusion right now.

"He tried to kill me." My voice low. "More than once. Sandor, I can't."

"Dana, he'll behave." I'd never heard that pleading tone from Sandor before. His voice was usually so chest-rumbling deep, it was weird to hear the plaintive rise on the word *behave*.

"You don't know that." There's no way he could, right?

"I'll talk to him," Sandor said. "He'll behave."

"Uh huh," I replied, walking back into my apartment. Neither Sam nor Gus had moved. They'd probably heard it all. Oh well. I handed the phone to Gus. "It's for you."

"Yeah," he said, flashing me a pointy-tooth victory smirk before turning away to focus on something Sandor was saying at the other end. "But—" Sandor's voice getting louder. "I was just—" Shoulders slumping, ingesting the words being hurled by his older brother. "OK, OK. Fine." Eyes down as he passed the phone back to me. "Your turn," he muttered.

I shared a look with Sam as I took my phone back. Still irritated, but it's not like we were married. Or even exclusive. Sam owed me nothing.

"Dana?" Sandor had been talking; I'd missed all of it.

"Sorry, Sand. Could you possibly repeat that?"

"Gustav won't try to kill you. Even if the deal is lucrative. He's going to behave on the understanding that he's under your protection."

I snorted. "*My* protection? Who are we kidding here?"

"You find a way to keep him safe," Sandor said, "and your debt to me is done."

Apparently with or without Pack protection, an over-sized Dana-themed apartment-sitting party package would also work. Anshell's cooperation with any such plan was still to be determined.

Until then?

The big blue demon was staying with me.

Fan*freaking*tastic.

Chapter Fourteen

"What the hell am I supposed to do with you?"

I stared at the blue-skinned, three-eyed assassin that spread nearly worthless cerulean diamonds in his wake to deflect threats, and would kill anyone if the price was right. His only allegiances, as far as I could tell, were to making bank (however the dimension he found himself in defined it) and to his brother, who was also my boss.

Yes, I owed Sandor my life many times over. At least the way he tells it. I was kind of oblivious at the time, sure, but apparently lack of awareness of an event in no way diminishes one's debt resulting from it. Sandor had never drawn a tit for tat line between everything he'd done and why I had a responsibility to help. But come on—I'm Jewish. I speak fluent guilt, with a practical working knowledge of both undertone and inference.

Bottom line: until we figured out who the cephalopod crew was representing, and how to get the bounty on Gus released, I was going to have a big blue shadow.

"I'll take the couch," Gus said by way of response. Because the sun was up now and who wouldn't be thinking about sleeping arrangements? "Better view of the door. Your building security sucks."

No kidding. If there was any kind of useful barrier

to entry, Gus might actually have been prevented from entering.

"See you in a few hours," I said instead, heading to my bedroom area. "Don't make me regret this more than I already do."

"Don't tell anyone I'm here and you won't."

The alarm on my phone went off at 2:45 PM. Had to be at work for 4:30 so there was just enough time for a quick set of pre-shower stretches, sit-ups, push-ups, squats and a Sun Salutation before I headed out.

Demon Blue was still sleeping. I kept my footsteps as silent as possible, his snoring shifting to a snort as I passed by. Paused to watch this beast who was an ally—however temporarily—but could just as easily flip to foe. The eyeball above his brows was sunken into his skull, the folds of flesh around it bunched into shadows lined with yet more shadows, and the skin glowed with a scarab-blue-freckled iridescence.

I probably shouldn't have kicked Sam out. But I was irritated on principle: my sort-of boyfriend not backing me up was *so* not cool.

Ignored that little voice whispering in my head. The one that pointed out Sam owed his allegiance and loyalty to Anshell, not me. That their bond pre-dated ours by a lot. That they were actually brothers-in-law from the time Sam spent married to Anshell's sister. Before she died.

Yeah. So maybe I wasn't being reasonable.

Still, I felt the way I felt. And we owed each other nothing I guess. My bed was my own, and the demon dangling his six-toed feet over the arm of my couch was mine to deal with as well.

Did I want to change the dynamic between Sam and me? The thought of exclusivity twisted hard in my chest, and my stomach clenched into a white-knuckled fist.

Yeah. Maybe status quo would be fine for a while longer.

It was weird showering, knowing Gus was there, but I had to trust that I was safe. Or at least safe enough. He could have killed me in my sleep, maybe, and hadn't.

I poked my head out of the bathroom. Fully covered in towel, or at least the pertinent bits.

"You staying here at my place the whole time? Or will your escort services extend to my shift at the Swan?"

Gustav's top eye opened while the other two stayed shut, sweeping across my mostly exposed bits from the top of my ears to somewhere around my knees. Clinical. Not sure whether he did human, or female, but I didn't appear to be getting any kind of rise from him. Did this species *have* sex organs? Genders? Too many questions suddenly.

He closed his eye again.

"Staying here," he grunted. "Safer. Less expected."

I nodded, then realized he couldn't see it. "OK," I said aloud as I retreated into my room to get dressed for work.

How did my life get so weird again?

Maybe "normal" was a delusion, an impossibility too many strive for and fail. Maybe this thing we call *normal* doesn't actually exist.

"Coffee," I said, staring at the Swan Song's coffeemaker and willing it to get itself ready without my assistance.

Sadly voice activation wasn't one of the machine's standard features, nor was it yet one of my superpowers.

So instead I cleaned and waited for the brew that is true to pour through.

Eight PM was late for me and coffee, even at work. But I'd been here a few hours, and I hadn't exactly slept well what with an assassin who'd tried to kill me crashing on my couch, and finding out that Alina was trying to convince members of the Pack to turn on me.

Maybe I'd take my caffeine with a shot of something. Bailey's? Pretty sure I still had a bottle in the fridge somewhere below and...*yes*.

"I'll have what you're having." That Irish brogue. *Again*. He thought his smile was charming but I sure as hell wasn't going to validate that ego for him.

"What do you want, Owain?" I poured him a coffee, added a shot of the creamy whisky liqueur. "I told you I'd think about your offer. It's only been twenty-four hours."

"Can't a lad share a pint," he took a sip, grimaced at the taste, "with an old friend?"

"We're not friends." Rolling the sweetness around my mouth, my tongue curling at the bitter offset of the charred liquid caffeine.

"Stop holding the past against me," he said, dropping the expected charm for something else. Something real?

No.

"Give me a fucking break," I said. "You left. Now you're back—and I know the back part has nothing to do with me. Us." I lowered my voice. My tone had the six-eyeballed Glo-var podlet, with her shiny mauve skull and eyes like blooming tulips attached to waving pink stems, craning her corn-husk-shaped ears to hear more. I shifted the angle of my body to block our conversation. Maybe I *was* a cat sometimes. Didn't mean I wanted anyone to suffer for that curiosity.

"Really? It's like that?" Owain actually feigned surprise. I knew better. You don't spend so many years shooting up the ranks of the Agency as an idiot. Even an idiot savant, which Owain definitely was not. Nope. He was just your normal, crème de la crap variety. Although not an idiot—fair is fair. No, he was the man who chose to leave. Leave *me*.

So yeah. It *was* like that.

Making his tracking me down with an Agency offer that much more curious.

"What do you want, Owain?" I couldn't even look at him, wiping at the already spotless bar counter surface, firm underneath hands that would otherwise belie my bravado with their tremors.

He didn't respond; instead he nudged his coffee cup to the side, a few inches to the left, and started drawing circles in the moisture with his index and forefinger. At least that's what it looked like from here. Something he used to do. Like doodles, only with water and hands.

"You happy here?" Owain looked up at me, stilling his finger sworls by wrapping his hands around his mug. "You did all that school, training, for what? So you could become Bartender of the Year in a mixed-species dive bar down by the docks? I don't get it."

"What's to get?" I stopped cleaning, clenching the edge of the curved surface, white-knuckled. "It's not forever."

"I've read the terms. It's a good offer from the Cinegon," Owain said. That would be the elite leadership team of the Agency's Ottawa office. "Good enough to get you out of this shit hole and back on the path you're supposed to be on."

"Oh?" My laugh, brittle, broke off a bit at the end. "What the hell do you know about my destiny? I'm not that sweet little innocent Dana you used to know. Shit changes."

"I can see that," he replied, holding my stare without flinching. "But so do people." He reached out to touch my hand and I jumped back. Out of his accessible range. "What, you can change and I can't?"

"Why would you?" I struggled to keep my voice from shaking. Still angry. "What would you get out of it?"

"You?" He glanced at me as I glared back, then looked away again. "Your forgiveness?"

"Bullshit," I said. "After all this time, you come back with an offer from your boss to get me to do a job—and all you really want from me is to pat you on the head and say *there there*, I forgive you, I trust you, everything will be rainbow-farting unicorns? Seriously? How stupid do you think I am?"

"You're not," Owain said. "Stupid."

"Gee, thanks for the validation," I said. "But I don't need your approval."

"Clearly," he said. No trace of flirt on now.

"Let me guess," I said. "Our past *connection* is a flag in both of our files. Someone Agency-side thinks I've got something they need to make a mission all it can be. But why would I help them out? Can't just ask. Hmm." I tapped my lower lip with my index finger, pretending I didn't know what I was going to say next. "Maybe sweeten it with a former lover. Things ended *abruptly* there, right? Maybe go, do a bit of give and get on the closure, see if you can ride all those untapped emotions with a deal and seal?" Owain didn't respond, looking down at his hands. "Yeah. Not much to say to that eh?"

"I'm sorry," he said. Then looked up again. Blue eyes cool, ice chips floating in a frozen martini. "That's what you want to hear, right?"

"Fuck you," I said. "And the horse you rode in on."

"That horse, I'll have you know, has an engine with power your truck can maybe glimpse at in a late-night pizza dream. And," he continued, "I paid for it in cash."

"Should I be impressed?"

"Hate me all you want," Owain said, "but this job will make you good bank. Don't throw the opportunity away because you're pissed at something I did when we were basically kids. Be smart."

"Like you?" Yeah, that wound wasn't close to the surface at all. Nope.

Owain leaned back, watching me. Evaluating. Then:

"You haven't made a decision about the offer yet," he said. I shook my head. "Because of me?"

"Not everything has to do with you."

"Then what?" Owain paused, looking up and to the left of me, calculating the variables. "*Not* me. But someone, or something." I stared at him, my lips pressed together without words. "You're not going to tell me."

"Been busy with the shit that's my life." I bent down to pull clean glasses out of the steaming dishwasher, the sanitize cycle done and cooling. Something to do. Easier than admitting the thought of working with the Agency had woken me up in a cold sweat three times last night. Even now, my stomach was churning at the reminder. Of who I'd been. Of who I didn't want to be again. Besides, it's not like I was about to tell Owain what was keeping me so busy these days. Or who. Last I checked, my potential re-employers weren't big on treating everyone with the kind of inter-dimensional equality for all approach we practiced at the Swan Song.

"What'll you have to drink?" Changing the subject. "I know how much you hate Bailey's."

This time Owain's smile was genuine.

"A pint," he said. "Something dark and sweet. Local. Surprise me."

I thought about what we had on tap. *Yeah.* Poured him a full pint draft of *Mississauga Gravelings.* A local stout made from chocolate, black tea, cherries, clover, apple peels, and a solid base of native burial grounds surface dirt stored in oak barrels. The distributor had thrown in a few cases of those green glow-in-the-dark plastic skeleton fingers to hook over the pint glass rim. Because that's what people want to think about while drinking—severed fingers. Then again, given our clientele, maybe it wasn't such a misguided marketing ploy.

Owain stared at the finger, then at me. Unhooked the digit and licked it clean, tongue around and along the side, pulling it out again with a tight suctioning *pop.* I couldn't look away. Until he rolled it around between his thumb and forefinger, raising the pointed nail to the side of his nose, and scratched.

I snorted and returned to filling the drink orders piling up, while he settled back into his seat, grin twitching. Yeah. Got me there.

Janey's most recent drink order had drained us of the last bottle of domestic vodka. Mixed with Smarnog lashes, cinnamon, fenugreek leaves, orange neon ear jelly squirts and a couple of shots of blue Curaçao, I couldn't afford to go dry on it.

Even better, here was my excuse to get away from Owain. Years of nothing then, what, I see him twice in as many days? There had to be something else going on.

I glanced over at his silhouette from the shadows of the Employees Only area. Still familiar, time distancing itself from circling the clogged drain of my memories. That way lay darkness and a remembered pain in my chest as his absence squeezed out my ability to breathe.

That was then. In the now I was doing better. Playing well with others, more or less, and I was even having relationships. OK, plural and OK, concurrent. Your point being?

What was Owain really doing here?

And why was the Agency so interested in me that they'd sent one of their more senior operatives as the lure?

Chapter Fifteen

"Dana." Sandor's basso echoed along the hallway, the exit sign's red light the only illumination other than the incandescent blue-white glow from his office. I hovered in the doorway, unwilling to explore Sandor's new language-of-guilt side further. Still, boss. I bit my lip and pushed myself past the threshold.

"What's up?"

Sandor studied me, standing there, and the outer edge of his left eyelid twitched. That was new. Then again I was feeling kind of twitchy myself. He was fiddling with his lower lip, pulling it out and down between thumb and forefinger, careful not to knock himself with those thick orange claws. His inner lip was paler, although still more orange than I'd ever seen it, and dotted with flecks of purplish Forget-Me-Not blue.

Sandor's transformation from Gustav's blue to this kind of toad-like green—I didn't know such a thing was possible. This was coming from someone who could sprout whiskers and claws though; surrealism could be relative.

"Thanks for hiding my brother," he said, abrupt, releasing his lip right before shaping the words and pushing them through. "It's not too bad, right? I know he can be a dick."

"He hasn't tried to kill me yet," I said, "so it could be worse."

Sandor started fiddling with his lip yet again, worrying at a non-existent flake of loose skin, before he noticed me noticing. He stopped, then made a show of rummaging in the top drawer of his desk. "I know I've got toothpicks in here somewhere," he muttered.

"Sandor," I said. "It's alright." He looked up at me. "OK, maybe it's not great. But I'm doing it. For *you*." I left out the part about who owed what to whom. Sandor nodded. "Did you find out anything more about who's after him?"

"There's this clan, west coast fuckers," he said. "Islanders. I spent some time out there years back—they grow some of the best psilocybin crops. 'Shrooms," he clarified, to my blank stare. "They also run these Ayahuasca camps out in the bush." Sandor paused. "Is it the bush if it's not around here and we're talking mountain-adjacent?" I shrugged. "Whatever. Anyway, I've been hearing rumblings that maybe they've got their twigs in this. Not sure why though."

"Are the octopod things that keep hassling us from that clan?"

Sandor shook his head. "Nah," he said. "These guys are more leafy/branchy. Big teeth. Think dryads, like those ones you read about in your sanitized-for-human-consumption fairy tales. Only smaller. More shrubby than towering hundreds-of-years-old-protected-by-granola-munchers oak."

"What did Gus do to piss them off?"

Sandor shrugged.

"So," I said. "'Shrooms, huh?"

Sandor shrugged, his smile sheepish. "What can I say? It was the '70's."

I narrowed my eyes, realizing in that moment I had no clue how old my boss was. I'd always assumed a few years older than my thirty-something, but I had no idea. Did his type age like humans? How long would they live—like us, or longer? Shorter? Was it rude to ask? Ugh. Probably.

"I'm guessing you already tried getting Brother Blue Dearest to share and got nowhere, right?"

"Useful exercise, that." Why would Gus help us help him with actual information? That would make things too easy. "So who are you avoiding?"

My turn to shrug.

"Girl, it's prime evening bar tab tip time out there, the happiest time of the night—your words, not mine."

"An ex." Voice clipped to strip out the emotions I didn't want to face in the mirror. "*That* ex."

Sandor grunted, sympathy crinkling his nose and the skin around his bottom two eyes. "He here to get you back?"

"Nah," I said, crossing the room to settle into one of the hot pink pleather armchairs. The silver duct tape covering that rip under my right elbow. Damage from a knife fight, or did the chair come that way as part of its second life? Dumpster Diving Special was my guess. "He offered me a job."

"Come again?" Sandor leaned forward. "What kind of job?"

"Agency."

All three of Sandor's eyes narrowed. "Agency," he repeated. "*That* Agency?"

I nodded. "They made the starting number lucrative enough to get my attention," I said. "Sending it with Owain, given our history, was their way of underlining it with a thick red marker."

"Blood like, as it were," commented Sandor. "You telling me I should start looking for a replacement smart ass to serve my drinks here?"

"Nah," I said. "I don't know. Owain says the terms are good, and I could use the cash, but I can't get the details until I agree. I'm not angling for a raise, by the way," as Sandor opened his mouth to protest, "although I wouldn't complain if you found your way to throw a monetary increase in my direction. I'm just not sure I want to be owned by the Agency again."

"Not sure?" Sandor snorted. "You like your freedom."

"No kidding." A grin to soften my words. Then: "I'm not sure I trust myself to go back. Also, why me? I'm hardly the only operative to quit. Easy enough to find someone hungry to get back on that payroll to do whatever dirty work they need doing."

"And the guy? Opportunity to work with him doesn't sweeten the deal?"

"I don't know," I said. Honesty because I had no choice. "It feels like someone wants me looking in one direction, at Owain, so I don't look somewhere else—maybe at the reasons for this sudden gig, or why I shouldn't get sucked back into that life."

"Plus," Sandor said. "Three guys might be too much even for you. Especially if one of them is the one who got away."

"Yeah, well, I can't see Jon caring."

"And the other guy? Your big cat?" Sandor raised an

eyebrow. *Just* one. Impressive. "He doesn't strike me as someone who likes to share."

"You're not wrong," I admitted. "But he's OK with Jon." Sandor raised a second eyebrow. "*Ish.* Besides, Owain only just showed up. It's not like anything's going on."

"Yet."

I stuck my tongue out at Sandor. Realizing after it was out that maybe giving my demon boss the raspberry wasn't the most respectful of acts. Whoops.

Fortunately, Sandor seemed to have rediscovered his sense of humor.

We both heard footsteps in the hallway, followed by a head of dreadlocks hovering in the doorway. *Janey.*

"Girl, you planning to come back and tend bar sometime soon? They be getting restless out there. And that fine drink of Irish ain't making to leave as long as you're back here." She gave me a smile she probably meant as encouraging, but the sour downturn of her mouth hiding her teeth suggested something else. Something meaner.

Sandor narrowed his eyes at her. He saw it too.

"Sorry," I said, hoping to redirect any rebuke from the boss—who, granted, could be a bit of a pushover with his female staff members. Fortunately, it worked. Sandor shut his mouth again and waited.

"So you're coming?" Janey wasn't letting me off the hook.

"Yeah." I glanced over at Sandor as I pushed myself up from the chair. "Later."

"Who's the guy anyway?"

I was surprised Janey cared. Maybe she was bored. "My ex."

"Which one?" Janey raised her hands in surrender at my glare. "Fine, fine. But seriously girl, ain't you already got two? What'chu need with a third?"

Fuck it. Janey already had a picture of me in her head, with all the preconceptions and assumptions that went with it.

I stopped her with the hand not holding the jug of vodka, palm to forearm, until she was looking straight at me. "Variety," I said with a grin that said naughty could beat nice any day.

That got a real smile from Janey. Finally. I was still echoing it right up to the point where I slid back behind the bar.

"Missed you," Owain said. His smile, that look—it was hard to breathe. Like a smoker who'd gone without for the magical three-day grace period and now wanted that glowing cancer stick in hand, its orange ember burning as harsh smoke was inhaled into lungs that craved it and more. Physically, emotionally, I couldn't go there again. And yet…

"Sure you did." I knew his words were bullshit and yet I allowed myself to be fooled by the veracity I wanted to find there.

"When do you get off?"

"Is that an offer?" The words smirking out before I had a chance to slam down my protective filter again. *Damn.* Hello old habits. Bad habits. *Remember why he's here and who sent him.*

"Wicked lass," Owain said, flashing me a grin. "Work."

"Work. Right." I couldn't help myself. "Soon. A couple of hours. Why?"

"There's a late gallery opening for a friend," he said. "Be my plus one?"

"You do art now?" That was new.

"I do all kinds of things now," Owain replied with a wink. "Don't worry, I won't bite. Unless you ask nicely."

I shook my head, trying not to laugh. Even though we were sliding back into old rhythms, and I couldn't stop it. Dangerous times indeed. Still…

"Fine," I said before I had time to think about it. Because fire was super pretty. And maybe I wouldn't get burned by it this time.

Chapter Sixteen

The gallery was in the middle of the city. Just west of
Chinatown, Kensington Market was a historic hub for
waves of immigrants who settled here before moving
out to the relative affluence of the suburbs. It was where
my mother's mother's family had grown up. Even now,
if you stripped back the layers of signage replaced by
Spanish and Portuguese and Arabic and Vietnamese,
you'd be able to see the Yiddish underneath.

But it was more than a haven for first generation en-
trepreneurs. It was also home to a community of artists,
buskers, junkies, skateboarders, students, stoners, poets,
writers, musicians and more, sharing the interlocking
laneways and street-art-covered alleys.

More recently, the urban cool elite—hipsters, digital strategists, those who'd sold a chunk of their souls
for a piece of the money pie—had started buying space
in the area's low-rise condos as they sprouted up. Concrete and glass boxes rising from the ashes of brick and
wood and dead weeds and turn-of-the-century squalor.

The gallery was in an older section of the market,
around the corner from the one-hundred-plus-year-old
synagogue that now doubled as a Korean community
center during the week. I almost tripped on the steep

slabs of stone, no handrail, leading to the cavernous basement hosting the showing. Owain steadied me with his hands on my shoulders. *Too easy.* I slid out from under their weight as soon as I hit the level ground of the entranceway.

The space reminded me of the subterranean bars of Madrid. Windowless and carved into stone, with reds and purples and blues and greens lit by a targeted white and yellow incandescence. There were a couple of bridge tables shoved together to create an impromptu bar, with pitchers of Sangria and bottles of wine ranging in shades from pale to lustrous. Smoke, too, and vapor. I stumbled again, this time on nothing; was the floor really uneven or was it all in my head?

"Let me get you a drink," Owain said, close enough to my ear that I could hear it over the murmuring of the voices around us. So many people in such a small space. I nodded my thanks to the place where he'd been and found myself in a room full of strangers, chattering and laughing, all elbows and asses that pressed in without ulterior intent around me.

I scanned the room taking shallow breaths. *There.* A gap in the bodies, off to the side and towards the back. So hot. Fans propped in corners beating fruitless air against the solid heat-emitting human barriers. Those closest got a breeze, felt some movement in the sweat bubbles slicking their skin. My skin.

Jon's gallery was the opposite of this. It was above ground, for starters. High ceilings, big windows, air-conditioning; even his busiest openings were more comfortable than this. Although arguably less gritty. A showing at Jon's was more glitter, moneyed with attitude, from this season's John Fluevog footwear to the latest haute-brand Queen West jacket or showpiece shirt. A chain carelessly draped from neck to belly. His clientele were the artistic elite and the patrons who financed them.

This place was more tattoos and piercings and collars. Leather and bare skin; muscles toned from work and not some gym, yet equally unconcerned with showing what they had. Vintage versus new with tags still on. I relaxed a bit. Here I could blend.

"Hope you like Sangria." Owain passed me a plastic cup of something red with stained fruit chunks.

"Thanks," I said, but he couldn't hear me so he shrugged and smiled. I raised the cup and tapped his, mouthing the word anyway. "Cheers."

"*Sláinte*," Owain replied, smile broad. We could be on a first date, or even a blind one. Awkwardness and distance and possibility coupled with *what ifs*.

We wandered from piece to piece, mounted on walls or as part of a floor installation. There were even a couple of dye-dipped popsicle stick floaters hanging from the nearly invisible fishing twine strung over our heads.

"What do you think?" Owain had downed half of his drink already; I'd been sipping at mine, more cautious. Even so, I was light-headed from the combination of heat and alcohol.

I stopped to look at a 3D mandala. Patterns on lines and shapes that bent and expanded into an abyss of infinity. "There's something about this one," I said. "I can't look away."

Maybe I could be arty, adorn my walls with the creativity of someone who was not me. I glanced at the price beside it: $1,600. Then again, maybe bare brick could be my personal artistic statement. A brand that says *I'm going to pretend blank is good because I can't afford anything else.*

"Owain! Ye arsehole." A burly man sporting a shiny purple dress shirt with sleeves rolled up to his elbows slapped my sort-of date on the back by way of greeting. Sweat dripped down, beading on individual eyebrow hairs and pooling in the dark smudges under his eyes. His accent said Dublin but his light brown skin suggested somewhere the sun shone hotter. "I thought ye weren't going to show."

"I told ye I'd be by when I could," Owain countered, smiling his deflection. "And here I am. Had to wait for the lass to get off work first."

The man spun to take me in, an overhead halogen bouncing shiny glare off his bare skull.

"So you're the lady our Owain has been keeping secret from us all these months." He grabbed my hand and started pumping. "Jasper. Jasper Dimenjian. Pleased to meet you."

"Dana," I said in reply. "But I don't think I'm her, whoever she is." I glanced at Owain, who shrugged. "We just ran into each other again recently. It's been, what, years, hasn't it?"

"Ah!" Jasper beamed. I wondered how much he'd had to drink already. "A toast to old friends then!"

"I don't know that we're—"

Owain interrupted by sliding his arm around my waist and kissing the side of my head. I shut my mouth again. That old familiar feeling. Him and me, together.

"To old friends," Owain said, tapping what was left in his glass with Jasper's and then mine.

Friends. *Sure.* We could be friends.

Jasper, the sweaty butterfly, spotted another pretty

flower across the room and flitted that way to pollinate artistic potential and scatter his seeds of lucre-based suggestion elsewhere.

I could feel where Owain's hand pressed the thin fabric of my tank against my skin, held in place by the slickness coating every surface of my body now. *Sexy.*

And yet...and yet...

Was I feeling the past or the now?

Owain angled his head as though whispering something in my ear. At the last moment, as I braced for the assault of sound to drown out all other noise, he shifted. Not quite touching. Did he say something? I had no idea; all I could hear was the rushing of blood in my ears and his closeness speeding the patterned beat of my heart.

My fists clenched and breathing was suddenly too hard. Solid bands of sweat and *run!* and ice that shivered its way along my spine to the tailbone below, trickling into the crack of my ass from behind. Everywhere a threat, everyone in this room of chattering laughing drinking debauching holding the potential for worse. I knew no one.

I forced one hand open to drag the strands of dripping hair from my eyes; saw blood streaking the inside of my wrist. My own: I'd punctured my flesh with my nails.

Self-conscious, I rubbed my palms against the black fabric covering my legs. Hiding it. Blood was such a good look for me, especially out and about amongst the norms. Not that I cared what they thought. What Owain thought. Right?

I pointed to the door and Owain nodded, motioning me to go first. Such a gentleman.

The air cleared as I ascended back to street level. *Relief.* It was still hot, but after the underground steam bath beneath us I'd have been happy with a few minutes in a meat locker.

"What happened back there?" At least he'd waited until we were outside to ask.

"I need something slushy and alcoholic," I said.

We wandered, the sidewalks lit by blue and red and yellow plastic lanterns casting lines and jagged patterns that muted the dirt and the garbage. Nothing could dull the smell though: alleyway urine, garbage cans stuffed early with compostable recycling. An all-you-can-eat cornucopia of culinary opportunity for the raccoons who eyed us from the shadows. Then brighter lights and wide boulevards of Spadina Avenue, with its late-night neon in Mandarin and Vietnamese and Korean, drawing us away from the quiet and winding dark of the Market.

We paused outside the rough wood-paneled façade of The Bubble Tree, its muted lights filtering onto the sidewalk as spray from the overhead air conditioner dusted us with the promise of cool relief. I glanced over at Owain.

"Fine with me," he said.

Twenty bucks in the palm of the hostess, delivered with a flirt and a smile, got us a seat at the quieter back area away from the other patrons. Not quite privacy, but not exactly public either.

"So," Owain said, when the silence stretched and got restless. "Seeing anyone these days?"

"What do you think?" After so long, some questions didn't deserve a straight answer.

"Right," he said, leaning back and crossing his arms.

"Not my business." Watching me in a way that said *I know how you sound when you sleep.* And yet here we were, sipping at bubble tea and chewing on our tapioca pearls, the chatter from the kitchen behind and the tables in front weaving around us as sweat dried against the backs of our necks.

"Make your pitch," I said. Leaving the past where it was meant to be. "I'll try to keep an open mind." Owain smiled, triumph in the creases of his cheeks. "Just remember—I had good reasons to leave."

He nodded. "Understood."

"OK then," I said, leaning back and crossing my arms. "Give it to me. Let's hear your case."

"Money." Owain held up a thumb to mark off his count. "Can't buy you happiness, but it sure makes life easier."

"Uh huh." Couldn't argue with that. "What else you got?"

"You went into the Agency to make a difference, defend that line between us and them." Owain's index finger joined his thumb in the air. "Now you can get back to doing that."

"There's no *us* and *them,* Owain." I couldn't help myself. "Different doesn't mean evil. Or even necessarily dangerous. They're just… *Other.*"

"The Agency has changed," he said. I raised my eyebrows. "Fine, it's evolving. There's more room for the kind of thinking you're talking about. Don't you want to be part of that?"

"Maybe," I admitted. "Anything else?"

"Backup. Safety." Up went his middle finger to join the other two. "We watch out for our own."

I snorted.

"Well, there's me," Owain said, bending his thumb in and holding up four fingers instead. "We make a great team, don't we?"

He was serious. Almost. I shook my head at him and smiled to soften my words. "You're not enough."

"Ouch, you pain me." But he was smiling. The wound wasn't fatal. "Then how about this," Owain said, suddenly serious, all five fingers splayed in the air. "You could finally find out what happened to your father."

I stared at him. Yeah, there was that.

Owain paid. We walked.

"The Agency keeps records," he said. Casual. "Classified doesn't mean gone. Someone knows what happened to your father."

I stopped, touching Owain's shoulder so he paused as well, turning to look at me.

"Do you know something?" My voice rising in pitch if not volume. "Did you find something out?"

Owain shook his head and glanced around, making sure we were still alone. So far so good. "Let's keep walking," he said. "We're not having this conversation. And no. Not exactly. But rebuilding your clearance levels might give you access to enough for a clue."

"So it wasn't an accident."

"I didn't say that," he replied. "Maybe it was. But wouldn't you like to know for sure?"

I nodded.

We turned a corner and it was the Market again, only quieter than before, with the streetcar clatter and traffic at our backs. Owain glanced over at me, then away, then back again.

"What?" Impatient with myself. Like we hadn't learned from experience.

"Nothing," he muttered. Then: "No, not nothing." Owain touched my hand and it was like it had been before everything happened; we were *us* again. Only not as young and not so innocent. And then he was pulling me towards him, his grip firm but relenting—I could have extricated myself at any time.

I should have told him where to go and how to get there in excruciating detail.

I didn't.

Because I wanted to taste what I'd been missing. Because sometimes I'm an idiot.

Our lips met halfway and there was nothing left to say. Tasting the salt and sweet of each other's sweat. There, by the steps of the old synagogue that now doubled as a Korean community center, in the shadow cast by its towering walls of stone. Where some of my ancestors had prayed, their names even now engraved in marble plaques on the other side of those locked doors.

I opened my eyes, saw Owain's gaze flick from me to somewhere over my shoulder. He gave a faint nod as his lips tracked from my lips to my ear.

"Duck duck goose," he whispered. Our old signal.

I nodded and counted out my response. *Blink* three... *blink* two...*blink*...

I dropped and spun, my back to Owain, as a blade I hadn't realized he was carrying arced across the space where I'd just been. A bald head, with its sunken eyes wrapped in pinkish/purple loose skin, rolled away from us as its torso, tentacles still flapping, fell limp to the ground.

At which point I realized *what* he'd likely just decapitated: a representative of that eight-limbed group I was supposed to be working with. This was *so* not good.

"Owain, hold up." Voice low. "Do you see any more of them?"

"Yeah."

I started to straighten up, my hands out where everyone could see them.

"Dana," he said. "What are you doing?"

"Watch my back," I said. Fully upright now. I knew where all my hardware was hidden, even if nobody else did. Yet.

"Always."

"Let's not over-promise. I'd settle for you being here for me right now." I scanned the street. Almost deserted, except for the leather-wrapped skinhead junkie slumped in the doorway of the nearest vintage clothing place. But I felt it. Heard the slithering, a squishing skitter displacing pebbles and dirt.

So I called out, gambling.

"My friend didn't know. I'm sorry." Silence. "He was defending me. Your compatriot," I started, then realized I had no idea what these squidly creatures called each other. Tried again. "They came upon us unannounced, in the dark. My friend's reaction can be understood, yes? He didn't realize you were here to talk to me."

"Dana?" Owain managed to make my name a multi-syllabic question.

I shook my head and didn't answer. Hoped he understood that it was best to let me handle this, if I could. Didn't really want to find out what would happen if I couldn't.

"You surprise me, *luv*," Squid D'Lee said, stepping out of the shadows. I'd never realized before how dark these streets were at night. As though the City had a dimmer switch on the overhead lights, and the timer went off at 2:01 AM. "And here I thought we'd become friends."

"What do you need, D'Lee?" He really had the worst timing. And what was with him and fedoras? This one was stormy grey. An indigo and azure feather, tucked into the side of the black bandeau, glittered as the squid rotated his head.

"Frank wants a status update."

"Really." My fingers threading through my sweat-dampened curls. "You couldn't have, you know, called or something?" I wasn't big on some of the social niceties required for participation in polite society—too much effort and tight pants for too little payoff. Even so, a bit of advance warning and maybe Mr./Ms. Headless-and-Amorphous over there would still be alive and flapping.

I made a point of staring at the head, then back at the live cephalopod again.

"Well," D'Lee said, inclining his head as though acknowledging my point. "We are where we find ourselves now. So let us confer a piece and then we can all be on our way." He glanced from Owain back to me, his grin all pointy teeth and stretched lips.

"Fine," I said. "What do you want to know? No, I don't have Gus and no, I haven't figured out where he is yet either. Feel better now?"

Squid D'Lee evaluated my words via long stare. I glared back, emptying my head of anything but the thoughts I *would* be having if I wasn't currently lying: annoyance, shopping lists, Owain naked, Jon with Claude on his knees in front of him, Sam looking down at me and me looking up at him from below...

It must have been enough. Squid beckoned over three heretofore-unseen minions to gather up the remains of their fallen comrade. How a gaggle of squidlets could do that was a mystery but at least it freed up my evening, so yay there.

"We'll be in touch," Squid D'Lee said, melting into the darkness.

Owain let out a low whistle and tucked away his sword.

"Now *that's* a story I'd be wanting to hear," he said.

Chapter Seventeen

You up?

I was blocks from my bed when Lynna's text buzzed
from the passenger seat where I'd tossed both phone and
messenger bag. Saw the message but wasn't about to
risk a ticket by texting while driving so I waited until
the first red light to respond.

Ya. Still out. You?

Just got off work, Lynna texted back. Hungry?

I could eat

5 mins @ the place on Dupont?

The light was changing.

See you there

You don't order salad at the Valiant. Sure, you could—
the place has been there since the mid-1950s, and
something raw and vegetable-based was probably on

the menu—but healthy eating wasn't the point. If you were at the Valiant, you were there to harden your arteries as much as possible in a single sitting.

Lynna and I did our part. Three eggs over medium for me, with sides of strip bacon extra crispy, hash browns and toast with both butter and jam. A quarter-inch-thick slice of grapefruit and a sprig of parsley for appearances. Lynna ordered a deluxe cheeseburger with fries and gravy. We split a side order of sausages, and bottomless refill coffees all around.

The key to any greasy spoon counter experience is to commit.

"Where were you coming from so late? Did you work to closing?" Lynna could cross-examine even with half an oversized potato wedge shoved into her mouth.

"Yes and no."

Lynna waved her fry at me to continue.

"Got off late, went to a gallery launch in the Market afterwards." I paused, knowing that if I shared the rest, there would be more questions. Maybe some I couldn't answer. "With Owain."

The partially chewed potato bit shot out of her mouth and past my ear to land, *plop*, on the green-grey Formica table behind us.

"*The* Owain?"

I nodded.

"The one who broke your heart? The reason you've resisted making any real commitment since then?"

"Resisted may be overstating things." I didn't disagree, not really, but I hated being pop-psyched.

Lynna nodded, letting that one go.

"So how was it? I'll bet it was super weird seeing him." She paused her stream-of-consciousness flow to dip another fry in the cup of gravy. "Did he explain anything? Give an excuse?"

"For what?" I wasn't bitter. Really. OK, maybe it was the post-endorphin-proximal-rush glow talking. "Leaving? Or coming back?"

"Both," Lynna said. "Either. Did he at least try?"

"So-so," I replied. Pushing my plate away; congealed, recently scalded grease curdling in my stomach with anticipatory gusto. "He came with a job offer, and an apology. I'm not sure I trust either."

"Don't blame you," said Lynna, switching to her burger. Thinking as she chewed. "How did he look?"

Trust Lynna to go there. Hell, who am I kidding? I'd already been there, and back, and holding a cup of Sangria. People on shaky milk crates shouldn't get too stompy.

"Good," I said. "He looked good."

"And?" With her free hand, Lynna did the *go on* wave. "How was he?"

"I just admitted he looked good. Nothing happened."

"Uh huh," she said. Grinning this time. Oh Great Lynna, all-knowing Sphinx of the multi-varietal hookup. I don't know why I even bothered trying to hide anything.

"Fine, we kissed. But that's it." My coffee cup plunked down for emphasis, *clink*; a bit spilled over the edge onto the saucer below. I grabbed a couple of aluminum-dispenser-boxed napkins to soak things up. That tiny bit of coffee splash required my full attention. Really. "And it was good."

Lynna snickered. "Is Owain sticking around this time? Undead with the boyfriend might not care much, but I'll bet tall, hot and feline hunky fine will."

"Total double-standard," I muttered. "I don't ask Sam about who he's with when it's not me. Why should it matter who I see?"

"It shouldn't," Lynna agreed. "And yet."

"Whatever," I said. "And no, I have no idea if Owain is going to stay. Guess we'll find out, eh?"

Gus was snoring on the couch when I got in. The only evidence I had that he'd moved at all in the last sixteen hours or so was that his head was where his toes had been, and instead of having to look at his ugly-ass feet, I was staring at poinsettia-red and holly-green wool footie slippers. 26°C in the shade and *now* he gets cold?

Gus cracked open his left eye with a groggy snort. Then the top eye, maybe to validate what the first visual suggested.

"Hey," he said, voice more croak than creamy smooth. "You usually get home this late from work? Didn't my brother let you off early because of me?"

I shrugged. What, I owed my dangerous loft guest a detailed itinerary and check-in on my life? I was thinking a hard *nuh-uh*.

"Things to do. Old friends to see."

Gus's nose, almost identical in shape to Sandor's tusky snout, did a nostril *flare/flap/flare/flap* sequence as he angled his head towards unwashed me.

"You *have* been a busy busy girl," Gus said. Chortled. Another nasal sequence. "Bacon and eggs and sausage and coffee—and you didn't think to bring anything back for your house guest? Some considerate host you are. I *do* need to eat sometimes." Was demon big and blue whining? Seriously? "And what were you doing in Kensington Market?" I stared at him and he started laughing. "Oh…"

"Shut up," I said, sinking into a chair. "Wasn't there anything to eat here?"

"No," said Gus. "Nothing fit for either non-human *or* human consumption. Speaking of," he said, stretching himself up to seated now, "how's your new whiskey-drinking norm with everything?"

"Everything how?" Regretted asking as the words passed my lips.

"He's cool with you being all you can be?" Meaningful look, which I purposely misunderstood. "Your variable existence?" I still played dumb. "Girlie, come on, you *know* what I'm talking about. Does new guy know you go furry? Or is he into that?"

"You're such an ass," I said. "Fine. No, he doesn't know. And I doubt he'll be around long enough to find out. He came back to offer me a freelance gig, nothing more. Happy?"

A long moment as Gus watched my face, the sudden hunch of my shoulders and the clenching of my fists.

"Are you?" His question was mild, but the emotion squeezing my chest, the surprise of tears shining in my eyes was anything but.

"I don't know," I said. How's that for spontaneous honesty? "New guy and I have history, and the end was not good. But whatever. Maybe things will be different this time around." Gus was silent. Couldn't read his face. "Or they'll be the same and he'll flake off again without saying goodbye."

"Harsh," Gus said. "He did that to you and you're even considering giving him another chance?" Shook his head. "If you want to be treated like shit, get Sandor to let me pick up the next contract that puts a price on your head. We could have a bit of fun together first."

I stared at him. Ice of the cold and disgusted kind now.

"No? Then have enough self-respect to kick this guy curbside before he worms his way in again and stabs you in the back."

"Do you know something?"

"Nah," Gus said, settling into the couch cushions once more. "But come on. You're smart." I opened my mouth to say something, shut it again with a snap. "*Be* smart."

"I need a shower," I said, getting up—and changing the subject. Getting advice from a demon who wasn't Sandor? The world was a weird and wacky place.

Gus wrinkled his nose. "Yeah," he said. "You do."

A quiet knock on the door before I was able to make it into the shower. *So close.* I inhaled deeply at the crack until I recognized the scent, then slid the barrier open.

"Hey," I said. "What're you doing here?"

"I came to check on you," Sam said. His nostrils flared, picking up on the mixture of scents embedded in my dried sweat, still tacky against my skin. Sam licked his lips, the aromas of bacon and sausage and eggs hinting at my recent breakfast; then, hesitating, as he caught a whiff of underlying Kensington Market and Owain.

"How was your night?" Pretending not to care about the smell of a new man on me, even though the clenching of his jaw suggested otherwise.

"Worked. Went to a gallery opening. Got jumped by tentacle guys in the Market. Good times." I kept my voice light as he passed me in the entranceway. Hoping that by not stirring the air currents much I could also avoid any awkward questions.

"You saw Jon?"

Even though it was clear I hadn't; I shook my head.

"Who then?"

"Owain. You know, the guy from the Agency." I hesitated, then barreled forward. "Unfinished business."

"Your ex," Sam said.

I nodded.

"*Unfinished* business?"

"He's trying to convince me to come and work with the Agency again, remember?" I left out the part where there was kissing.

Sam nodded; I got the sense it was a topic he'd circle back to. Then I guess he processed the pertinent details of the rest of my evening. "Wait, you got jumped?"

"Squid D'Lee and some backup muscle," I said. "He wanted a status update on my supposed search for the big blue blob crashing on my couch."

"I heard that," Gus grunted from said couch.

"D'Lee should have called first," I continued, leaning up against the wall outside my bathroom. "We were startled, and Owain didn't know I knew them, so he kind of overreacted. Beheaded one of them."

Sam started laughing. Oh sure—it was *so* funny when we pissed off the cadre threatening me with amputation. Why not. I crossed my arms over my chest, accidentally shifting the towel's coverage; suddenly I was flashing a lot more leg than before. Sam's *hey how are you* smile went somewhere deeper, darker.

"Where were you off to before I got here?" Like it wasn't obvious.

"Just the shower." I tossed him a grin, arching my back for full effect. "Feeling helpful?"

Sam's grin widened, all thoughts of Owain gone for the moment, as he leaned his forearms on the wall beside my head and angled in for a kiss. *Oh.*

"I can be very helpful," he whispered in my ear. And then, his tongue along my neck, trailing lower along the exposed skin of my shoulder.

Clearly Sam had forgotten the big blue elephant in the room.

"Don't mind me," said Gus, who apparently did want to be minded. Sam stiffened. "I'm always happy for a good show."

Sam growled and swiveled his head to stare at Gus, a cross between *back off* and *I'd like to see you try it*.

The demon smirked and raised his hands. "OK OK," Gus said. "I'll just head out for a bit, see if I can find a hot dog cart to eat." He edged towards the door, keeping all three of his eyes on Sam, before he ducked through the still-open entranceway and closed the door behind him.

I got the water going as Sam made sure the front door was locked.

Turned around again to see he had peeled off his shirt and was working on unbuttoning his pants. He didn't join me in the shower though. Maybe he was waiting for a direct invitation?

"I'm dirty," I said, dropping my towel and waggling my eyebrows. "I've got a lot of last night to wash off." I turned to step into the shower and then, oh whoops, my washcloth fell. I'd better bend over to pick that up.

Behind me, Sam chuckled.

"You go ahead," he said. But when I went to pull

the curtain closed, he said: "No, leave it open. I want to make sure you don't miss any spots."

This was new. I tried not to feel awkward as I sprayed water on myself. Gliding the soap over my skin, lathering up my hair, before turning my back into the spray again to rinse off. Sam hadn't said a word, and I couldn't open my eyes at this point until I was sure there was no residue left to sting.

I turned off the water and reached for my towel.

"Wait," Sam said. So close that his heat along my spine made me shiver. Naked himself now. "You missed a spot." He turned the water on again, tugging at the towel in my hand until I released it.

Sam lifted the nozzle and ran the droplets across my back until I was slick with liquid before placing it back in its cradle. And then he was behind me in the shower, pressing me against the steamy tiles. His hands snaking up to cup my breasts before sliding lower. Those fingers. That mouth on my neck, my shoulder.

I spun around, reclaiming myself; my own fingers making use of the running water to create a little friction of my own. Sinking to a crouch as Sam moaned above me. *Yes.* I thought maybe he couldn't last, his eyes closed and his breathing shallow, until he pulled me up again.

More.

Sam reached back and turned off the water, stepping out of the tub and extending his hand to pull me out with him. I watched as he moved, tracking him, until our hands touched and I was out of the tub and against him. Precarious balance. The rug beneath my foot slid and I slid with it, towards Sam, his back against the door and my chest pressed against his.

I wanted...

"Sit," I said, my palms on his shoulders and pushing down. Kissing his ankles, the inside of his knees, moving higher. I paused to reach into the cabinet under my sink for the box of emergency condoms I was pretty sure I'd left there. My hand touching air. *No!* Come on.

"Wait." Sam leaned to the side, finding his pants and reaching in for his wallet. The ultimate *in-case-of-emergency-break-glass* supplies. He must have been a Boy Scout because he came prepared.

He got distracted on his way back. There may have been bite marks. On my stomach now, as Sam kissed his way along my spine. *Yes. There.* I could feel where he touched but didn't know what he was going to do next before he did it. Until I heard the telltale crinkle of the condom wrapper.

"I like it when it's just us," he whispered in my ear. And then the weight of him was against me, pressing down, pinning me with his body as he kissed the back of my neck and wrapped his arms around me.

And then I knew exactly where he was.

"So tell me more about this ex."

We'd showered again, dried off, and were leaning over the kitchen counter drinking coffee. Sam had done the honors while I got dressed.

"What about him?" My eyes narrowed at the unspoken undercurrent. Guess Sam had decided now was a good time to revisit the topic from earlier. "Is there something specific you want to ask me?"

"Why'd you split up?"

Great. The can of worms I wanted to re-open and

maybe spread on toast with some Marmite. Because why not.

"We split up. He left." Hoping Sam would leave it at that. The silence stretched, longer, until I finally caved and filled it. "He left the country. Chose an assignment back home in Ireland over staying with me."

"Was it serious between you guys?"

I nodded, swallowing down the lump in my throat. "Yeah," I said. "We lived together, worked together. Met each other's families. The subject of marriage and kids and a picket fence in white came up. So yeah, it was serious." I took a long gulp of coffee, the taste of bitterness and tears on my tongue. "And then it was done."

"Do you trust him now? Would he have your back?"

"Maybe," I said. "Maybe not. He did last night when we got attacked. Why?"

"OK," Sam said. "Hear me out on this. Ezra Gerbrecht has close ties with the Agency, right?" I nodded. "And so did your father." I nodded again. "Wouldn't it be easier to find out what's going on over there from the inside?"

"Unless they figure out I'm not what I used to be and they decide to turn me into a pin cushion, or pump me full of poison, or find some other way to make the rest of my life a living hell." You know, like those nightmares I still had. Sweat beading on my upper lip as I clenched my fingers into fists that drove nails into claws into the soft and fleshy part of my palm.

I jumped up and started pacing. Big cat, small cage. Sam watched as I stalked from one end of the room to the other, then back again. Waiting for me to wind myself down. Finally pulling me down into his lap and wrapping his arms around me when I didn't. Kissing the side of my head and stroking my hair, soothing, before he continued.

"How closely would you have to work with this guy?"

"Who? Ezra?" I twitched in his arms. "Hopefully as little as possible."

"No," Sam said. "Your ex. Owain."

"Um," I said. "Closely maybe? With him bringing me the offer, he might be positioning himself as my handler."

Sam tensed beneath me and I pushed myself back to look at his face. Waited for him to meet my eyes.

"Is that going to be a problem?"

"Depends," Sam said. "Does he still have feelings for you?"

I laughed, short and sharp in the octave of hurt major. "No idea," I said. "Does it matter?"

Sam didn't answer, not directly. Instead: "Do you have feelings for him?"

Right. Sam didn't like to share, and Jon was already pushing the upper limit of his willingness. Even though I didn't ask Sam who else he was sleeping with. Even though there were no numeric limits on our arrangement.

Yup. And the view from where my head was lodged firmly in my ass was great too.

But I couldn't lie. I respected Sam too much for that.

"Maybe," I said. Even though I knew it wasn't what he wanted to hear. Even as the muscle that jumped in his cheek as he clenched his jaw against my words said plenty.

Chapter Eighteen

"Anyone home?"

I knew there was—I'd seen my mother's car in the driveway—but I figured it was only polite to call out when entering someone else's home using a key. Maybe she was busy. Or had a friend over. Or had been abducted by creatures with tentacles who walked on dry land. Or…

"Dana!" Mum was fully dressed and holding garden shears. She put them down on the kitchen counter before wrapping me in a solid squeeze.

"Hungry?" Once she let me go, I motioned to the bag of food waiting for inspection.

A dozen Gryfe's bagels, a tub of Western Creamery cream cheese, and a package of Kristapson's smoked salmon (the good stuff). Oh and did I mention those cheese blintzes from Harbord Bakery? With the sour cream?

"I could eat," she said, her smile almost as wide as it had been when she saw me. "That's a lot of food. Are we expecting anyone else?"

I surveyed the pile of ingestible comfort in front of me. She wasn't wrong. "Leftovers?"

"My freezer thanks you," Mum said.

* * *

"Are you OK?"

We'd done the small talk, caught up on family gossip, and now Mum was watching me absently shred what was left of my second bagel into a series of tiny crumb piles.

"Owain," I said. "He's back. And he brought an offer from the Agency with him."

I couldn't tell Mum about the offer details because I didn't know what they were. I hadn't read it yet. The decision wasn't whether or not I agreed with the terms, not really; it was about me, and the Agency, and was I ready to go there. Could I live with myself if I did.

Owain had suggested working my way back up to classified-information-accessing levels. He didn't explicitly say he'd help me find out what happened to my father, but there was the definite suggestion he might be able to nudge me in a useful direction.

What was the value of knowledge? Was the potential to up-end buried history worth the risks? Could he be trusted, especially after all this time?

Mum remembered Owain. The parts I'd told her; her curiosity about the bits I'd left out. Owain was the kind of grand passion that spawns emo poetry and maudlin drinking songs. I still remembered the way he'd watch me across the flickering candlelight at the pub where we'd share a pint, one of our traditions after a run well done. A little something to ease the adrenaline hangovers.

Owain and Mum had met. We'd been together long enough for that; days and nights and plans made and futures discussed. But then he got an offer he wanted more than me.

I probably should have gone with Owain when he asked, but that was then and I'd had reasons not to go. *Ezra.* He'd given me a big promotion and put me in charge of a project I couldn't turn down. Kind of like the overseas offer he made Owain.

Owain's new job would take him back to Dublin, where his family was, then to Germany and Switzerland and beyond. It was danger and adventure and everything I knew Owain had been craving. Maybe if I'd been a different person, I would have been willing to put his career ahead of mine. Maybe if he'd been a different person, he would have prioritized my career over his. In either revisionist history scenario, there was a chance we'd still be together. I might still be normal. *Maybe...*

"Playing the *what if* game is pointless," Mum said, reading the expressions on my face. "*Coulda woulda shoulda*—you'll drive yourself crazy."

"I know," I replied. "But what if I chose wrong?"

"What if *he* did? What if there were things at play that made those so-called decisions inevitable?"

I stared at my mother. Could she be right?

"What aren't you telling me?"

"I don't *know* anything," Mum said. "But think about it. The Agency. So many fingers and pies. Look at what your father did. Ezra Gerbrecht. Two men among many who were supposed to protect you."

I leaned back in my chair, appetite gone, staring at my wisdom-spouting mother.

"You have no way of knowing whether the decisions you made back then were your own or whether you were manipulated into believing they were. Once you accept that as a possibility, then you have to extend that same benefit of the doubt to Owain. You both served the same masters."

"Holy shit," I said.

"Indeed," Mum replied. "Of course, Owain stayed with the Agency all these years. You didn't. It changes a person. I've seen it."

My father. Who'd lied to the woman he was supposed to love. The man who'd altered my blood in an Agency lab, and inked a target on my back.

Well. Can't say my father never gave me anything.

He'd also given me a secret room. Yes, my father had somehow created an area above my old bedroom that defied the dimensions of time, space and square footage.

I'd stumbled on it a few months ago, and I'd been trying to follow the breadcrumb clues he'd left me ever since.

Blood—*my* blood—was the way to get there. Didn't want to think too closely how he'd managed to do that. Instead I climbed onto the ballerina-pink sateen chair in the middle of my childhood closet, pricked my thumb with my earring—*ow!*

—and tried to think of England while scattering three drops of blood onto the wooden frame above me.

"Good luck," Mum said from below. I'd forgotten she was there. "Hope you find what you're looking for."

Me too.

I wanted to spend some time exploring the maps in the flat file drawers but my mind kept wandering.

Seeing Owain last night. Being with Sam today. And then there was Jon.

Going back to the Agency and hoping I could make it out alive.

Choices. Desires. Ramifications.

I bit my lip and tried to focus.

"So, Dad," I said to the silence of the room. "How are things?" I want to say that if I squinted hard I could see him standing in the corner, smiling with pride. Except squinting made my brain hurt and it was pretty much me, myself and, oh yeah, I up here. Even if my father had hidden something useful, it didn't mean I was having any luck finding it.

Still, I experimented. Like I did every time.

"Map on my back," I said. Nothing. *"What'cha gonna do with all that map / all that back with all that map?"* Words set to the beat of a Black Eyed Peas song had me wanting to blast some music and dance, but otherwise sparked no magically useful response.

Served me right, looking for someone else to save me. I was a big girl. I had a brain. I could totally figure this out for myself.

And yet, there I stood, uninspired to do anything other than deal with the overall grit buildup in this place. Yup. I came, I urge-to-danced, and I cleaned. Because sometimes it's got to be done.

Or so I hear. The urge doesn't strike *that* often.

Sure, it felt like someone could have been watching me. But I didn't *see* anything, and I was making a conscious choice in that moment to believe only what I could see, hear, smell, taste or touch. Anything else required faith—not my forte—or at the very least a viable alternative working theory.

Didn't get much sleep last night, what with Owain

and then breakfast with Lynna. And that couch looked so soft. I didn't need to be anywhere for a while…

I closed my eyes.

Ow!

My back was on fire. A shiatsu pinprick pattern of pain I'd felt before, but only once. That night on the beach. Under the full moon, in the chill of the summoning, as the portal gaped its maw to grant all manner of beasts and monsters and nightmares passage through the sharpened gaps in its ephemeral gorge.

Except that the sun was still up and I hadn't summoned anyone or anything.

I tore off my tank top, then my bra, then my legging crops. Too much fabric. And what the hell was going on here?

I skidded over to the exit and pulled the lid back, calling down for my mother. To her credit, although her eyes widened at the scene, all she said was: "What can I do?"

"Take some pictures of my back? I'm gonna want a visual." I tossed her my phone, camera activated, after helping her up into the attic space. "Also, could you please describe what you're seeing?"

Mum moved around behind me, and I heard the *click click click* of the shutter capturing the moment. Fuck, that hurt. How did I make it stop?

"Could be the sun," Mum said. The floor beneath us groaned as she changed position. "It's shining directly on your back." I grunted. "Try moving into the shade."

I did. Nothing happened. And by "nothing" I meant I was still being stabbed by hundreds of tiny fairy blades all at once. Or acupuncture needles, assuming they were being shoved into my flesh far deeper and rougher than the instruction manual recommended.

"Anything?" Mum's voice rose on a question mark. I shook my head. "Maybe try the opposite end of the room. Closer to the books and papers."

"Nope, still hurts," I said, trying it. "Light still on me?"

"It is," Mum said. "How odd. It's following you." She sighed. "I'm so sorry, *Danyankeleh*, this isn't the life I would have chosen for you. Or you for yourself."

"*Danyankeleh*," I repeated. "Since when do you call me that?"

"What, your nickname?"

I turned to see my mother, frowning, perplexed. "It's what Dad used to call me. Not you. *Danyankeleh*."

The bookshelves started rumbling, and the drawers of papers and topographical etchings flew open. Sheets flying in a breeze that didn't exist. Mum and I looked at each other, and I nodded. Hoping she understood. Mouthed a *3-2-1* countdown and then...

"*Danyankeleh, Danyankeleh, Danyankeleh, Danyankeleh*," we said together. A wet sucking sound as the overhead lights flickered. The bookshelves shook, rattling the contents, and a new wooden box came flying off and at my head. Super-cat reflexes: I caught it millimeters before it smacked me in the nose. Back pain suddenly gone.

"Dana," Mum said, voice tight. Tighter than before. "Look at your arm."

I expected fur, claws—the usual.

Instead I saw...feathers? Curved orange talons where my fingers were supposed to be? What the hell? Maybe not all the shifters I knew stuck to the same features each time they transitioned, but I'd never seen anyone go outside their species before. Not even Anshell, although of anyone I wasn't betting against him on that nifty superpower.

"No," I muttered. Trying to find a focal point in my head, channel everything into that tiny pinprick of white light and then shove it through to find the other side of my increasingly questionable sanity. Hoping it would all come out normal and smelling of lilacs and roses and lavender the other end.

"*Danyankeleh.*" A voice from the shadows.

"Stuart?" My mother cut through the magical thickness of the space in this room with pain and loss suddenly not quite so of the past. *Of course.* She would recognize the sound of him faster than me.

I didn't know where to look first. My father? Mother? At the grotesque claw that was more dragon Celandra than anything I recognized on myself?

Fuck it.

I snagged my tank and somehow got it back over my upper half, only then turning to look where my mother was staring. Green static fuzzing, flickering, around an outline. So familiar. He opened his mouth, shaped the two syllables my mother hadn't seen from him in over sixteen years: *Hannah.*

Grief and loss shoved down and away. Buried but never quite left behind.

"Stuart!" My father, his transparency solidifying as we got closer.

"Hannah." His voice repeating. The name echoing tinny as though bouncing along the accordion pleats of an aluminum foil sheeting vent.

"Dad?"

His head swiveled towards the sound of me. I could still see the orange flowered curtains through his opaque transparency.

"*Danyankeleh*," he said. "I'm sorry."

And blinked out of visible existence again.

Chapter Nineteen

"I don't know what to do with this," Mum said. "We buried him. Is he a ghost? I don't understand." I squeezed her hand as her voice rose. "What is he doing here now?"

"I have no idea." Then: "You said we buried him, right?"

Mum nodded.

"OK, I remember the funeral and the *shivah* and all that. But we didn't do open casket. I know there would have been *shomerim* there, guarding his body from the time he died to when we—" I swallowed down the marshmallow thickness expanding in my throat, even so many years later. You never forget the sound of dirt hitting a coffin. "When we put him in the ground. But what if something happened? Between when you identified the body and when we did the thing at the *feld*?"

"I never saw his body," Mum said.

"Wait, what? How did I not know this?" Useful information that could change everything.

"Well, you were young," Mum said. "And it happened badly, and far away. His remains needed to be identified before they could be shipped back to us here."

"But didn't he die in an accident? Something to do with work?"

"Yes. Work," Mum echoed. "*Agency* work." She gave me a look that said *figure it out*.

I didn't like where this was going. History—that reality fabric of a past I'd thought I knew—was reinventing itself on the fly.

"Who identified him?"

"Your old boss," Mum said. "Ezra Gerbrecht."

Ezra, my mentor. Substitute father. The man who'd handed me over to Alina and tortured me for information. Then rescued me from some nameless monster *not* named Alina. Abducted me twice. Who, in the space/time continuum of maybe twenty-four to forty-eight hours, had presented himself as a befuddled old professor suffering from early-stage dementia, the steel-trap-minded senior-level leader of the Agency's Canadian Bureau, and as my father. Which one was the real Ezra?

Then there was my actual father. Another riddle to unravel. First: was he actually dead? Recent evidence suggested not. Second: if he wasn't dead, who or what had we buried? And finally, if we accepted the increasingly plausible possibility that my father was still alive, then where the hell *was* he?

"I'll bet those Agency labcoats know something," Mum said. Blunt with a lip-twist of bitter lemon. "Not that they'd tell us. Not after all this time."

"I could go back. Take the freelance job, trust Owain, gamble on being able to get close enough to the right clearance levels for some answers."

"If you need money that badly, I'll give you some." Her eyes suspiciously shiny again. "You don't need to do this."

"It's not the money," I said. Pacing now. "Although

that would be good. What I need is information, the kind I can't seem to get anywhere else."

"You said you were done."

"I know." The same way we both knew what I was going to do next.

"Promise me you'll be careful." Biting her lower lip, the pain a reminder of what she was holding back.

"I promise."

"I'll bet someone there could figure this all out," Mum said, changing the subject; pretending she believed me, pretending she cared enough to sacrifice me for whatever "this" was.

I nodded. And hoped I'd be able to escape the bowels of that hell twice.

The *Danyankeleh* effect had shaken loose two maps and a box of letters still in their original envelopes. Correspondence between my father and Ezra from a different time. I scanned through pages of family news, tidbits about mutual friends, rambling sentences on gardening and growing, an exchange of recipes and some offhand comments about astronomy. Innocuous.

Now I saw them for what they could have been then: communication between two men so close that either one could have covered for or caused the other's disappearance.

"Was Dad a gardener? I don't remember him much with pots and dirt," I said. Testing that theory.

"Gardening?" Mum laughed; a short bark. "No. The closest your father came to outdoors living was that old charcoal hibachi. Pretty sure the filthy thing is still in the garage. He'd stick whatever he could find on metal skewers then throw them on the grill. At least half the time they'd end up blackened char—completely inedible—and we'd order a pizza." Her shoulders un-clenched, the memory tugging a smile from the creased edges of her mouth.

"So he had no interest, as far as you know," I scanned the last three letters I'd opened, "in seed va-rieties, cultivating clippings of leaves or branches, or cross-pollinations of any kind?"

Mum was staring at me now.

"I have no idea what the two of them were talking about, but Stuart could barely boil water for pasta. And we've already established what happened when he got involved with that hibachi. Those weren't instructions for grilling, were they?"

I shook my head.

"Then they couldn't be recipes for any kitchen I can think of."

"And the stars?"

"Still no idea," Mum said.

I looked at some of the so-called constellations Ezra and my father had been going on about. Funny names. *Dog's Breath Passage. SMERGH.* Acronym or actual name? *The Eightway. Bucket of Gorp. Zarcon Loubitz.* Googling on my phone wasn't helpful either—whatever these were, nobody was tracking them online. Although we were talking about Ezra and my father—they'd go old school on anything important anyway. Still, none of this made any sense.

I took pictures of the letters on my phone, just in case. Made a list of the odd names, recipes and grow-ing instructions I was finding in those old letters. There had to be a connection.

What was I missing?

I saw new maps in layers of tissue-thin sheets atop the scored oak tabletop, scattered by the wind that had blown through earlier. I was no cartographer, nor was I a geography specialist of any kind, but the terrain seemed off to me. Like I was looking at distorted reinterpretations of the same space looping over and over again.

The table had been outfitted with four L-shaped brackets I'd thought were for show. My cursory eyeballing assessment suggested the edges would line up with the maps. But why guess?

I grabbed the sheet closest to me and, pushing the others aside, lined it up with the corner guides on the table. A *click* as the page snapped into place. *Huh.*

From underneath, the solid wood table began to glow as though the map was an x-ray image and I'd attached it to a lit panel.

I grabbed the next-closest map, the one marked *Bucket of Gorp*, and lined it up with the flèches before smoothing it down with flattened palms on top of the first one. This time lines curved and points of circled interest levitated off the pages; glowing sapphire snakes and stones of lake-bottom murky greens bordered in goldenrod yellow. The buzzing in my ears mirrored the vibrations against my hands from below.

"Let me try," Mum said from beside me. I jumped at her words; I'd forgotten she was there.

Mum lifted the next sheet in the pile: *Zarcon Loubitz.*

"Do you feel it?" Maybe if it buzzed for Mum too, I could validate my reality.

"Feel what?"

I touched her hand, the one holding the parchment,

and her eyes widened. Energy from me to the map with
her as conduit.

"What *is* that?"

"I don't know," I said. "But I think it has to do with
these pages."

Mum handed *Zarcon Loubitz* to me. As soon as I
settled it into place on top of the other two sheets, colors and lines sprung up to dance on the page; worms
crawling over each other for freedom.

One thing was clear: I was the key. My touch was
a living flesh and bone divining rod for something I
hadn't been able to figure out—yet.

I hoped what I was touching was paper. Tried not
to focus on the shade variants of the ink, the texture of
uneven surfaces rubbing under my fingertips, the recognition that these maps could have been etched onto
something that shed in layers and maybe hadn't come
from a tree.

My imagination was made up of memory and recon-
structionist history and nightmares. Sometimes I forgot
how to tell the difference between what really happened
and my any-time-of-day-as-long-as-it's-inconvenient
imaginings of terror. Blind obedience was no excuse. I
focused on my breathing, counting with numbers that
stumbled backwards as I pushed them uphill, until the
white humming of my vision receded and I was back in
the room. The maps were sheets of paper, nothing more.

"Honey?" My mother touched my shoulder, light,
and I started. I'd forgotten she was here again.

I nodded. I could do this.

Maybe I needed to think about this differently. Seven
sheets, seven layers. How many *Danyankelehs* did it
take to unlock a dimension? I felt like I was looking at

things beyond 2D or even 3D. Was there such a thing as 5D, 6D or 7D outside of hair dye colors?

The individual elements from the maps continued to float several inches above the stack of pages. I saw mountains and skies and rocks and paths. Water, snow and ice. Snaking rivers of color woven through a loom with skeins of potentiality strung an infinity of lifetimes ago.

I touched the apex, one finger only, and a point of light appeared above it which spawned two more and then two more again. There was an answering stab of pain from my back. *Damn.* And here I'd thought it was safe to put my shirt on again.

I drew my index finger along one of the shimmering, undulating snakes and shivered, an answering sensation of touch along my back once again.

The maps in front of me were linked to the tattooed dots on my back. I could only assume that my father had done it, although I had no idea how.

No wonder Alina and who knows what else was after me for my skin. The information I wore was dangerous. Exactly how dangerous was still a big unknown.

To find out more, I needed to get closer to the source: my father. And since I couldn't reliably do that, I was going to need Ezra.

And for that, I had to rejoin the Agency.

Chapter Twenty

Managed to get through my shift at the Swan Song, albeit on auto-pilot.

The headlining group was a synthpop cover band trio called Depeche Load. The colored films we'd added to the overhead lights at their request rotated, casting a flickering glow of cotton-candy rainbows over the room. There was an adoring gaggle of pig-tailed fans in white-and-blue Japanese schoolgirl outfits clustered near the stage, their skirts at least a handspan above their knees with white socks pulled up to a handspan below. They were joined by another cluster of bolero-wearers in tuxedos, suspenders and undershirts.

There were gigglers with Adam's apples, and tuxedo-wearers with breasts. At least two breasts, maybe more. There could even have been tails but I wasn't going looking.

The combination of music, lights and high-pitched laughter was giving me a headache. OK, maybe my head was still spinning from earlier in the attic, but the squeals passing for singing weren't helping. Plus the hangers-on kept coming up to the bar and ordering crazy drinks to match whatever *Yu-Gi-Oh!* character's card they happened to be holding.

The latest one was a classic: Blue Eyes White Dragon. I went with a layered test tube of shots for that one: Mexican *Ricacha Horchata* for a creamy cinnamon/vanilla/raisin base, then some Dutch *Bols Blue* for an orange kick, topped with some kind of chocolate liqueur imported from parts unknown. Possibly using ground parts unknown as well. A Sandor cost-cutting special. Everything alcoholic went better with one of those tiny paper umbrellas, right?

From what I could tell, the *Yu-Gi-Oh!* drink connection was actually part of some kind of city-wide scavenger quest for Pride-friendly experiences. The Swan Song wasn't physically near the bars and clubs that catered to the hetero-adjacent crowd, but considering the range of clientele we got in here it's not like a bunch of norms were going to faze us no matter who they fooled around with. We were safe. Relatively speaking.

Still, between the techno and the weird drink orders and the part where it was getting close to my getting-off-work-and-going-for-a-run time, I was definitely tracking on a minute-by-minute basis.

Something I didn't recall doing when I was with the Agency. *Don't think about that.* Owain wasn't wrong when he pointed out how I was wasting my training and education pouring liquid inebriation for anyone who paid. Had it bothered me before he'd said something? Sure, I guess. On my dark days. But the part where my work didn't tend to give me new nightmares made up for a lot. I could look at myself in the mirror and not hate the person I saw staring back at me.

Could I go back there and still live with myself?

Could I live with myself if I didn't?

* * *

This time, the run was uneventful. We ran, we flicked
water at each other; there were birds and rabbits and
mice. Nobody crashed our party, and I was able to take
a break from my indecision for a couple of hours.

Bliss.

The moon was starting its downward descent as we
wrapped things up. Sam had something to take care
of with Anshell, or maybe he was still bothered by our
last conversation. You know, the one where I'd admitted to residual feelings for Owain, despite him having
ripped out my still-beating heart with his bare hands
and kicking it to the curb as he left. I knew I shouldn't
care about Owain anymore. Just as I knew what Sam
really wanted was me, and all to himself. I probably
shouldn't have been so honest. Sam wouldn't meet my
eyes now, keeping his distance all of a sudden. Giving me the nod instead of a good-night kiss before we
headed back to our separate vehicles.

Human form reminded my muscles that my mind
was still restless. I needed to talk with someone who
didn't have a vested interest in the outcome, and who
was probably still awake. Not Sandor. And Lynna was
up north in Collingwood on a shoot until tomorrow.

Good thing I had options.

Jon kissed me on both cheeks, Euro style, before folding himself into the chair opposite me in the all-night
café on Charles Street. Just a few blocks west of the
Guy Watching Central strip, the heart of Pride celebrations, the restaurant was almost completely full. Almost
everyone seemed like they were on something, fingers

and palms and thighs touching over and under their tables around us.

My vampire companion licked his lips, savoring the energy, before focusing back in on me again.

"What are you having?"

"Chai soy latte," I said. "Extra cinnamon sprinkles on the foam. Thinking about a side of poutine with something extra for protein on top. What can I get you?"

Jon waved over the waitress, who suddenly found our table irresistible and the man sitting at it even more so; she couldn't stop staring at him now that she'd noticed his existence. I'd forgotten the impact of Jon's charm on the unsuspecting. We hadn't made it out much lately.

His drink, a steaming cider with a stick of cinnamon, appeared in less time than it took to brew my latte. Guess someone was motivated. The poutine with two forks arrived shortly after.

"What happened?"

"Am I that transparent?"

Jon eyed the poutine, then me, raising his eyebrow to punctuate his point.

Oh. "I guess I am." I forced out a small laugh I wasn't feeling.

Jon waited as I poked at my curd-laden mound, swirling a fry in the gravy before finally sticking it in my mouth and chewing.

"I'm thinking of working with the Agency again."

Jon blinked. I'd said something unexpected. "Why?" He didn't know much of my history, but he'd heard stories of what they could do to a supe. "Life's gotten too boring?"

"Sure, that's it. I want to go back and risk my life for a cause I'm not sure I believe in because, hey, it's better than switching up my workout routine. Makes perfect sense."

"Then why?" Jon leaned forward. "You won't be safe there. They don't know what you are now, correct?"

"Of course not."

"Tell me then. Why would you risk yourself? Is the money that good?" It had been a while since I'd seen Jon actually get this worked up about something. He was vibrating.

"Yeah." I reconsidered. "I mean, yeah, the money is good, but that's not why."

I told him what happened in the attic. The maps, and my father. How things were getting weirder and I needed information from the only source I could think of who might be able to help. *If* he felt like it. *If* I could create a scenario where maybe I trusted him, even if only temporarily.

"You think you can get answers there if they believe you're one of them?"

"Yeah."

"And your old partner, your ex—what was his name, Owain?" I nodded. "He'd have your back?"

"Honestly? I'm not sure," I said. "Maybe?"

I know. Glowing endorsement of fealty and fidelity. But I didn't lie to Sam, and I wasn't about to start with Jon.

"You're right though," Jon said. "Fastest way to get the information you need is from the inside out. Doesn't mean I have to like it."

"I'm not thrilled about it either," I said. "But at least its freelance. No contractual obligation to mortgage my soul for a millennia or anything."

"And your first born?" OK, now Jon was joking. I was pretty sure he was joking.

"Nah, they don't do that anymore."

The silence stretched, companionable, each of us lost in our thoughts. Then:

"You coming over later?" Because there was that between us, no matter what else was going on.

"Not tonight," I replied. Maybe I'd regret it.

Then I remembered Jon was still seeing Claude, his not-so-ex.

Maybe I wouldn't regret it at all.

Chapter Twenty-One

It was daylight, and coffee. Should be safe.

Of course, this *was* the Agency we were talking about.

"You've read the paperwork?"

"Yeah." I'd skimmed it. Lots of wherefores and here-tofores and non-compete clauses that I'd scratched out and initialed on the version I'd printed. Because yeah, sure, I was going to sign away my rights and protections based on one of their boilerplate agreements. I was trusting that way.

Right.

Owain put out his hand for the document and started reading, pausing every minute or two for a sip of coffee. Espresso, no sugar. Tough guy. But then, caffeine wasn't about the joy for him—it was medicinal, practical, and he'd determined it to be the fastest way between tired and awake.

As he read, I entertained myself with sugar packets and wooden swizzle sticks. I'd gotten the frothiest of café lattes, sprinkled the foam with brown sugar that melts into a crumbled shell, and now I was bored. It was either that or notice new flecks of grey nestled into the red curls cropped short above Owain's ears. Laughter lines around his eyes etched deeper than before, and a scar the size of my thumbprint under that jawline I used to be able to trace from memory in the dark. The way my chest clenched when he glanced my way. How part of me still waited for him and wanted him back even though I knew we weren't right together anymore.

Better to build forts out of paper, sugar and disposable cutlery.

I had a good bridge system going and was working my way up to a crystalline catapult defense when Owain put the stack of paper down again.

"Have you looked over the job?" If he noticed what I'd been doing, he opted to keep his opinions to himself. "You're briefed on the target?"

"No." Whoops. Should I have broken the seal? "I thought we had to settle terms before I was privy to those kinds of details."

He chuckled, took a sip of his murky caffeination to cover it.

"I forget that you've been gone awhile and need to get your clearance levels back," Owain said. "You're right—even if you tried to break the seal, all you'd see would be a supermarket flyer PDF. I've got to put this through first."

"Does this mean you're my handler?" Yeah, that would work well. My ex knowing all the quirky details of my current life circumstances. "Or are you just my first point of contact?"

"Higher ups are still working that out," he said, meeting my eyes. Evaluating. My own eyes looking back at him were cool, or at least I hoped they were but who knows. Could we work together again? Really? Someone somewhere thought this was a good idea?

"Any higher up in particular?" *Don't say Ezra don't say Ezra don't say Ezra.*

"Was there someone in particular you thought would care?" Owain's voice was deceptively even. I knew his tells the way he knew mine—he was fishing for any triggers I may have developed in the lapsed years between us. Like I'd tell him.

"See much of Ezra these days?" Fuck it. Sometimes the best response was the real one.

"Of course," Owain replied, narrowing his eyes. "You don't? He was your mentor—and you're in the same city. You two haven't kept in touch?"

How was I supposed to respond to that? The Ezra we knew may or may not be dead? Or that he could maybe shrug into and out of a flesh suit that looked like his old self but sometimes used the voice of his long-dead friend Stuart? Oh, wait, maybe Stuart wasn't dead either. That some version of Ezra had worked with an entity named Alina, who'd been raised in a bleed and feed ritual four months ago, and together they'd taken turns torturing me? It was all very confusing.

So I shrugged instead of explaining.

"We see each other occasionally," I said.

"Lots more opportunity for you to catch up soon. I'll let you know once this has been processed, and we can talk specifics." Owain downed the last of his coffee in a single gulp. "If there's nothing else?"

"Actually, there is." Could I ask? And if not Owain, then who? "Have you ever heard of something called *Zarcon Loubitz*? Or *Dog's Breath Passage*?"

"That's pretty random," Owain said, leaning back again. Suddenly less interested in leaving than he'd been thirty seconds earlier. "And no, I haven't. Why d'you ask?"

"Found some old letters of my father's, and he mentioned those. Made no sense to me but I thought maybe you'd know more."

He nodded, understanding without having the panoramic view. Some things he still remembered.

"Like maybe they're connected to his accident," Owain said. Not a question. "And you thought I might know something more about it, what with me being a Company man myself. Yes?"

I nodded.

"Even if I did—and I don't—you'd need clearance levels to find that kind of thing out." He gave me a look that involved raised eyebrows and a faint smile to soften that edge. "You'll be wanting to be careful who you ask once you're back with the Agency. Last thing you need is for history to repeat itself."

I narrowed my eyes at him. "Is there something I need to know?"

But then Owain was all charm and brogue and white teeth and that *c'mon let's get into trouble for a while* grin. I wasn't getting anything else out of him tonight.

I'd noticed that exercising more this close to the full moon helped me control any residual restless, trouble-causing energy. You know, the kind that might out me as something other than what I needed to be when re-entering the belly of the Agency beast: normal.

Owain said he needed a couple of hours to put everything through. It wasn't even ten o'clock and already the pavement was shimmering in heat that was only going to get worse. Sure, this was Canada, home of the winters that made you want to hide out for five months until the snow melted and the sun did something other than make you squint. But June in Toronto was rarely a moderate experience either, with consistent daytime temperatures over 30°C (86°F), and this year was coming in right on steaming cue.

I could have gone back to my apartment, showered, maybe taken a nap. Except there was Gus and the smell of his feet and, oh yeah, the possibility I might let him know I'm back in with the Agency and any judgments he might choose to share on the topic. Not that I cared what he thought. Still, I wasn't in the mood to rationalize or defend my actions. Especially to him.

So I headed over to Hart House, adjunct to the University of Toronto downtown campus and home of my first Agency test with Ezra. My day pass got me access to the House's exercise facilities, a saltwater pool with high glassed-in ceilings and the potential for ghosts wandering the halls. One of these days I should really spring for a membership. Still, after half an hour of jogging around the track, some weight training and then laps in the pool, the urge to be all I could change into subsided. *Hallelujah.*

It also helped me sift through the information I had so far. My father had been working on something that required maps with a cipher, and that cipher seemed connected to whatever he'd tattooed on my back. He'd either kept it from the Agency as a whole or it was uncommon knowledge—my proof of that was Owain's blankness when I'd asked him about specific places mentioned on the maps. Sure it had been a gamble. Didn't make it any less of a useful exercise.

Also didn't mean Ezra was ignorant of the meaning,

or the significance, of whatever my father had been working on. This casual contract arrangement with the Agency could still put me in Ezra's crosshairs, even with other people watching; we were living in a post-truth reality where anything was possible. Even more so in the covert ops field.

I had to stop what I was doing—soaping my armpits—to put my palms flat against the beaded white tiles and concentrate on my breathing. Ezra was connected to Alina in my mind, and that part of my mind ran screaming from what it had seen. *Breathe.* It was just me, and water, and I was safe. *For now.* No. *Focus.* Counting backwards from one hundred; harder than you'd think. Then the alphabet as the water ran cold. Teeth chattering. Until my thoughts were my own again.

I rinsed off the last of my shampoo and stepped out of the enclosure. Oh yeah, becoming a double agent had been *such* a good plan.

But maybe evil Ezra was just the façade, and underneath it was my father's old friend, the one who'd brought me jumbo sucker swirls as a kid. Looked out for me when I was starting out. It was possible that reality as I knew it was fluid, right?

If that was the case, though, then what was Ezra's tie to Alina? And how was Alina connected with my father?

I'd missed three calls while sweating out my personal demons: Sandor, Anshell and Owain. The unholy trifecta of Dana Responsibilities.

Nothing from Sam.

Sandor had left a message asking me to come in for early afternoon, reminding me that I'd booked off as of 10 PM for tonight's Pack run. Anshell was checking in—personally!—to see how contact with the Agency was going. Of course he already knew; it wasn't the kind of thing even I'd keep from the Pack Alpha. And then, finally, Owain. Paperwork was filed and let's get together to go over the assignment.

The snowball that was my life. Here's hoping it didn't crush me as it rolled down that hill of inexorability.

Sitting across from Owain in a boardroom surrounded by grey cubicles and flickering overhead fluorescence, I tried to remember why I was doing this. Curious about the gig, even though I didn't really want to work for the Agency again. *I didn't.* Still, I wouldn't mind being one step ahead of the bad guys for a change. Figure out who's up to what from the inside, rather than standing on the other side of the door trying to see in through the reverse peephole.

Maybe this would be the time I kept the Agency from sucking the marrow from my soul.

I took the tablet Owain handed me, pressed my thumb against the flickering oval, and broke the seal.

Dumb fucking luck.

The target was my own diamond-spewing couch surfer under tusked nepotistic protection: Gus.

I realized Owain was watching my face for any kind of reaction, so I did my best to paste on a professional *let's get this done* expression. But could I really take on this gig now that I knew who the target was?

The old Dana would say sure, why not. A demon was a demon. But now? Some of my closest friends and playmates were something decidedly other than norm. And that big blue guy crashing at my place as a favor to his brother—my boss, and also my friend—was maybe even sort of growing on me. OK, so it wasn't super-nutrient-rich soil that sprouts green in like ten minutes. But it was there.

Plus, if I didn't accept the contract, the Agency would put someone else on it. Even if I was super unproductive with my results—after all, it'd been a few years since I'd done any tracking—it could buy us all enough time to get Gus to safety, maybe even clear his name first.

Was I really going to double-cross the Agency and get away with it? The thought alone was fantasy magic land to the power of *who-the-hell-do-you-think-you-are?* The part where I was still considering it notwithstanding suggested a grip on reality that was slipping into the same range as *do-you-hear-voices-not-your-own?* No way I could do this. Could I?

But what about the part where change can be effected better from within than without. What about that?

Maybe.

If I just could figure out *how*.

Chapter Twenty-Two

"We need to talk."

"Have you ever noticed how no good conversation has ever started with those four words?" Gus had a point. Didn't change my need for him to share and care.

"Fine, let me be more specific. We need to figure out a plan."

"Oh?" Gus leaned back, clasping his hands behind his head and letting me in on all kinds of armpit stench. "I'm feeling Thai. Count me in for a large Chicken Tom Yam Kha from the place down the street, would you?"

"Yeah, they do a good one…wait, no. This isn't about lunch." Even though my stomach was growling and some veggie spring rolls would totally hit the spot. "Did you know you have two contracts out on you now? And those are just the ones I know about."

Gus stared at me and did a long blink. All three eyes went blank, chilling me despite the heat warring with the air-conditioning, and I remembered my temporary roommate was a merciless killer for hire.

"Are there now," he replied. "Do tell."

I reminded myself he'd promised Sandor not to kill me. Or hurt me. I was pretty sure about the not hurting me part.

"There's the cephalopod crew. You know about those guys."

Gus nodded.

I took a deep breath. "They're not the only ones. I just landed a second freelance contract to bring you in."

"Did you now," Gus said, bringing his arms down slowly to rest at his sides. It lowered the stench factor in the room again, so yay there, but also meant he could get to any weapons that much faster if he chose to break his promise to Sandor.

I watched his index finger twitch, and I leaned back myself, moving my own hand into range of my nearest weapon.

"And what do you plan to do about it?"

"Honestly?" I pasted on a cocky grin I wasn't feeling. "I think we need to figure out who keeps placing bounties on your head and get them to stop."

Gus relaxed a bit, his shoulders lowering to somewhere not quite so close to his cheekbones.

"Yeah," he grunted. "You gonna bring me in if we can't?"

I raised an eyebrow at him. "You gonna let me?"

"Nope."

"Then," I said, "we'd better figure out a plan B."

We agreed that Gus wouldn't kill me as long as I didn't double-cross him and turn him in to either of the ones who wanted his ass in a sling. So I figured it was safe to take a nap before another shift at the Swan.

"Hey good-looking. What time do you get off?"

I tensed, then forced myself to unclench before turning around, ready to do a verbal smack-down on the cliché hitting on me. Because come *on*.

The glint of white teeth, set in a mouth so familiar I could taste it even now, flashed me a smile.

"Hey, Owain, what can I get you?"

"Jamieson neat. And thanks."

I poured while I waited for him to tell me why he was really sitting at my bar. Let's be serious—there's no way the Swan Song was going to become his regular watering hole.

"I want to go out with you again." He was abrupt, downing half his drink in a single gulp after spitting out the words.

"What?" Maybe I hadn't heard him right.

"Let's do something. It's still early." It wasn't that late yet, maybe ten o'clock, but the more Owain drank the deeper his Irish brogue would get. At least, that was old Owain. This new guy—I couldn't tell if he was faking it for my benefit, whether this was part of the welcome-back-to-your-old-life plan, or whether there was a small part of him that still had the conscience to feel bad about what he'd done to me.

He reached over and put his hand on top of the back of mine.

I had no idea what to do.

"This guy bothering you?" Sam dropped into the seat one over from Owain, enough room for weapons to be drawn if necessary. Then he reached over into my space to snag himself a bottle of whatever domestic beer I had in the ice bucket for easy access, twisting open the cap and tossing it back onto the counter. Making it clear that he had capital *P* privileges in this establishment, and with this particular bartender.

Ah, testosterone. So ready to rise to any possible occasion.

"Sam, this is Owain. The guy I told you about." I turned to Owain. "Owain, this is Sam."

Sam raised his beer to his lips, eyeing the competition, and nodded a greeting. Owain lifted his near-empty glass in a mock *cheers* before echoing the nod. Because words were just too much effort sometimes. Uh huh, that's it.

Wait, let me tell you about this amazing piece of Florida swampland I have for sale…

"I was just asking my old friend Dana here," said Owain, laying on the Irish for effect, "if she felt like going out again later. It was great *craic* the other night."

"Again?" Sam looked at me, not Owain. What could I say? I shrugged.

Sam's lips pressed together, remembering how I'd smelled when he'd dropped by the next morning. Before I'd had a chance to shower. His eyes cooled as they flicked down to the bowl of pretzels then back up again to me as he realized Owain must have laid hands on me. Sam hadn't asked before because he hadn't known to ask, because under our current arrangement it wasn't Sam's place to ask.

I could tell he wanted to ask.

"Dana, can I see you a moment?"

I nodded, catching Janey's eye and waiting until she'd set up behind the bar for me before leading Sam towards the quieter hallway leading to the storage room.

"What's up?"

Sam leaned one shoulder against the wall and took my hand in his, looking down at me. Literally, not figuratively (I hoped)—he was almost six feet tall to my

five-foot-four. *Home.* Sam's touch always felt like home
to me. Scared the crap out of me, that. I tried to smooth
any emotions from my face before I looked back up at
him.

"That's your ex, Owain?"

"Yeah." I gave him a teasing smile. "Jealous?" Hoping that making jokes could take the sting out of the
green-eyed beast I knew was lurking behind his words.

"I get that you have to work with him," Sam said,
not answering my question. "But do you need to spend
time with the guy outside of that?"

"Uh…" I didn't know what to say. I knew what I was
supposed to say—that Sam had nothing to worry about,
or that it was none of his business—but I couldn't force
out the words. Admit the truth; I cared about how Sam
felt, and there was a reason for that. Emotions stuck in
my throat no matter how much I wished in that moment I was normal and could say what should be said.

Sam couldn't hear any of my internal monologue
though; I didn't say the words out loud.

"Have you slept with him since he's been back?"

"No," I said.

"Are you planning to?"

"Uh…" It was no use. Whatever I was thinking,
whatever I was feeling—there was nothing I could say
to make this conversation stop.

Sam slammed the wall with the heel of his hand.
Whoa. And still I couldn't force the words he needed
to hear past lips too scared to make the right sounds.

"That's it," Sam said, spinning on his heel and heading for the door. "I'm done."

I wanted to call him back, but couldn't. It was all I
could do to watch him leave.

* * *

"So that guy is one of your new friends." Owain eased back in his chair and took another sip of Jamieson. Pretending to ignore the way I kept blinking the shiny from my eyes. "Isn't he part of that shifter clan, the Moon with Seven Faces?"

I nodded.

"You've been keeping some interesting company since we parted ways."

What could I say? By Agency standards, I was sleeping with the sub-human enemy—whether Owain knew it or not. By Pack measurements, I was playing with the kind of fire that flame retardants can't touch.

"Supes aren't the enemy," I said.

Owain turned to watch the couple at the far end of the bar who were draped around each other in an undulating mass of legs and beaks and fingers and eyeballs. There was moaning, the picking of nits out of each other's sparsely spiked hairs, and a purplish puddle of gelatinous slime under their chairs. We'd be using bleach on the floors tonight for sure. Owain raised his eyebrows at me, smirked, then took another sip of his drink.

"Right," he commented, looking away again. "Perfectly normal." Let's humor the crazy woman holding her shaking-loose marbles in one hand.

"It's Pride month." I shrugged. "Shit happens."

Owain shook his head. Not the Dana he thought he knew. But maybe he'd only seen who he wanted, expected, to see. Maybe he was One Who'd Gotten Away for good reason.

Even now, here, I was shielding my new reality from him because it was safer.

Which pretty much said it all.

* * *

Faced Sam a few hours later at the Pack meet. From a distance. I ran with Annika, stayed where I could be seen, and shifted back the moment it was OK to do so.

Grateful that this was the last night for a few weeks I'd need to do this.

Chapter Twenty-Three

Three knocks.

The camera angled towards the door swiveled, flickering red then green. Locks, automatic, slid and clicked from closed to open—*one*, *two*, *three* and then the final deadbolt turn to *four*. On that *four* count, the light overhead blinked out with the ticking hum of a plastic kitchen-timer dial reverberating against a metal oven surface. Counting down, but to what?

The locks clicked back into place behind me.

I wanted to call out. And yet it felt wrong, somehow, to make noise here where the dark was thick and tasted of sweet chocolate orange.

Instead I followed my breath towards the light. Air cool on the back of my neck with the welcome relief of an air conditioner's blown kiss.

"Close your eyes." Jon's voice, husky, pitched low and close to my ear.

I whipped my head around, left and right. Nothing; only the flicker of a candle on the other side of the room tricking my pupils into seeing what wasn't as it appeared.

"No," I said. My stomach quivered. Why did I do this to myself?

"You say that as though you have a choice." Dark pressing in around me as headlights from the sporadic traffic, passing by beyond the glass, flickered against the closed blinds and kept going.

"I always have a choice," I said. Because between us it was true. "I'm sorry. I guess I'm not in the mood tonight."

"Are you certain?" Jon drifted into the space in front of me. Tempting me with proximity.

I bit my lower lip and shook my head.

"OK," he said, dropping the I'm-a-sexy-vampire-come-to-seduce-you routine. "Wine?"

"Yeah." I cleared my throat, because I wasn't completely unaffected. "Yes please."

"Tell me what happened with Sam." We were sitting together on orange-and-purple-and-turquoise-threaded bolsters scattered on the polished wood floor, our backs against the rough wall of century-old brick. Jon rolled over on one side to look at me, his head propped against his palm.

I thought about changing the subject. But what was the point? Jon and I were friends who happened to get naked together, and he could read me—no program guide or translation app needed.

"I think Sam is dumping me," I said. Tears in my eyes all over again. *Damn it!* I blinked them back, turning my head away so Jon wouldn't see. "I couldn't tell Sam I was completely over my ex, and I couldn't promise him I *wouldn't* sleep with Owain either—even though I haven't since he's been back. And I'm not even really sure I'd want to, even if I could."

Jon rolled onto his back and laced his fingers together under his head. Not looking at me.

"What did you expect?" Jon's bluntness was unusual.

I sat up; all the better to see his face. All of it. Nuances, tells, words spoken through body language rather than anything I could hear.

"What are you talking about?" Blunt is as blunt does. Theoretically. "Do you know something I don't?" Damn it. I sounded like an insecure emo teenager. *Do you think I'm pretty? Am I loveable?*

"Sam never wanted to share you," Jon said. "I was already here, so he dealt with it because he wanted you." His voice was mild, but there was a bit of kick to the aftertaste. Wait, Jon was feeling possessive too? All of a sudden?

Maybe it wasn't so sudden. I had to be honest, if not out loud then at least to myself. But in Jon's case the moral high ground was a lot more crumbly.

Why did it always have to be about people, emotions, as possessions?

"Claude," I said. His asshole sort-of-ex boyfriend, who'd scratched me. A single-word reminder of why Jon and I were on a care-and-share-with-limitations basis.

"I know. So, about your new old friend," Jon said, changing the subject abruptly. We'd slaughtered the topic of him and Claude, burning and burying the bones already. "He's with the Agency."

Not even a question. I nodded anyway.

"And you're still planning on working with them?"

I nodded again. "It's not the wisest idea," I said, acknowledging the potential for danger, torture and possible death-by-skinning scenarios. "Owain says things are different now. Maybe this time I can avoid some of the crap that happened before."

"Things that wake you up sweating and screaming?"

Shit. Jon had noticed.

I guess it'd be hard to miss.

"They don't know about me," I said. "My blood work from seven or eight years ago would still be on file somewhere, but they don't know what Claude did to me." And there it was again. That chasm of past. I pressed my index fingernail into the pad of my thumb, right hand and left, palms upturned; a yogic pranayama *Gyana Mudra* to bring me back to the now. "They don't know I can shift into a cat."

"Good," Jon said, not bothering to pretend. "And if you're told to bring in someone you know? A member of your pack? Or a friend?"

"Or friend with benefits?" I kept my voice light, fingertips brushing along his shoulder, the benefits of this friendship—or some of them—catching in my throat.

Jon caught my hand, arm across his chest, and kissed the palm heart I'd offered him without realizing it. The inside of my wrist. His lips, so cool; iced relief from the heat that penetrated even the air-conditioned chill of the room.

"You're safe," I said. Brushing my lips against him as my hair tickled the space where Jon's shirt opened to his bare chest. "I would never," I said. "No matter what they offered. No matter what was between us. You're safe." My teeth, crescent ridges of indentation, pressed against the undead flesh of his neck made pink again from the blood of the living. He moaned. "From the Agency at least."

But I was in control, and this was as much as I could handle.

Left with that emptiness inside I still couldn't touch. A heat, a brush of fur on fur. Craving someone that was missing, someone who was *else*.

Chapter Twenty-Four

Life was weird, Owain was back, Sam didn't want to deal with me, and it was possible I'd be shifting into something new and far less cat-like very soon. But at least Jon and I were still friends. Even if the benefits part was in question now.

If you can't be with the one you want, enjoy the one you're with.

Danyankeleh.

I jumped, swerved the truck; almost hopped the curb and hit a fire hydrant, veering at the last second to a screeching brake-slammed pause before continuing. Good thing it was 5 AM early. Not too many people on this particular road just yet.

The whisper came from right beside me.

The truck swerved to the right as I stared. At the last moment I braked, hard, then pulled over into the strip mall parking lot in front of a twenty-four-hour coffee place. This time the fluorescent-orange-pop-and-maraschino-cherry-red cab I cut off blared its angry horn at me in punctuated bursts of surprised frustration. He screamed something unintelligible at me as he sped past my open window.

I glanced over to the passenger seat and almost lost

the long-since-digested contents of my stomach before refocusing on what was in front of me. Swallowed thickly.

"What do you want, Ezra?" Because that's who I saw.

"Not. Ezra." The form of my mentor went staticky, then translucent, the lines blurring between the man who had molded me and the man who should have been there to help. Another flicker of blue/grey/yellow and then it was Ezra again, even though the expression on his face was one I remembered seeing on my father. I think. Whoever he was reached out without making full contact; even so, all the hairs on my arms and the back of my neck spiked up. Like dragging a magnet through sand, targeting the black bits and leaving the rest behind. I had no idea what my father or Ezra or whoever this was wanted. The goose bumps prickling my skin were not forthcoming with answers.

"Dad?"

He nodded at my question mark, the edges of what made him recognizably him firming and fuzzing at his attempt to make tangible contact.

"Not Ezra?"

He shook his head.

"Can you prove it?" Torture me once, shame on me; torture me twice, well, I must be a fucking idiot.

"I can't," he said. Then: "Wait. You found my room in the house. I saw you there?" Not quite sure, even though it had been less than a day since it had happened. Upstairs, in the space that shouldn't exist. "And Hannah? Your mother was there with you?" My confirmatory nod eliciting a tender smile and several rapid blinks. "She looks good. Older."

"We all are." As I took the leap of hypothetical belief. "Dad. What are you doing here? And why do you look like Ezra?"

He shrugged, his outline flickering as my father/Ezra faded and the grained surface of my vinyl passenger seat became more defined without its opaque overlay.

"My old friend comes to visit me sometimes," my father said. "We've shared many things. Years. Sometimes Ezra is with me and sometimes I'm with him."

I stared. My father, who was either dead or he wasn't, kept using words in a sequence that made no sense to me. Was he dead? If so, was this his ghost? Did I believe in ghosts?

But if he *was* a ghost, why did he also look like Ezra? Was Ezra also a ghost, or was I reading the situation from left to right when I should really be going right to left?

Fuck it.

"You're not making sense," I said.

"You found the maps?" Because when faced with a reality challenged, why not change the subject altogether. "I felt it, you know. The lines and the patterns joining together. Showing. Telling. The path from you to me and back again."

This didn't feel like the sharp-minded, senior-level science specialist I'd remembered my father to be. The logic over emotion birth partner to Mum I'd seen in that spirit-walk flashback Anshell and I had gone on a few months back. Dad reminded me more of the Ezra I'd seen in his native university office environment. Befuddled. A stereotype of the absent-minded professor.

Except my father wasn't a professor, and he also wasn't Ezra no matter how much he currently looked like him. Right?

Maybe I could play along while I figured this one out.

"Why are you here?" Motivation prioritized over identity. I could do this.

My father didn't answer, although he did twist in his seat to watch me.

Great. We were going with attempted mind reading over oh, say, anything in the helpful-answer category.

"The Agency finds you interesting," he said finally. Hello random observationalist. "I used to work for them. Did you used to work for them as well?"

"Yeah."

"It was real then. Not imagined," he said. This was feeling more and more like a conversation with Celandra.

"No," I replied. "I *used* to work for them. With Ezra. He trained me." Watching the face he presented for any flicker of emotion, recognition. Instead I saw frustration purse his lips and tighten the creases around his eyes. As though there was something there, he could *feel* it, if he could just focus hard enough.

I thought maybe he was going to soil his pants from the effort. Then I wondered whether ghosts still did that. Which brought me back around to one of the many as-yet-unanswered questions: was my father, if indeed it *was* him sitting here beside me, a ghost?

"The Agency has made you another job offer," he said. "A new one. A *now* one. Are you going to take it?"

"How did you…?" No point in asking questions he wasn't willing, or maybe equipped, to answer. "Where are you that you're able to keep track of my job offers?"

"I'm here," my father said. "Also there. Where you are and where I am, but only sometimes at the same time. Keeping track of the *whens* and *hows*, the intersections, it confuses me sometimes. Those times I forget.

What is real and which is that thing I shouldn't confuse with reality. But also the questions you're asking aren't quite the right ones. You need to ask to understand. You can't see. Although you do see through me. Because of where I am, where I've been, and where you need to be."

"Where do I need to be?"

My father blinked a few times. I couldn't tell if he was surprised or perplexed by the question.

"Here," he said, as though the answer was obvious. "Where else would you be?"

"With you?"

"Oh no," he said, blinking at the rate of a computer screen refresh. My eyeballs hurt watching him; I was still too young for eyestrain, right? "*Nonononononono.*" His voice rising in both pitch and volume. "You can't be here because then why am I here? It does not make sense. Can't happen. Won't happen. Right?" Expectant, but of what I wasn't sure.

At least he hadn't started singing. Or dancing naked in the moonlight, like Celandra. Things that couldn't be unseen that I'd prefer not to see in the first place.

"Dad, are you dead?"

"No," he said. Confident in that answer at least. "I'm very much alive. Why do you ask?"

"Well," I said. "The Agency told us you'd died. We had a funeral. Sat *shivah*."

"Oh," he said. I couldn't tell whether he was surprised or whether he was beyond all that. "Was it a good turnout?" *There*, that dry sense of humor I remembered.

I nodded.

"Dad, what happened to you? This is all kinds of crazy." I skipped the part where that adjective fit him as much or more than the current situation.

"I'm not entirely sure," he said. "I've been trying to retrace my steps, deconstruct the outcome from all possible triggers. Ezra and I were working on something. Testing. And then something happened, a big *boom*, but for me it's also a big blank. I can't see how it happened, or exactly what. But the outcome put me here and you and your mother and everyone else I knew there. Or here. It's all very confusing sometimes."

"I get that." Because it was obvious.

"*Danyankeleh*," my father said, turning in his seat to look at me. "Will you be taking that job at the Agency?"

I shrugged.

"You can't trust anyone there, you know. Your friends are probably not the friends you think they are."

"Understatement," I muttered.

"But," he continued. "You'll be able to help me if you're part of the Agency. Track down the information I need to figure out how to get free again."

Of course. This was the man who'd tattooed baby me for his own still-to-be-determined purposes, lied to my mother about it, and put a magical bull's-eye on my back as a result. The father who'd put his needs above the safety or interests of his family—you know, those people he was supposed to love and protect.

No wonder he wanted me working for the Agency again. Why was I even surprised?

I shook my head rather than share my thoughts out loud on the irresponsibility and self-absorption of this particular parent of mine. Had he always been this way? I'd never noticed before; maybe I'd been too young. Then again, time could have shaped his psyche along new neural pathways. It *had* been sixteen years. He'd been who knows where doing who knows what. For all

I knew he was dying each night to be reborn the next day. OK, I didn't really think that, but anything was a possibility until the actual truth was somehow revealed.

I wanted to put my faith in the man who looked and sounded like my father. Hug him and get his approval, praise for the things I'd done and the person I'd turned into. But this was also a man who'd betrayed me before he even really knew me, using me as a tool to effect his own ends. His and Ezra's. They'd both allowed my mother and me to believe Stuart Markovitz was dead. And now he was back, although not really, and I didn't know whether my father had ended up where he was now by accident or design.

And you wonder why self-reliance is my faith. At least if I disappoint myself, I'll have only me to blame.

I flashed, uncomfortable now, to how things had been with Owain. How his not being there left me twitchy and wanting more. A familiar feeling. I expected him to vanish the way my father had.

But I didn't say any of that. I might care, but it wasn't something I was about to share.

Instead: "There might be another way."

My father's eyes narrowed within Ezra's face. Irritated? The way his eyebrows scrunched around the furrowed trio of lines etched above the bridge of his nose reminded me of my former mentor's piercing intelligence. That focus as he reassessed all the possible factors he could nudge around the playing board. For Ezra, there was always the game. Had it been the same for my father?

Was it still?

"Who are your allies, little girl?"

My blood chilled; this voice was not my father. I

blinked and saw Ezra. Blinked once more and *she* was beside me. The last someone I wanted to share space with—ever.

And why was she here, now, when moments before I was looking at Ezra and talking to my father? How were those three connected?

I didn't say her name. The utterance could make things worse, and I wasn't in a gambling mood. Instead I leaned over and turned on the radio; I needed to do something with my fingers that wasn't me tapping out my nervousness to the beat of my rattling breath of fear. Death metal blared through the crackling speakers and I jumped. Forgot that the U of T station went particularly experimental when they figured nobody was listening. Or, you know, too drunk/baked to care.

Whoever was sitting next to me now was not appreciating the staccato beats and guitar string slides punctuated by a falsetto peak that could have been a note-based ice pick stabbing directly into my eardrums.

"Turn that down." Ezra, exasperated. *Interesting.* Exactly how many consciousnesses were there occupying the same space at the same time? I wished I'd paid closer attention in physics class. There was a formula, somewhere, where all this made sense. Right?

And what did the music have to do with it all? Had I just accidentally discovered a way to switch the skinsuit channel?

"Maybe," I replied. Fake it till the crazy goes away. "Who am I going to see in your spot if I do?"

Ezra chuckled as pride played hide and seek with his smile.

"Good girl," he said.

"Ezra," I said. "Please. Where did my father go? And *her*?"

At my vague reference to Alina, Ezra shook his head and looked over his shoulder. Nothing there; his shoulders lowered, unclenching inch by *move-it-faster-already* inch. Interesting.

"It's me right now," Ezra said. "Stuart comes to visit sometimes too."

"You're tripping me the hell out, Ezra," I said. Mentally cataloguing the location of my nearest weapon. "You show up, you vanish, and in between you're speaking in riddles or tongues, and maybe you're torturing me or maybe you're saving me. Calling you inconsistent is an understatement. What do you want? Seriously? And what the—my father? Skins? What the hell is going on?"

Ezra started laughing. Apparently my outburst was his version of good stand-up. Tears rolling down his face, droplets dangling in the ridges and shadows of his cheeks before he brushed them away with the back of his spider-web-patterned hand. On the inside of his right-side wrist, to the left of the streaked blue veins, was a thumbprint-shaped tattoo. Inked in grey and smudge, lines and sworls contrasting against his pale skin; a police blotter imprint of something someone wanted to remember. I tried to see whether his thumbprint matched the markings. They were different, I thought, but I couldn't be certain from this angle.

Let's assume dissimilitude. So then why? What was the significance?

I reached out, the tongue of a snake tasting its prey; not quite as fast as I now could, but not so slow that Ezra had a chance to stop me either. Touched the symbol with my index finger and felt a jolt. My heels ached. Instinct: I tried again. This time my thumb lined up with the print on Ezra's wrist. My entire body contracted beneath my skin.

Forced my focus through that pinprick of light Anshell had taught me, clinging to my humanity even as the cat clawed its way through my throat and I swallowed back the yowl that would end all questions while shredding any last bits of my peace. My thumb was on fire, but the flames were invisible even as the pain was anything but.

I held on.

Ezra's face contorted, curving in on itself.

"What have you done?" His voice becoming distant. I expected him to disappear, even as I held his wrist, but instead he solidified once more, Ezra as Ezra; only the changed expression giving a clue that anything was in flux.

And then he was my father again.

"Good," Stuart said with Ezra's mouth. "You can let go now," he added.

I glanced down as I loosened my grip. The thumbprint was still there.

So. Much. Weirdness.

"We don't have much time," he said. "I think. It's hard to know for sure, but it felt as though I could be here for longer this visit. So ask me. I'll give you what I can."

Deep breath. Let's do that thing that makes no sense. *Carpe diem*, fish of the day and all that.

With my luck, I'd be shifting into that next anyway.

"Where are you when you're not physically here?"

"Wrong question," he said. "The more pertinent inquiry: how can someone be in two places at once?"

I waited for him to respond. If my father wanted to be asking the questions, he could damned well share some answers too. But he was still playing paternalistic teacher, a trait I'd never realized before how much he shared with Ezra.

But I was far from that little girl in a pink frilly dress, knee socks and white patent leather shoes who always did what she was told. If I'd even been that before.

"Stop," I said. "We don't have time for games. Again: where are you—right now?"

"I'm sitting next to you," he replied, brushing off my irritation and tone as inconsequential.

"And?"

"I'm also in an alternate dimension," he said with an exhale that lasted many more consecutive seconds than the average breath should take. Maybe I should have kept track, but I lost the count after ten.

"So you're here but you're also there." I calculated the possible if/then scenarios in my head. "How did you get *there*, the place that isn't here?"

"I don't know," he said. "Last thing I remember was being in the lab with Ezra. Then nothing. Then *not* here."

"Why are you here now? Not before?"

"I tried, *Danyankeleh.* So hard. So many times." He brushed a tear from his cheek, impatient to dismiss the show.

"What changed?"

He shrugged. "I have no idea," my father said. Then: "Ezra. I think Ezra found a way to make the barrier more permeable."

I nodded. I had an idea how he'd pulled that one off. One word: Alina. "Tell me about Alina, Dad."

Sudden stillness where before the energy had twitched. His index finger touching his lips together as they shaped *ssh*.

"We do not speak her name," he said. "Especially so close to the inter-dimensional divide. Especially you must take care."

"Why, Dad? Why me?"

"Because you hold the key to unlocking the dimensions for good. In your veins. On your back."

"Does she know? Has anyone told her?"

"I did," my father said. Right before he vanished, still wearing Ezra's face.

Chapter Twenty-Five

I was knocking and knocking; I couldn't stop. Even when my knuckles started to ache. Even when my skin tore and blood trickled across the back of my hand and down into the cracks of my skin. Even though I knew what and who I smelled like. Even so. Forgetting I knew where they kept the spare key. Rousing whoever I could on the other side of that door to let me in.

It opened and Sam was there. Shirtless. His neck and cheeks flushed red through his overnight stubble as his eyes widened and his shoulders went tight. Taking in the wild mess that was me in front of him. I couldn't tell if he was worried or annoyed I was here; either way, when he stepped back from the doorway, I followed him inside. Clicked the dead bolt behind me. Can't be too careful these days.

"Anshell?"

"Out," he said.

"Back soon?"

"Maybe." Mr. Non-Committal all of a sudden.

"I need to talk to him." As if that would help move things along.

"Got that. He's still not here."

"Can I wait?" This monosyllabic Sam wasn't my favorite version. Although maybe that was the point.

"Suit yourself," Sam said with a shrug.

Mr. *I-Can't-Be-Bothered-To-Care* headed upstairs, ostensibly to his room and back to bed. I hesitated a few beats before following him up, my palm flat on the door—just in time to keep it from being shut in my face.

Sam didn't fight me; instead he turned to flop back onto the bed, his head propped by pillows still indented from where he'd left them minutes before. I tried not to think of the times with me, there with him.

Instead I shut the door behind me. Old habits. But instead of joining him where he lay, I sank into the nearby yellow flower-dotted armchair. Only one t-shirt was draped across the back. Must be laundry day.

"This feels weird," I said, watching him breathe.

"You reek," he said by way of reply. "Jon?" My turn to shrug. His nostrils flared and his eyes turned questioning. "There was an old man? Men?" I shook my head. "What have you gotten yourself into this time?"

Sam had no right to judge—he was *this close* to dumping me. He could keep his judgments to himself.

"Do I owe you an explanation? Thought you didn't care anymore."

Sam narrowed his eyes. "Never said I didn't care."

"This, what we're doing right here—"

"What, communicating?"

Sure. Communicating. That's what it was.

I tried again.

"All of this." I did a vague *etcetera etcetera* wave to encompass our current state of fun. "This wasn't our deal. It's not like I ask you who you sleep with when I'm not around."

"So ask."

"I don't want to." Sharper than I'd planned. Sam's eyes narrowed at my tone, the first hint that there might be more to my *don't ask don't tell* than I'd let on.

"Have you ever thought about actually making a choice?" Sam jumped up and started stomping around his room, opening drawers and then slamming them shut again. I wondered if he was going to break anything; I'd heard some definite glass-on-glass contact that last time. "Everything isn't always about you."

"I think about others plenty." I did, didn't I?

"And me? Do I factor into your life at all beyond a quick fuck?"

I smirked. Couldn't help it. "Quick? There's nothing quick about what we do together."

Sam's lips twitched, even though he was still irritated as hell.

"Seriously, Dana," he said. "Do you think about me at all?"

"Of course I do." More than he realized. More than I felt like sharing right about now.

"I can't keep doing this." Sam's hands clenching and unclenching. He couldn't look at me.

"Why not?" My voice rose. "I thought we had something good. Why do things need to change?"

"Because they do. I'm not playing here."

"Never said you were." It was like pushing words past a mouthful of chewing gum leftover from last year's Halloween haul. You know you shouldn't, but you want it, and then it's there and sticking to your teeth and you're looking for a way out without gagging. "I'm not either, you know."

"Not what?"

"Playing. I care about you," I managed.

That got his attention, as Sam's gaze turned back to me, his eyes softening at the creases. Then: "You came here for a reason, right?" Sam's subject change was abrupt. But hey, if he was willing to go there, I wasn't going to stop him. "You needed something? What happened?"

So I told him. About leaving Jon's, although I skipped the details of what we'd been doing beforehand; about who'd shown up as I was driving home. What they'd said. Wanted. My words putting distance between now and the topics I wasn't yet ready to revisit with Sam.

"So the Father of the Year prize *won't* be going to Daddy Markovitz," he said.

"No kidding. One minute he's helping me, and the next he's helping himself. Makes me wonder about all of it. The maps, the room, all of his *Danyankeleh* warnings—and for what? A means to an end? Keep me in circulation so I can get him what he needs?" I picked at an invisible ball of thread at my knee. "I almost prefer Ezra. At least he's honest about his self-interest. Mostly. He doesn't try to remind me I should love him first."

"What do you think of the alternate dimension theory?"

"I think it's possible," I said. "But if it's true—and why would he lie about that?—then that meat suit he was wearing must be a portal of some kind. Or the tattoo. Or maybe both?"

"Perhaps," Sam said. "If tats are involved, it's the second time he's used it. More than once could be a pattern."

It took me a couple of beats to make the literal dots connect. "Oh," I said. "My back. Right."

"And both sets of tats," Sam continued, "combined with something to do with your blood, could be connected to accessing a portal. Maybe the same portal."

"Nothing good came out of it last time." The room was warm, even with the overhead fan on, but I was shivering. Teeth rattling together. *Never* was too soon to see Alina and her cadre of death and dismemberment again.

I was gripping the arms of the chair; deeper as my claws slid into the upholstery and started shredding. My face itchy where the whiskers poked through, hairs raising into a cowl behind and around my neck. A spiked leather collar, except the points were my hair and the leather my skin. Choking me. I couldn't breathe. *No.* My eyes catching the light in the shadows, more contrast than when I'd walked in. The rise and fall of air filtering through Sam's lungs. His blood as it rushed through the arteries and veins.

His eyes, watching me.

I focused on those eyes. The energy flowing under his skin, matching mine. His pulse. Sam did a slow blink—no threat here, at least not to me. A man. Another blink and he was an oversized orange feline stretched across where the man had been. And then he was on the floor, in front of me, rubbing against my legs. Purring. Sharing his warmth. His peace.

I gave in to the feeling then. Allowed the waves to roll through me, tickling my toes as my bones broke and reformed; fur and sinew and fat and muscle softening the internal blows. Within and without. I released the terror that closed my throat and turned my eyes, my attention, inwards, backwards, facing places I did not want to see. My own fur warming me now.

I let it all go.

Sam's head bonked mine, but gently, and he made a small chirping sound in his throat. Because I was no longer human on the chair but rather a grey shaggy feline with tufts between her paws and an even larger ginger cat licking at my face.

Our fur had changed colors. I remembered in the part of my brain where I stored such information, like which underwear I had on or what the capital of Canada was, that I didn't always look like this. I'd seen Sam with white fur before, or maybe it was black. None of that mattered. I knew *him*, as he knew me, and it had nothing to do with appearances or words or colognes or cars.

He was as I saw myself. The other half of me. The part without which I was the lesser, somehow missing. A longing, a need I realized I hadn't felt before. When we were. Before we weren't.

Fuck. Me.

Sam nipped at my ear; this was new. Grabbing my attention with a sudden, different kind of craving.

I butted his head with my own, gentle. Sliding myself alongside him. I looked over and he was watching me. Intent. Prey? I watched him too. Backing away, towards the bed.

Turning at the last moment to jump up. Enveloped by his scent; man and beast and lavender detergent and cardamom chai tea from the last time I'd stayed over. I knew them all; rolling from side to side, spreading the scent of me into his sheets until he and I blended together. No beginning and no end.

The bed sagged as Sam jumped up beside me.

Touched his nose to mine, a greeting without threat. Lying down to stretch out alongside me. Nuzzling in. The man inside the beast soothing the beast inside me.

Energy crackled and my fur staticked out in all directions as the cat behind me became man once more. Stroking along my side. Under my chin. Making me purr as he nuzzled in closer and wrapped his arms around me. Holding me without holding me down; I could leave at any time.

My choice.

I chose to stay.

The transition from full cat to full human was harder for me. Less practiced. I breathed Sam in; his lips on the back of my neck the touch point from one form to the next. Mostly there. Not quite. My tail twitched between his legs and I realized that somewhere, somehow, he'd shed the track pants from earlier and was now naked. With my tail tickling his balls.

Whoops?

Based on the growing hardness behind me, Sam didn't mind.

Easier to focus on that as the fur along my spine, my torso, receded with each inhalation back into my pores. Smoothing and stretching to pinkish. My arms outstretched; starting as fur and pads and claws, devolving into skin. The dual scent of Sam, confusing, with two distinct strands to follow.

As my cat dissolved and my human pushed through, I realized I'd left my clothes somewhere as well. Glanced over at the chair, the floor beneath it. Oh. Yeah.

Too late; we were fully skin on skin now. Against. Between. His lips on my neck, his fingers interlacing with mine. *Want.* Extricating his left hand to drag light

fingernails down from under my chin to the dip between one breast and the other. Brushing the back of
his hand against nipples straining to reach it. Palm flat
on my belly, pressing me into him, as his fingers fluttered towards somewhere hotter, darker. Wet.

"Please," I whispered. And then: "Yes."

I heard his bedside drawer slide open. The crinkle
of the condom wrapper, a pause as he rolled it on and
then Sam was inside me. Whole again. His touch sparking mine, skin on skin, thrusts that pushed beyond and
more and crested before receding.

No more fear.

I was home.

When I woke up again the sun had moved midway up
the sky. I was on my own in the tangle of sticky sweat
and sex and 600-plus thread-count Egyptian cotton.

Thought maybe I smelled the oily rich tickle of
fresh-ground coffee from downstairs. I salivated, licking away the salt and sweet from where it beaded on
my upper lip. The pressure on my bladder made a com-
pelling argument for getting out of bed and I padded,
naked, to Sam's solid dark stained-wood chest of drawers circa sometime early mid last century. I'd done it
before, but I wasn't sure how he'd feel about me doing
it now. Considering.

My hand hovered over the handle. A girlfriend could
do this.

Could I?

Instead I grabbed the top sheet from the bed and
wrapped it around my torso, tucking the ends into the
fabric before bending down to scoop up my discarded

clothing from earlier. Shower. Definitely. An experimental armpit sniff confirmed it—I reeked.

Several glorious minutes later, I'd scrubbed and lathered and rinsed away Jon, and Ezra, and my father, and Alina, and Sam. Alina. *No.*

The water was a relief. Hot was good; the liquid mixing with my lather/scrub/rinse/repeat allowed me to release the surface layers of the last several hours of my life from my skin. If only it had the same effect on my memory. Those places I went when I didn't want to, dangling in my mind by bloodied fingernails that shred to the quick as they scrabbled at the edges of that waking nightmare pit. The one where screams and groans and my own past inaction grasped at my ankles with bony fingers as I backed away and tried to forget.

I giggled, hysteria wrapped in nonsense, the sounds bouncing off the tiles of the bathroom; I slapped my palms flat over my mouth to muffle what I couldn't control. Too many keen listeners in this house. I had to be careful. Couldn't let them know what I was thinking, how far from the confident Warrior Dana I'd slipped.

I was gasping now, taking tiny breaths close together, spinning while standing still. I slapped my hands against the wall now, hard enough to displace a thumbnail of grout; somehow I forced myself to lean rather than form a fist and punch it through. Pounding in my ears. *Breathe.* I had to breathe.

A soft knock on the door.

"Dana, it's me." Sam's voice. I could focus on that. "Can I come in?" The rope of sound to anchor me back to a reality that was real and not made up of my terror.

I didn't trust my voice. Not yet. But I craved the

sound of his. Stabilizing. Making me whole. Until I could breathe again, the scent of him calling to me even as his voice grew quiet again. Waiting.

"Yes." I managed that. It took a couple of tries.

The door clicked open and Sam slid in, shutting it behind him. Had I forgotten to lock it before? Or was he particularly handy with a penny or maybe the dull edge of a butter knife?

Sam eased back the fabric shower curtain, all rubber duckies and neon-striped blue and orange and pink fish, releasing the steam I'd collected in my nook. I was shivering despite the heat. Sam saw it all. Then reached back to grab the plush purple towel—Anshell got only the best—and turned off the tap before wrapping that towel around my shoulders. Patting me down as my tension eased under his touch.

So different from the last time we were in the shower together.

"Better?" Sam angled his head down to catch my eye. He smiled, but it was hesitant; unsure of which Dana he was seeing behind the wild eyes that stared back at him.

I realized he'd seen me, *this* me, before. On the beach. Two nights ago, when Alina had decided to pay me a visit.

And he hadn't left me behind.

Even now Sam was here, despite having no responsibility to stay. He owed me nothing.

And yet.

I definitely owed him.

My breath was still shaky as I forced a smile to lift the edges of my mouth. Tentative. I wanted it to be real but wasn't sure I could sell it yet. I mean, I *was* naked and wet and coming off a panic attack.

But Sam's warmth rubbing along my arms helped. Not sexual. It was something more. My breath steadied and the ambient temperature of the room normalized with my own basal thermostat. I counted to twenty to be sure.

I knew Sam was watching, cataloguing details in his head. I couldn't help it. Whether I wanted to or not, I had to trust him with my secret.

"Come here," he said, and I left the relative safety of the tub for the security of his arms. Sam kissed the top of my head, his lips coming away wet; my forehead, and then my eyelids. Cheeks. Jawline. So soft. Brushing against my mouth with his before pulling away to lean back against the sink counter. Wrapping his arms around me as I pressed my ear to his chest, tuning the tempo of my breath with the pumping of his heart. Tears unshed, but only with effort.

I tried not to think of the life flowing with that beat; how I would feel if that pulsing proof of vitality were to end. I couldn't. He couldn't. My breathing shallowing again as I struggled not to drown in the blackness that reached across my chest, along my arms, around my throat until there wasn't enough air and I was choking.

Sam stroked my back. Soothing, the way I remembered my mother's hand as she tried to ease an over-tired toddler to sleep. Calming my mind with her motions; a sense memory responding in kind to Sam's touch.

"You're safe," he whispered into the drops of wet beading on my ringlets of hair. "Everything is fine. Everyone is safe. I'm here. It's OK, you're OK." Moisture leaking from my eyes, mixing with the wet dripping from places the towel had not yet tamped down. Marking Sam's faded grey cotton t-shirt with the damp thumbprints of my tears.

I didn't cry. And if I did, it wasn't in front of anyone else. The whole tree/forest/did anyone hear it thing. Right? So I wasn't crying now. Never mind those feelings that demanded to be heard. I shoved them down, hard.

My chest hurt from the pressure. I pushed away everything I didn't say, wanted nothing to do with, squeezing my eyes shut as I clenched my fists. Scented blood. I'd cut into the lines of my palms with curved claws arcing from my fingertips, embedding them into my flesh.

And then there was the pain.

"Shit," I muttered, my mind abruptly my own again. "Let go," I said, louder. "Please."

Sam released me, stepping to the side and settling himself down on the closed-lid toilet seat. Watching as I ran cold water on my hands until it ran pink, then clear, and my partial paws became fully human fingers once again. The clouds in my brain breaking up and freeing me from their fog.

Until I was normal again. *Me.* For now.

"Do you want to talk about it?" Sam's voice was level. No judgy vibe.

"I really don't."

"I've seen it before." Sam wasn't looking directly at me. No non-verbal signs of aggression; I was willing to bet he was doing it on purpose. Suggested he'd had practice. Not his first rodeo at the Skittish Feline Corral.

Was it wrong for me to hope it was going to be his last?

"I've got some tricks," I said. "Tools. For when it gets bad."

"You've been treating this yourself? No help?"

"The internet is a beautiful thing," I replied. "Everything from instructions on bomb building to treating PTSD in the comfort of your own home." I tried on a half smile, lightening my words without committing.

Sam nodded. "There are other things you can do," he said. "Pack things. Stuff you won't find online."

"Sam, you can't tell Anshell. You can't tell *anybody*." My voice shook. "If anyone found out, I'd be a target. I'd be screwed." My eyes, begging with the words I wouldn't allow myself enough rope to say.

Sam didn't say anything himself for several long moments. Then:

"I'll keep your secret," he said. "But only as long as nobody's safety is compromised because of it. Not yours, Anshell's, the Pack's or mine. Best I can offer. But you have to deal with this."

"I *am* dealing with it." My tone snapped along with my patience; I softened it. "I'm trying," I said. "Doing the best I can."

"I know. And you can do it. But everyone needs help sometimes." He caught my eye, reinforcing his words. "You're not alone here."

I nodded. My head wanted to believe him; the rest of me, those dark places where the monsters hid, whispered Sam would leave at the first sign of real trouble.

Except he hadn't. Not yet, anyway.

No. He was ready to dump you when you couldn't tell him you wouldn't sleep with Owain. That you didn't still have feelings for the man who had broken your heart.

I'd added a third variable to the already-precarious balance of me with both Sam and Jon.

I was such an idiot.

Except Sam hadn't gone far. He was here in the bathroom with me, making sure I was OK; knowing I wasn't really.

"I'm sorry," I managed, turning to face him. Owning it. "What I said about Owain."

"Don't," he said. "It's done. My problem."

"No," I said. Voice soft, husky with tears I swallowed back down again. "Mine."

A sharp look, then, as Sam opened his mouth to say something—the opportunity lost with three sharp raps on the bathroom door.

"All good in there?" Anshell. Guess he was back from his run. Or whatever.

I glanced over at Sam.

"Are we?" I waited until he shrugged his acquiescence. "All good," I said, louder. Pretense only. Anshell could have heard me if I'd whispered.

"Kitchen when you're ready," our Pack Alpha said.

Anshell was reading the paper when we made it downstairs about five minutes later. Old school. Maybe Anshell owned a tablet, but if he did he certainly wasn't using it to avoid getting newsprint smudges on his fingers.

Two mugs, a carton of cream along with the sugar bowl and two stainless steel teaspoons with a winding rose pattern were arranged *just so* to the side of the already-full coffeepot. Anshell had one of those higher-end models, the kind that grinds the beans thirty seconds before brewing. The smell alone was enough to take me to my happy place. I could almost forget the crazy that had brought me here.

I settled in opposite Anshell. Sam hooked the chair between Anshell and me with one ankle, since his hands were now full with two bowls of some kind of fruity cereal and two mugs of coffee. Somehow he managed to balance them all until after they made contact with the table without spilling anything. Impressive.

Sam nudged half of his collection over to me. *Considerate.* I nodded my thanks because I suddenly didn't trust my voice. Instead I forced my eyes down to my bowl. The spoon. That growling stomach that said *feed me*, and getting some cereal into it pronto.

I took a sip of my coffee—*bliss!*—and then one more to prove to myself that I wasn't ruled by my stomach. Point made, at least to myself; I scooped up my first spoonful of sugary crunchy bits covered in milk and started chewing.

"Dana had an interesting drive over here," Sam said, prompting me. He gave good deadpan when he wanted.

"My father," I started. "I don't think he's dead." My coffee suddenly fascinating between my hands. "He seems to be stuck in some kind of alternate dimension. Or maybe it's parallel." I took another sip, grimacing at the greasy film of cream that had been so enticing moments earlier.

"Explain," Anshell said.

So I told him. About my visit from my father. Then Ezra. Then Alina. The surprising accidental side effect of death metal music forcing her out and allowing Ezra back. The skin. The riddle of that thumbprint tattoo.

The person who'd tipped off Alina about me in the

first place; about the inter-dimensional power in my blood, and my splatter-dot back tattoo.

Daddy Dearest.

"Nice," said Anshell. Yep, that was my Pack Alpha—the Grand Master of Understatement. "And what of that job offer, the one delivered by your ex-boyfriend?" Anshell paused, waiting for me to fill in the missing name blanks. Sure. Why not hang out all the dirty laundry on the kitchen table at once.

"Owain McCready," I said. Not looking at Sam this time. "But you knew that. And yeah, I took the gig. Ezra's fingerprints were all over this, even if Owain was the messenger. Fastest way to figure out what's going on is with a guided tour, a swipe badge and proper clearance."

"You haven't told them about being a shifter, have you?" Sam knew the answer but asked anyway. For Anshell's sake I guess.

"No," I said. "I like my freedom, and prefer not to be sliced open and experimented on. What, you thought I left because I didn't like the brand of rice pudding they served?" Shook my head. "Most of the agents were good people. Or seemed that way. But the science wing—I couldn't be part of what was going on there." Swallowed the lump of bile that threatened to push its way up my throat and out my nose. My hands balled into fists and I dropped them into my lap so we could all pretend not to have noticed.

"Not even this Owain?" Because some of my secrets were also Anshell's and those of the Moon with Seven Faces Pack. A moment of misplaced trust could cost us all.

"Especially Owain."

Sam narrowed his eyes at that, recognizing my tone for what it partially was: shame. Embarrassment. Discomfort with who I was and what I'd become. Even now. And then he surprised me—reaching over to squeeze my hand.

He understood?

"What about the demon?"

Right. The one still crashing on my couch.

"The Agency wants him, the octopods want him, and they're both looking to me to make it happen. I can't hand Gus over though, no matter now annoying he is, because I promised Sandor. Right now, I'm avoiding all of them and pretending to have forgotten my extensive search and target retrieval skills. But it's going to get very old very fast if I can't think of a new storyline." I looked at Anshell. "Any ideas?"

"Working on it," he said.

Chapter Twenty-Six

"I'm taking a shower and then you owe me drinks, dinner *and* dessert," I said, stomping towards the bathroom and dripping octo-slime all over my floor. It had been another wild night at the Swan. Celandra had been there, and Frank, and a whole lot of spewed ink from body parts I didn't want to think about too closely.

Gus was preening in front of my full-length hallway mirror. He'd changed out of his customary flannel pants, t-shirt and hoodie for something a bit more leather daddy. Currently he was admiring the separation of his mottled ice-blue ass cheeks between the black leather straps dividing them.

"Nice," I commented, midway to cleanliness.

"You think?" Gus angled in the opposite direction, hiking the waist and evaluating the impact of this alternate posterior vantage point when perked up from below even as the crack strap helped to lift and separate. Guess he'd decided to harness his assets for the night.

I nodded, checking out the view from a few different perspectives. "You've definitely got the ass for it. Where are you going?"

"It's Pride," said Gus. "Church Street? There's gotta be a beer tent out there with my name on it."

"What about the part where there are two separate contracts out on you—that we know of? You think it's safe?"

"Well, seeing as you're holding both contracts, I think I'm good for now." He twisted again before leaning forward and checking himself out one more time. "Plus it's a capture out on me, not a kill," he said. "If it was a kill, they'd have hired someone like me rather than you and I'd be dead already."

"And that's a good thing?" Considering what I knew about the Agency's experimentation techniques. "Aren't you curious who wants you and why?"

"It'd be a long list," Gus replied. "Life is short. I want to have fun fun fun till they try to take my T-Bird away."

"Have you ever gotten a capture gig?"

"Of course," Gus said. "Got my claws wet on a few. Still pick them up now and then to keep sharp. Harder than kills. All that transporting. Those octo-dorkers who caught you and Sandor for a while—they're the go-to's for snatch and grabs these days. It's their thing."

"And what about the norms?" I was genuinely curious. "Aren't they going to notice a six-foot-five blue demon with tusks and an extra eye walking down the street in leather chaps?"

"People see what they expect to see," said Gus. "Besides, it's Pride. I wouldn't be the only one in costume. With all the intoxicants floating around out there, chances are nobody would believe what I am even if they saw past the veneer."

"Still," I said. "I want to stop being bodily threatened every few hours because of you. I'm going to try to deal with the Agency myself." Gus's eyes narrowed. *Whoops.* Had I forgotten to mention that? "But these cephalopods," I continued, pretending not to see his implied threat. "They're a nuisance and they're getting destructive. Celandra diverted the last attack, but they still broke stuff at the Swan." I crossed my arms. "Don't care about me? Whatever. But this is your *brother*. You need to make this stop."

"Agency contract?"

"Yeah," I said. "Remember? I'm sure I told you. The Agency wants you as well *and* they offered me the gig."

"Aren't you out of that game?" Gus started fiddling with his crossover lace-up suspenders, all leather straps and brass rings. Somehow he kept missing the fastening. *Interesting.* Suddenly my proximity made his fingers twitch in a fear response he couldn't control fast enough to hide.

"I was," I replied. "Doesn't mean the offer isn't tempting."

Gus stilled, scary silent, and I was aware all over again that I was sharing unguarded space with an assassin who'd almost ended me a handful of months earlier. Forced myself to breathe, keep my voice light. "Don't worry," I said. "I have enough nightmares. I took the gig to buy us time."

Gus gave a single nod. Nightmares probably weren't a problem for him, but I think he believed me. Maybe there was something he'd read in my file for the original Dana *dunzo* contract that suggested trusting me was worth the risk.

In truth, in that place deep down where I kept my secrets, I couldn't swear that this Agency gig would be a one-time thing. Too much family history there, and I had too many questions. Just because my father had tattooed a demon bull's-eye target on my back, and at least one version of Ezra appeared to be in cahoots with my personal nightmare Alina, didn't mean everyone who worked at the Agency was evil, right? Maybe change could happen from the inside?

Or maybe I was spinning rationalizations to avoid the practical reasons for my decision to to take on this job. Sure, partly, it was to protect Gus if I could. But I also needed answers that Owain had hinted the Agency might actually still have. And while I was getting that information, I might as well get paid for it.

Fortunately, Gus couldn't hear my inner monologue. "What's the bounty?"

I walked over to my bag, found the offer and passed it to him.

What the hell. I could do full(ish) disclosure.

Impressive what a demon with such thick fingers and angled nails could do with a touch-screen tablet designed for much smaller hands. Guess it's true what they say—it's not the size of the appendage but what you do with it.

Gus's eyes narrowed at something in the bottom corner of the scroll. I leaned over his arm to see. The authorization code?

"Does that mean something to you?" I'd often seen it on assignments, but always assumed it was some kind of randomly generated number like a password or an invoice.

Gus nodded once. Curt.

"Tells me who wants me. And why."

"Show me," I said.

A grey-blue-ridged nail tapped the first four digits of the eighteen-character string.

"SCOV," Gus said. "That's a requisition code. Tells

you the department it came from. SCOV is Science and Covert Affairs." My old department. I kept that part to myself. "Those next four characters—that's the clearance level of the person initiating the request. 1103. Someone in upper middle management would be my guess."

"Does everyone in the Agency get this kind of clearance code? I don't remember having one."

"Of course," said Gus. "But until you're at a certain level, you wouldn't know about it. Maybe they didn't trust you as much as you thought."

"It's possible." I pointed to the last string of letters and numbers. "What about these?"

"79Z3," Gus said. "Highest-level approval. Buck stops here code."

"You recognize it?"

"Yeah," Gus said. "Your old pal Ezra Gerbrecht."

Fuck.

"I see." I was impressed with how level I managed to keep my voice. Even though I was screaming and pounding my fists on the wall inside my head. "What does he want with you?"

Gus scanned the screen with cool eyes, crunching the alpha-numeric string into possible if/then scenarios. A decisive nod as the most logical outcomes fell into pattern spaces in front of him.

"Cover story would be genetic sample gathering," Gus said. "Take a few skin scrapings, harvest a few of the twinkly bits. All very humane treatment for demons in case anyone checked into the records later."

"But?"

"Animal testing. That's what I'd be to them. Needles,

cages, sharp blades and no skin." Gus looked away. "You worked there. You know."

I swallowed the lump in my throat as a droplet of sweat trickled its way down along the side of my neck to drip, awkward, into the crevice between my breasts. I did know. The tubes, the screams, the pleas for help I couldn't answer without ending up in a cage myself— or dead.

"I can't let you take me in," Gus said.

"Even if I'd turned the gig down, which I didn't, you know they'd just send someone else. And if that person failed, they'd try again. And again. No—we need to do something different."

"Such as?" Gus scratched the outer nostril ridge of his nose, an unconscious tic I'd seen Sandor do more than once. "I'm not sending someone else in my place, if that's what you're thinking."

"No." I suppressed a shudder, counting to five in my head as Gus watched. If he recognized what he was seeing, he kept his observations to himself. "But maybe we could negotiate an alternative, something they want more than you. Or at least that they'd be willing to settle for."

"And that would be what?" Gus's laugh was more of a bark. "There's a reason I know those codes. It's me they want, and not just for skin scrapings. There are bodies, and I know where they're buried."

"Then why not just put out a hit? Dead demons don't tell secrets." I paused, thought about it a moment. "Usually. And what about the Squid faction—are they a backup crew? Agency hedge-betting?"

"Unlikely," said Gus. "Tentacles are too much for those pocket-protector normies. Freaks 'em out."

"Owain seemed to be dealing with it OK," I commented, the beginnings of an idea percolating; not quite ready to spew grounds or steam just yet.

"Your ex...*whatever*?" Gus chuckled.

"Shut up," I said. I was pretty sure Owain was ex all of it, but maybe those feelings—the ones I *was* hoping we both still had—would convince him to help me out of this mess.

Owain was willing to meet for coffee before my shift. After I'd showered, changed and burned the clothes I'd been wearing. The octoplasm was starting to smell more like celery mixed with leeks and rotting fish. Plus it had soaked into the fibers of the fabric.

"Try vinegar" had been Gus's parting words as he headed off to Church Street to find the fun.

Yeah, I was going to get right on that.

"So you have questions about the job?"

Owain leaned forward, playing the side of his pint glass as though holding a clarinet and not a moisture-beaded vessel of potential intoxication. Fingers thrumming across sweat and ice and dark rooms with cool kisses. *No.* Remember the now.

"Yeah." I picked up the pack of matches lying on the table; Spotted Dick or Duck or Fox. Rolled them over and under and through my fingers as I rifled my brain for the words. "Do you know if this is a straight-up snatch and grab? Or could the Cinegon be good with something else. Like, instead of the target."

Owain took a sip of his ale, watching me. "Where is he?" Reaching out a hand to touch mine; a calculated move. Or maybe he was hoping to induce telepathic connectivity between us through touch.

I shrugged, meeting his eyes even as I pulled my hands back to drop them into my lap.

"Still looking."

"Uh huh." He shook his head, a smirk playing on his lips before he hid it with a strategic sip of his drink. "You're sticking with that story?"

I nodded.

"Fine. Would it help you to know why the Cinegon wants this asset?"

"Yeah," I said.

"Let me see that offer again," Owain said. Of course I still had it with me; protocol dictated that the missive was never off your person unless or until you declined, completed the job, or were dead. Even I remembered that part. Anything less and you became the target. No thanks. "Right, see here?" I didn't, but I also didn't stop him. "That's the options area." He looked closer. "It's changed a bit since you were with us. This is a capture 'with residuals' job."

"Meaning?"

"Meaning you can capture all or part of the target and still have the job considered delivered in full. 'Residual' might mean the fee is pro-rated—" His voice trailed off as he scrolled down. "Right, yeah. Here." Owain tapped absently on the screen as his brain processed if/then scenarios until the one that made the most sense to him clicked into place. "So this guy shoots off something when he gets cheesed off. There's a note here about it but it doesn't make much sense. Mice chips?"

"I'm supposed to hunt down a large rodent and scoop

up its shit? I know the Agency wants me to prove how serious I am, but come on."

Owain shook his head, a half smile tickling the corners of his mouth.

"It's probably a typo," he said. "Unless you have some *inside* knowledge of this Rodent of Unusual Size?"

I shook my head and did wide-eyed innocent. Pretending Owain didn't know me better than that.

"Right," he said. Playing *Let's Pretend* went both ways today. "So here's what I might do. Find the target. Get him angry, so angry he spits out whatever it is the Cinegon wants to stick in their test tubes. But angry means a fight, and maybe the guy was too much for you."

"Ohhhh," I said, my own smile hitting my face. "Right. Because I went after him on my own. No backup."

"Right," said Owain, leaning back in his seat again.

"Thank you," I said. Raising my own glass in a toast. "Cheers."

"*Sláinte chugat.*" He took another sip, casual, like the answer wasn't a big deal either way. "Have you thought about your future plans? Career-wise, I mean."

"Meaning?" As if I didn't know. Owain had given me the tat, and it was time to serve up the tit in return. "You want to know if I'm thinking of coming back to the Agency full time?"

"Are ye?" Owain watched my face over the rim of his glass for anything my words might not convey in full. Surely my tells had changed after all this time?

"Stop pushing," I said. "Let's see how things go this time around first."

Chapter Twenty-Seven

"So about that Agency job," I said, propping my feet up on Anshell's coffee table. "Owain came up with a workaround."

"Really," said Sam.

"Yeah. He clarified the terms of the contract." I flicked a glance at Anshell, who gave me nothing, then back at Sam. "So I *could* capture Demon Blue and deliver him to the Agency."

"Which you're not going to do?" Sam made the question a statement. Just in case.

"Right," I said. "But what if I could get Gus to spit me some of his blue diamonds? I could say we fought and I lost but hey, nifty shiny stuff, and that might just be enough. Plus Owain said he'd sign off on it. There's no guarantee the Agency won't send someone else for Gus later, but since this is a Covert Science request, it might be enough for now to just get them some organic matter to test."

"And you're not curious what they're looking for?" Anshell's voice was mild but I wasn't buying it.

"Curious? Sure," I said. "But they're not going to let me in on their little secrets from out here. Belly of the beast and all that."

"What about *your* beast?" Sam's point wasn't an un-reasonable one. "How long will you be able to hide that?"

"I'll do it for as long as I can." Because really, what choice did I have? "Staying freelance helps. And I'll make sure to be busy around the full moon. Female troubles, sore foot, visiting family—whatever it takes."

"And Lazzuri will back you up?" Sam didn't sound so sure, but he was willing to be convinced.

"Don't see why not. Reduces the number of inter-ested parties after him by half," I said. "Then again, he's an ornery bugger. He might refuse anyway purely because he can."

"Assuming Mr. Lazzuri is willing to go along with your Agency plan, that leaves us with our tentacled bounty hunter friends," said Anshell. "We've been mak-ing inquiries through channels. It's a curious thing. No-body knows who hired them."

"Is that normal? I mean, for you to have zero intel?"

"No," said Sam.

"Implications?" I was curious—was there a limit to Anshell's reach as Alpha, or was there more to it?

"It increases the odds that this is not local," said An-shell, "In fact, it might be quite the opposite."

"So, uh, foreign?" I bit the inside of my cheek to control my smirk.

"Or inter-dimensional." Anshell ignored my attempt at humor.

Wait. The quest for Demon Blue could be coming from an alternate realm?

There were dots, and I needed to be connecting them. Who did I know who hopped between planes of existence?

One: Alina. But if Frank and Squid D'Lee were working with her, they would have used that big bad demon stick by now—and to inflict pain extremes on me. Which meant, as much as I'd like to blame her for all the recent bad stuff I'd been through, she probably wasn't the *It* in this particular game of tag.

Two: Celandra. Or at least I suspected it. Although she wasn't consistently lucid enough to ask, plus hiring out for dirty work duty didn't seem like her style. Celandra was also friends with Sandor—and loyalty wasn't just a word for her.

Who else was there?

Ezra. He'd known enough about Demon Blue's existence to authorize the freelance capture gig I'd gotten. But that was through official channels, and i was on two legs as far as he knew; I couldn't see Ezra contracting out the work to anything less than humanesque. And cephalopods were about as non-mammalian as you could get. If Ezra needed something like this done, he'd go through the Agency to get it. Why pay out of pocket? He had the clearance levels to pretty much authorize anything he wanted. And what he'd wanted was me.

He wouldn't need to hire a backup crew with tentacles.

Technically, I should be able to hop between dimensions, what with the tattoo on my back and the maps in the attic. But if I wanted to nail Gus, I'd do it myself and I'd do it here. I hadn't located another portal, and while I continued to search, that search had so far been of the fruitless variety.

There *was* someone else, though. Someone I kept forgetting about, as though his existence itself was protected by some kind of *Keep Away* spell.

"My father," I said.

* * *

It made sense. We all agreed.

"Plus," said Sam, "have you noticed how those tentacle guys never actually *hurt* you? They threaten, they restrain, they inflict pain-based motivation on the rest of us but you? You keep walking away. Not a scratch."

"It would certainly reinforce the hypothesis that whoever hired Squid D'Lee and the cephalopod crew included a specific note about you," said Anshell.

"As in suction cups off the girl?"

"Something like that." OK, that *was* Anshell trying not to smile.

But then I remembered it was my father we were talking about. Messing around with my life again, albeit from a distance.

"For the sake of argument," I said, "let's say my father somehow hired Squid D'Lee and his crew to capture Gus. And the contract does seem to be of the 'capture' rather than 'kill' variety for them as well. What would both Ezra and my father be hoping to achieve? And why wouldn't they be working together on this?"

"You don't know for sure they're not," Sam pointed out.

"True," I acknowledged. "But then why bother with two contracts?"

"Unless it's some kind of competition." Sam jumped up and started pacing. Every bit the big cat in the too-small enclosure at the zoo. "They worked together in that Agency lab, right? Before the 'accident'?" Sam actually air-quoted the word *accident*. Cynical much? I must be rubbing off on him.

"Right," I said instead. Wondering where he was going with this.

"And now, by his own admission, your father is stuck in an alternate zone of existence?"

"Yeah, something like that," I said. "And?"

"What if that's the common denominator?" Sam stopped his back and forth momentum to plop down across from me on the coffee table. "Not Gus. What if everything that's been happening is to get you to open another portal?"

"But then why would Ezra care about any of this? And what does it have to do with Gus?"

"Perhaps at this juncture we should ask Gustav Lazzuri ourselves," said Anshell.

The Village was hopping.

In the days leading up to the parades, the City had closed off Church Street south of Bloor so that there were at least ten city blocks of pedestrian-only traffic. On either side, between the packed sidewalks and the even more densely populated thoroughfare, the road was lined with vendors, hawkers and food trucks. Everything from t-shirts and temporary henna tattoos to poutine to cock rings and baskets of free-from-the-City lube packets. If you could imagine it, there was a reasonable chance someone somewhere had it for sale at a special "Pride" price.

Every few blocks were the beer tents. This, in addition to the bars packed in at a higher-than-normal density within a block of the Church and Wellesley Village epicentric intersection.

We found Gus at the third one we tried. I still couldn't believe nobody had noticed there was a tusked demon in leather gear who sneezed blue diamonds, but whatever. Guess people really do see what they expect to see. Unless that worldview is forced askew, whether they want it to be or not.

Gus was standing with his back to us at the bar, chatting up a guy almost half his size, with carrot red manga hair that stuck out in all directions. That was pretty much it for hirsute coverage though; the rest of the guy was freckled pale and hairless as far as I could see. Which was actually quite a bit given that all he was wearing was a red leather thong, matching spiked dog collar and gold lamé flip flops.

I could tell it was Gus by the twinkling blue sheen of glitter he'd sprinkled on his ass cheeks before heading out.

"Over there," I said to Sam and Anshell. Who suddenly seemed overdressed for the occasion in t-shirts and jeans, even when paired with low-key brown and navy-blue fabric/rubber flip flops of their own.

"Gustav," Anshell said, touching him lightly on the shoulder. "A word?"

Gus narrowed his eyes at the interruption, tensing for a fight; his shoulders dropping to a more relaxed warrior stance once he realized it was us. Not quite luaus-and-coconut-pineapple-drinks-with-paper-umbrellas-and-Hawaiian-shirts-on-the-beach relaxed, but enough that the risk of him ripping our heads from our shoulders decreased significantly.

"In private?" Anshell added that last bit when Gus didn't move from his new playmate right away. Maybe Gus was worried someone else would lay claim to the baby-faced manga man if he stepped aside, even for a couple of minutes.

Gus's reticence held moments past the point of casual. Yep, we were definitely interrupting something. *Oh well.*

"Hi," I said, reaching across to shake palms with the new boy. His flesh was clammy; I couldn't tell whether it was stress sweat or just the normal kind that seeps from all living surfaces in 38°C with the humidity. "Dana. And you are?"

"T… T… Troy," he stammered. "How do you know Gasper here?"

Gasper, huh?

"From here and there," I said. "Do you mind if we borrow him for five minutes? We'll bring him right back."

Troy's upper lip twitched and he blinked seven times in succession. Nervous tic? Or was he counting it out?

"What do you say, Daddy?" *Daddy? Ick.* "Tell me what you want me to do."

Gus leaned over to whisper something in the shorter man's ear while stroking the back of his neck. The blinking became more rapid; this time I counted fourteen blinks in fourteen seconds or less, eyes darting up and around, seeking out gaps in the overhead tent. At least that was my guess. If I was playing capture the tongue with a blue demon twice my size in assless chaps, I'd be wanting an exit strategy too.

But then Troy's eyes fell to Gus's black, thick-soled lace-up motorcycle boots, and I realized that whatever fight he had left inside had fled, leaving the flaccid bound shell of resistance behind. Gus waved over one of the staff loitering by an open flap, blowing smoke into the already heavy air, his or her tight t-shirt and baggy cargo pants suggesting female but I couldn't be sure.

And really, did it matter?

I couldn't hear what Gus said, but the end result was a short stool that had Troy at eye level with one inch above the surface of the bar's counter. He could see what was going on around him, but there was no way to pretend he was doing anything but obeying an order designed to demonstrate who was in charge—and who wasn't.

OK, sure, there were games to be played in private. Danas in glass houses and all that. But this kind of public display of obsequiousness? *So* not my thing.

Anshell raised an eyebrow, exchanging with Sam a look so fleeting I couldn't catch it, but otherwise went with poker face before sliding into a table towards a darker, less densely populated edge of the space. Sam settled in beside him, making sure he had a clear view of all possible avenues for both incursion and escape.

Me, I waited until Gus picked his spot—across from Anshell—before dropping into a fold-up chair to Sam's left. It meant I was facing away from the primary entrance/exit more than I would have liked, but I trusted Sam and Anshell to have my back. Or at least to give me a heads up if lives were in danger.

You know. Pack business.

"What did you find?" Gus looked from Anshell to Sam to me and then back again. "I *know* you didn't interrupt my Pride experience just to have a beer and get ripped off on the cover charge. Right?"

"Nothing concrete. Not yet," said Anshell. "But," he continued, "we were wondering—have you ever had dealings with a Stuart Markovitz?"

Gus leaned back, crossing his arms over his pierced-nipple-ringed chest. Dude was seriously going for the full experience here. Eyes flicking to me and then back again.

"Her father?"

"Right," I said, since Sam was keeping his words to himself for some reason. "Ever do a contract for him?"

"No," Gus replied. He didn't even have to think about it. "But isn't he dead?"

"Not as much as you'd think," I muttered. Gus raised an eyebrow. "I've been seeing him around so I'm thinking not so much."

"Re-animation? Or are you sure he's back?"

Re-animation was actually an option?

"I wouldn't call my father 'back' exactly," I said, keeping the rest of my thoughts to myself. "I think there's some kind of inter-dimensional airlock situation, or whatever the technical term for it is, happening. It's hard to tell. Dad pops in, fades out, comes back as someone else—and he doesn't make consistent sense even when he's the guy whose DNA I share. I think maybe he has early-onset dementia or something."

Gus nodded. "Yeah," he replied. "Realm hopping can be hell on you norms. Or," he corrected himself, "those of you with human-based biology. Humans, shifters, that kind of thing. You know—you lot."

I gaped. Shut my mouth again. "This is what happens to anyone who jumps dimensions? Like, once? Or does it need to happen on repeat somehow?"

"The more you do it, the worse it gets," said Gus. "How do you not know this? It's portal jumping 101." He narrowed his eyes, looking at each of us for ignorance confirmation. "Why do you think our friend Celandra is as bat-shit as she is? IQ nearing 200, almost that old in human years and, what, you thought maybe she'd gotten a bit feeble-minded in her advancing age?" Gus snorted. "Hardly."

"You do it," Sam pointed out. "And you seem relatively sane to me. How's that work?"

"Different physiology. Doesn't affect me."

"When you did contract work for the Agency," I said, trying hard not to stare, "did they run any tests on you first?"

"Nah," said Gus. "Subcontractor. No long-term responsibility for them and no stupid medical tests for me. Same reason you're doing it that way, am I right? Wait…" His voice trailed off as his mind cast backwards through times past. "I did take a few dimension-hopping gigs for the Agency. Snatch and grabs mostly. That's when I started noticing what portal crossing did to the mental grips of my packages."

"Did you ever say anything to whoever had hired you?" No way Anshell's question, however casually he posed it, was anything other than a cover. He wanted to know whether perceptual travel jetlag was a commonly known side effect.

"Nah," Gus said again. "Kept that bit to myself. But it was pretty obvious. I'd deliver the packages, all of them valued assets before I got to them, and they'd be making with the rambling verbal diarrhea by the time I brought them in. I'm too expensive to waste on non-threatening cleanup."

"Your Agency contact," I said. "Are they still there? Do you know?"

"Yeah," Gus replied. "Your friend Ezra Gerbrecht."

Was *everything* connected? Because otherwise coincidence was a super-contagious virus around here.

"Weird dude," Gus continued. "Always with the small talk. How was your trip, any issues, what did you eat—that kind of thing. Like he was making con-

versation, trying to act all *whatever*, but really he was
filing every detail away somewhere in that brain of his."

"That would be Ezra," I said. "How much does he
know about what you can do? Or your existential resistance to crazy?"

"It's not like the guy asked," said Gus, shrugging.
He glanced over at his slave of the hour, making sure
Troy was still squatting on the stool. Amazingly, he
was. "But isn't he genius-level, that guy? Wouldn't take
much to figure out the differences by looking."

"So then one might safely assume that Ezra Gerbrecht, who is still with the Agency, might have noticed
you suffer no ill effects by either moving between or
spending time in alternate dimensions." Anshell seemed
to be thinking out loud at this point. "If you were a scientist by nature, and you discovered a non-human with
the physiology to keep his mental acuity despite dimensional travel shifts, wouldn't you be curious? Want to
study the phenomena closer?"

"I didn't offer," said Gus. "And he didn't ask."

Sam was nodding now.

"Of course," he said. "And if the guy *had* asked?
What would you have said?"

Gus's stare reminded me of the frosty hoar that had
ice-burned my last phone, the same chill that held me
by the throat as it tried to choke the life from me. And
still I lacked the answers I needed for that single question I'd asked: *why?*

"I'd have said fuck you," Gus replied. "Fuck you, the
horse you rode in on, and the next several generations
of its offspring." He was watching Anshell now, grin
stretching into a slow leer. *Right.* He must have known
Anshell was also equine by now.

Anshell ignored the jab.

"You would have declined his request then." Hello stating the obvious, my Alpha. "So if Ezra Gerbrecht wished to study you, it would have to be without your permission. Correct?"

"Damned straight," said Gus. "Oh." Realization hitting, getting through even his thickest of skulls.

"So that explains the Agency snatch-and-grab gig they're outsourcing to me," I said. "But what about the cephalopod crew's contract? Ezra doesn't like dealing with anything that can't walk on its own bipedal appendages. Legs," I clarified. "So Gus there would be acceptable, but those eight-limbed guys wouldn't. Too *foreign.* And yes, in case you were wondering, Ezra is a big-time specist."

"So if Gerbrecht didn't hire those squidly guys taking apart my brother's bar to get at me, then who did?"

"Our only guess is the other person with a personal stake in making inter-dimensional travel safer for humans," I said. "My father, Stuart Markovitz."

We had no proof. It was still just a hunch.

But it was the most plausible one we had right now.

Ran into Jon and Claude on the way back to where I'd parked my truck.

OK, not so much ran into as spotted ambling towards, holding hands while Jon whispered in Claude's ear and Claude slid one hand down the back of Jon's pants, laughing. Not sure what I'd expected, but more broken up and less casual comfort wasn't unreasonable. Personal opinion. You know, given that Claude had scratched me into active shifterhood and then tried to kill me repeatedly.

Anshell and Sam had already left, so the awkwardness was left for me to enjoy all on my own.

"Hey, bitch," Claude said by way of greeting. "Slumming it?"

"Go fuck yourself," I replied, all pleasant voiced and smiling. "I didn't realize you two were still hanging out." That last part aimed at Jon.

Jon shrugged. Great, fine, we were all adults.

And I was such an idiot.

Sure, emotionally unavailable was my comfort zone. Owain. My father. Others. But with Jon I'd gone all over-achiever: not just emotionally unavailable but also physically—apparently I'd been sharing him with his asshole of an ex all along. Which I guess made Claude more *current* than *ex* actually.

True, he'd been sharing me with Sam and sort of that one time with Owain as well. Glass houses—check. But come on. What was I so afraid of?

Don't answer that.

Did I care if Jon saw other people? Not really. But that he could have fallen back so easily into old patterns with someone who'd tried to kill me was not something I could live and let live about. If it was up to Claude, I'd be dead where I stood even now.

It wasn't about monogamy. It was a matter of loyalty.

And Jon's wasn't to me, not when it came to Claude. But I didn't say any of that out loud.

"See ya," I said instead, turning to go. What was there to say? Jon and I would still be friends. But those side benefits?

Those were done.

Chapter Twenty-Eight

Sometimes you have to go back to the source. And while you're there, sharing some hot chocolate with a friend you've maybe seen naked wouldn't suck. Especially if the friend was hot, and the source had central air-conditioning.

"So this is where you grew up, eh?"

Sam was lying on his back, temptation and muscle tucked into pink and frills and florals. High school Dana, the one who'd decorated this room, would have been glued to the doorway with dry mouth and pounding heart. I was less of a chicken-shit now, experience breeding confidence. Relatively speaking. Still, the incongruity of the warrior among the petals, fabric though they were, was jarring.

"You promised not to tease me." I waggled my finger at him.

"I did no such thing," Sam said, pushing himself up on his elbows to grin at me. "You have officially lost your right to bug me about my sheets. Because," and he waved his hand over the bed, then to the curtains beyond. "Behold the field in which I lay, and lo but it is covered in girly flowers which milady pretends she cares nothing for. And yet. Behold."

"I'll be holding something," I muttered, but couldn't help smiling back. Sam's humor was infectious. Being around him, just us, felt *good.*

Adding to the pink in the room, hello large relationship elephant that we weren't discussing. The part where maybe we'd sort of broken up. Even though we'd turned around and slept together one more time after that.

Nope, things weren't confusing between us. At all.

I perched on the edge of my bed, closer to Sam's feet, opening my mouth to take a bite from the awkward topic. Sam got there before I did.

"Come here," he said, holding out his hand.

I drew back instead, spine to baseboard, as far away as I could get without leaving the bed. Shook my head.

"Not a good idea," I said. "You keep talking about walking away from *me*, remember? What are you playing at here?"

"So you *do* care?" Sam quirked a half smile to soften his words. Watching my face, my eyes, my lips.

"Stop screwing with me," I said. "We're all about Pack business now right? Nothing more?"

Sam shrugged, leaning back into the palms of his hands.

"Let's see this secret room of yours," he said instead. Changing the subject. "Your mom doesn't mind me being here?"

"A strange man in her house? Without her express beforehand permission? The horror!" My turn to grin. "Of course she's also up north at a friend's cottage so that point is moot. Besides, she likes you."

"I give good parent," Sam said, pushing himself up to sitting.

"Among other things," I muttered, heading to the closet. No idea if he heard me.

Probably best if he hadn't.

"Have you tried reading any of these books?" Sam was peering at the shelves on the far wall, inspecting tomes I'd suspected were only there as a distraction from the box of treasures unknown. You know, that one on the top shelf my fingers never seemed quite able to reach no matter how far they stretched—or what piece of furniture I stood on to get there. Also unseen, since I hadn't been able to actually confirm its existence since that first try when thick frost on glass panes was still a thing. As opposed to the air-conditioned condensation the windows had now.

"Not really. And I want to take a closer look at those maps," I said. "Who knows? Maybe Daddy Dearest will show up and actually stick around long enough to answer some questions this time."

"Don't suppose you could call him?"

"Nah," I said. "That would be too easy."

Sam left the books behind and drifted towards the table where I was. Guess *The Beginner's Guide to Quantum Physics* wasn't as catchy a topic as he'd hoped.

"Are these the maps?" A rhetorical question as he spread the parchment sheets across the table for a better look. "How do we make them light up again?"

"Watch this," I said, moving the stack to one side and pulling out only the bottom sheet, moving it to line up with the edge of the wooden *L* page holders. Touching my index finger and forefinger to the mottled surface. "*Danyankeleh, Danyankeleh, Danyankeleh.*"

The lines on the sheet lit up, golds and browns and blues. Sam exhaled on a whistle.

"Never dull around you," he said. "Hang on." Looking closer. "See that line here?" He pointed to a gap in blue, and what I was guessing was either a road or a shoreline. "Looks familiar." His eyes went up and to the left, as though he could visualize that familiarity in a way that aligned it with something he recognized. "And you believe something here points to a portal opening?"

I nodded. "I think it matches one of the patterns on my back," I said.

"Take off your shirt," he said.

I stared at him, cool.

"What? I've seen it before. Hell, I saw it yesterday—*and* at a much more stimulating angle."

"That was then," I said. Weak attempt at dignity. As though that ship hadn't sailed, sunk and been resurrected to sail another day.

"OK," he replied. Not pushing. "Would you be comfortable raising your shirt a bit? Just so I can see? I won't touch—promise." Sam paused, that *let-me-charm-the-pants-off-you* grin playing across his lips. "Unless you want me to touch. Then all you have to do is ask."

"Bite me," I said instead. "You want me, you don't want me. Make up your mind. Otherwise I've got things to do, and they *don't* involve getting naked—partial or otherwise—with you."

"What makes you think my mind isn't made up?" Mild. Not pushing this time. "I see what we could have. But until you get there, I've got things to do. So do you."

"Pack business, for example," I said. As opposed to the bit where I wasn't going to be sleeping with Jon anymore.

"Exactly," he replied. "So allow me to help. Let me take a look."

I huffed, but Sam was right. This might go faster if he could see my back and the maps at the same time.

"Fine," I said, leaning over the desk, palms and forearms flat on the surface. "Look away."

I felt the air behind me shift as every hair on my body strained towards him. Who was I kidding? There *was* nobody else. Not like Sam. *Damn it*.

His touch was light as he held the hem of my tank between his fingers, lifting the fabric, so slow, up towards my shoulders. Careful not to make actual skin-on-skin contact. Respecting my boundaries. Respecting me.

Sam's breath ran hot along the underside of my shoulder blade as he leaned in, closer, to get a better look. In my mind, his tongue was trailing down along my spine, his breath blowing soft heat as his fingers traced patterns between my dots. In my reality, his left hand lay flat against the desk for balance, close to my waist but not touching. Fantasy had his hands grasping at my hips, pulling me closer as he bent me over further. And reality?

"This bit here," Sam said, tapping lightly below my shoulder and then on the top layer of the map. "That is definitely the shoreline up from the Pack house."

"Where that last portal opened?"

"Yeah," he replied. "So let's put this map on the bottom." I watched as Sam placed the first sheet in the center of the table, lined up with the guides. Nothing happened. As soon as he touched the parchment, the lights faded and it was just black lines on a page without any glowy context.

I reached across and touched my index finger to the

un-inked corner. "*Danyankeleh*," I said, and waited. When nothing happened, I followed it up with "*Danyankeleh. Danyankeleh.*"

The map lit up again.

I stood up, my tank falling down to my waist again, and spun around.

"Ta da! It's magic," I said, my arms out in a mock almost-pirouette that ended with a flourishing wave and me over-shooting the turn to stumble forward into Sam's arms. Yeah, my dance career had been short, unremarkable and possibly involving a pumpkin costume. Or maybe a flower.

Sam caught me before I fell, his arms around my waist and his hands flat against the recently bare flesh of my back. Drawing me closer before either of us really realized what was happening. A reflex. Being together as natural as breathing.

I stared at him and him at me. As though either one of us could resist. My hands snaking up and around his neck as Sam, after the barest of jaw clenching/unclenching hesitations, leaned in to brush his lips across mine.

"*Danyankeleh*," he said, kissing my mouth. "*Danyankeleh*," kissing one eyelid and then "*Danyankeleh*" again for the other.

It was a term of endearment, I got that, but that it was one used primarily by my father was icking me out.

"Please stop," I said.

"This?" Sam ghosted his lips across the crease of my neck.

"No." I shook my head. "Not that."

"How about this?" Sam went lower, first with his mouth and then with his fingertips, into the crevice between my breasts. Down to my waist, both hands now,

pushing the bottom of my shirt up, higher, palms gliding over my breasts.

"Mmmm," I replied. Because words were hard now.

"So then *don't* stop, is that what you're trying to tell
me?" Sam had my breasts freed now; everything was
Sam and his thumbs and his tongue.

"No," I said. "Yes. Don't. Don't stop."

Sam chuckled and I could feel his vibrations through
my palms lying flat against his chest. Even through his
t-shirt, which I decided then and there was altogether
too much fabric. My own hands under, travelling higher.

"Off," I said. "Take this off."

He reached back and pulled the cotton material over
his head, tossing it to the side.

"You too," he said, and I pulled my tank the rest of
the way off, followed by my bra. Because occasionally
I can be obedient too.

"What else do you want?" We were standing there,
half-naked, waiting for one of us to make that next
move. As the air behind us shifted and settled.

And the sound of someone clearing their throat from
the far corner of the room. *Fuck.* We had company now?

I bent down to grab my tank before spinning in the
direction of the sound. Sam was already three steps
ahead of me, less concerned about upper-body modesty
than I was, growling like the big cat I knew he could be.

"*Danyankeleh.*" I saw Ezra clearing his throat, but
it was 100% my father in there. Nope, not awkward at
all. "I see you've brought company. Care to introduce
me to your friend?"

"Dana?" Sam wasn't doing anything without con-
sulting me for *what-the-fuck-is-going-on* clarification.
"Do you know this man?"

I sighed.

"Yeah," I said. "Sam, meet my father, Stuart Markovitz. Don't let the Ezra Gerbrecht appearance throw you. Dad, this is Sam."

I figured no last name on Sam was a good thing— no last name, no lingering after-effects or startling popping-in unannounced (elsewhere) visits.

Sam nodded to my father, who returned the nod; no handshakes were offered on either side. Was this a shifter custom I still wasn't aware of? I watched the wary tension in Sam's shoulders, the way he'd angled himself between Daddy Dearest's position and mine, and I realized it was Sam viewing my father as a potential threat. To me, the man's daughter.

My *pater famiglia* didn't seem too concerned, if his smirk was an indication of anything.

"So, my dear," he said instead, dismissing Sam from conversational relevance. "I see you've found the maps. Anything I can do to help you on your quest for enlightenment?"

"Tell me what these have to do with me," I said. Wary. "That would be a great place to start."

"What have you deduced so far?" Still trying to turn opportunity into a teachable moment.

"Well," I said. Eyeing Sam, letting him know with a nod that all was good. For now, at least. I watched as he moved to the side and leaned the ass I'd been so ready to grip moments earlier against the edge of the table. "These maps seem tuned into me specifically. Am I right?"

My father nodded. "Technically, anyone of the blood," he said. Correcting me. "You, me. Except I'm somewhere else so it has to be you." His eyes filming over with an opaque sheen before he blinked it away. "That's why you have to be the one to do it. Because I can't."

"And why would I *want* to open another portal? No good comes of that."

"Because I promised," my father replied.

"Who? Ezra?" Irritated. "I'm sure he'll get over it."

But my father was shaking his head.

"It's not that simple, *Danyankeleh*," he said. "Alina is owed her due. We made a deal, Ezra and I. Help her open a portal gateway, facilitate her ability to connect with the one she seeks, and then she helps me get home again."

"You seem pretty comfortable here in your attic," I commented. "What more do you want?"

"Stop pretending to be less than you are," Dad snapped. So there *were* limits to his patience. "You know that this, me being here, is temporary. My physical body is trapped in an alternate dimension. I'm getting old. I want to come home."

"And you're sure Alina said she'd help?" Sam's skepticism wasn't unreasonable. Mine was standing right there with him. "Was it a *by-the-way* thing or is there a written contractual agreement?"

"A handshake deal," my father admitted. "But she'll keep her end of things."

"And you know this how?" Forgive me if I wasn't in a trusting mood when it came to the most recent demon responsible for torturing me. "What *exactly* did you promise her in return?"

My father just watched, waiting for me to make the connections.

Sam got there first.

"You," Sam said. Voice clipped with disbelief. "Your father promised Alina you."

This wasn't the father I remembered. Or maybe it was and I'd forgotten.

The man I'd called Daddy held my hand when we crossed the street. Made me toast with peanut butter and banana, circles arranged into a happy face with eyes, nose and mouth; a Saturday morning treat so my mother could sleep in. Sitting beside him on the cracked cranberry leather sofa in his home office, looking through the books spread across his coffee table, while he worked on other books and with other stacks of papers at his nearby desk. My area held puzzles and maps; I never really knew exactly what he was working on.

While my father sat, several feet away and muttering to himself about I don't know what, I'd be tracing my fingers over the maps in front of me. Sometimes the surfaces would look like rocks from our driveway, multi-faceted grey and pink with shiny bits that twinkled when I held them up to the light. Other times there would be ribbons of blue meandering across the page. I liked to imagine that those were rivers feeding into places with sharp smells and strange animals and people who laughed and danced and spoke in strange tongues. Sometimes the maps would be black like the chalkboards at school, with smatterings of white pinpricks and lines that led to nothing; sometimes the only contrast differentiation would be the absence of color from a comparable absence of pigment.

"What if I told you," he'd say, when I'd get restless with waiting, when all the puzzles in the world weren't enough compared with scraps of attention from my father. "What if I told you these were maps to other worlds?"

"You mean the moon?" At age nine, the world was a literal place for me. There was what I knew, and everything else. The moon existed. Other worlds did not. A simplicity in belief and understanding.

"Like the moon, yes," my father had said, changing the subject after that. Maybe he was going to tell me about his theory of alternate dimensions. Classified hypotheses he was forbidden to discuss outside of the lab. Or maybe he'd been wanting to tell me about the dots on my back, and why they mirrored some of the details on the sheets in front of me.

But then he died, and his stuff was packed up, and I went on with my life.

Except he hadn't died. He was sitting here, in this room that shouldn't exist, talking to Sam and me about how he had sold out his daughter to evil in order to ensure his own freedom.

Me and my future therapist were going to have lots of material to work with. Assuming I lived that long.

"Tell me about your deal with the Cephalopod Order," I said. Because now, in the present, I couldn't afford a time-out to deal with my feelings of betrayal or hurt or unresolved daddy issues. "Why is Gustav so important to you?"

"I've been in this holding dimension too long," he said. "My mind is not what it was. It's a side effect of this kind of residency. I've managed to introduce a mutation into my blood that slows down the deterioration, but it's not enough. Either I make it back home soon, or I come up with a way to reverse this dimensional damage, or I lose my mind. There are no other options left to me."

"So," I said. "Gus."

"Correct," said my father. At this point I was using the term *father* loosely.

"Did it ever occur to you to just ask him for a few specimens to help with your research?" It was hard to keep the emotion out of my tone, and my tongue accidentally slipped too far between my teeth, biting down. I tasted blood.

"No," he said. "Mercenaries require payment for all services provided, and I had nothing to give since I was legally dead. No access to my old bank accounts, investments—nothing."

"Then how are you compensating Frank and the squid? Freelancers need to get paid too." Sam wasn't wrong there. D'Lee didn't strike me as someone who gave charity time to clients.

"Easier," my father replied. "They're helping me on spec as an investment. If I can find the mutation and fix it, they get a cut of whatever profits I make off it plus unlimited access to the formula."

"If D'Lee's crew was able to bring in their captures still lucid," I said, "they'd be able to charge premium rates."

"Precisely," said my father.

"Especially if they were the only ones in the market who could do it. But then what about Ezra?" I wasn't sure I wanted the answers, but we'd come this far. "You guys were such close friends. Why not work on this together?"

"Alina doesn't do octo-pedal seafood," my father said. I thought maybe he was joking but the delivery was deadpan. "Also my good friend Ezra can't be trusted all of the time to do the right thing." My father paused, considering his choice of words and the possible meanings which could have been construed by this sequence. "Perhaps a more accurate phrasing might be that my good friend Ezra, when faced with a choice, can most frequently be predicted to take the series of actions most beneficial to Ezra himself."

"So now we know why you guys have been friends so long," I said. Nobody laughed. OK, maybe it wasn't funny to anyone but me. "What exactly was the plan?"

"Trust me," said my father. Oh yeah. Like *that* was going to happen. "I wouldn't let Alina do anything to you."

"She wants to skin me alive," I said. "She and Ezra abducted me and tortured me for information. For fun. She's trying to force my," I stumbled, changing the word *Pack* at the last moment, "friends to spy on me to help her on pain of death and agony to anyone they cherish. She's a bad-ass demon, or at last something not from here, so I'm guessing less than full-on mammalian but more than your average creature from outer space. How am I doing?" My father didn't answer. "Last I checked, she had Ezra in her thrall and I've seen no evidence that you're not similarly smitten. So tell me again. How exactly could you prevent Alina from doing me harm, even if you were inclined to lift a pinky finger to help me?"

"I'm hurt," said the man whose DNA I shared. "Don't you know that blood is thicker than water?"

"So is Jell-O," I replied. "Still doesn't explain how you're planning to protect me."

"I won't have to," said my father. "I've already given you all the tools you'll need to protect yourself." And then he started giggling. No longer was it the chuckle of the sociopathic adult with whom I shared biology. Sam and I were now sharing metaphysical space with someone who should really be thinking about padded rooms and possible *not-for-recreational-use* restraints.

If this was symptomatic of inter-dimensional dementia, here's hoping it wasn't contagious. Did the shared skin suit insulate the wearer from the scrambled brain effect at all? Or was it more of a biological airlock situation, a living and breathing container, connecting realities A and B?

My Ezra-wearing father pushed himself to standing, launching forward from the crushed velvet chair of fluorescence where he'd been sitting up to this point. Started clapping his hands and stomping his feet to the beat of what I assumed was the music in his head. Spinning closer and closer, his arms held high and bent at the elbows. I could see that same thumbprint tattoo etched into his inner wrist as before. The one that seemed to respond to my touch, an on/off consciousness switch of metaphysical transmogrification. Wondered if I stuck my thumb in ink and rolled it onto paper whether the patterns would match. No time to check. I caught Sam's attention, motioning towards the insignia with my chin.

Lightning-quick, my hand was out and gripping my father's wrist as he danced past. It was good that he'd lost his lucidity for a while. Maybe the speed of my reflexes wouldn't register.

I pressed my thumb against the tattooed imprint on

his wrist. That jolt of energy again, one I was starting to recognize as a shifter-on-shifter connection, except this time it felt more personal, as though keyed to a frequency only I could access. Was that even possible? Electricity, the hairs on my arms and the back of my neck standing to attention; a growl in his throat as Sam neared us. Arms outstretched to catch my father if he ran.

But he didn't. Instead, Stuart the Currently Not So Mentally Stable opened his mouth and let out a howling that escalated to a nails-on-metal-siding shriek before leveling off to an in-heat caterwauling. *Right.* My father had shifter blood in there too.

And here I'd assumed Ezra had been operating out of a sense of specist superiority all those years. My father was his closest friend—and vice versa. No way it could have stayed hidden for so long. Ezra must have known.

And just like that, my twenty-twenty hindsight rearview mirror perspective shifted forty-five degrees to the right.

"Quiet," Sam said, his voice deepening; suddenly the man I'd seen repeatedly naked was transformed into the man who was second only to his Alpha. Sam commanded attention; I couldn't stop looking at him, craving his words, needing him to tell me what to do next. Feeling his energy beating against the buzzing hive of my father's fragmented power even as I stood at the periphery. I shook my head, loosening Sam's hold. Realizing that, like Jon, Sam could have exercised his will over me at any time—and hadn't.

My father was experiencing no such surge of free will. Which was probably a good thing, since it meant that horrible sound coming from him cut off as well.

The silence was abrupt, even though it had been there all along; a layer of gooey, sticky peace underlying the cacophony of *shut the hell up* sound.

Sam glided in closer, dipping his head down to stare directly into my father's eyes. I wasn't sure whether he was trying to touch any lingering lucidity, or whether his goal was to push back the long hairy fingerlings of reality gone on walkabout that made up some of the sketchier bits of Stuart Markovitz's mind.

My father was giggling again. Submitting to Sam's dominance without understanding what he was doing, or why. I wasn't positive he even recognized Sam's power for what it was.

Something different. I reached towards the edge of the map table where I'd left my phone; grabbed it and flicked the camera to active. With one hand I held up my father's wrist and with the other I zoomed in and snapped a series of stills from various angles. Sam watched while I did it, but only with partial bits of his attention—his main concern was my father and what he might do next.

It was good to have backup.

Sam's lips were pressed together and turned down at the corners; a bad taste on his tongue, or maybe a rancid odor disturbing his equanimity. I didn't smell anything. My father must have bathed recently, or perhaps sweat and mildew wasn't an issue in whatever reality he found himself stuck. I still wasn't clear on the *hows* and *whys* and *wherefores* of inter-dimensional travel.

Was it even travel? Or was it more of an astral projection kind of thing? Remembering that what I was looking at, *who* I was seeing, might not even be one person. My father, Ezra, Alina—it was getting pretty crowded inside that flesh suit.

And who was in control?

I still had my secret. While my father, in his more lucid moments, had probably guessed at my shifter potential, I was pretty sure that whiff of possibility hadn't made it yet to either Ezra or Alina. But with Alina's ability to single out and threaten Pack members—and I had no reason to think that my perspective-altering seclude-and-scold encounter had happened only to me—it was a *when* and not an *if* scenario now.

"I'm going to try something," I said, and in my mind I saw fur and flesh with painted nails and pinkish pads. Felt that now-familiar rushing underneath the surface of my as-yet-still-human skin, tickling, before waves of fur rolled across my forearm from just above my elbow to the tips of what had been my fingers but were now paws. I held up my curved claws, a semi-circle of lethal pins, admiring the patterns they cast against the shadows.

The inked skin may have been shaped into a human-sized thumbprint, but when I smacked my paw against the spot it somehow expanded to encompass what would have been the heel of my palm in human form. My father's eyes snapped wide as my claws made contact and pressed into his flesh. Not far. Not enough to draw blood, unless he moved. But he felt it, and he felt me. The glimmerings of lucid thought peeked through the slats of his mind.

I wasn't sure, if I was being honest, whether I preferred my father coherent or dementia-addled at this point. Coherent meant the potential for answers that made sense, but that came with a side order of self-interest and uncertain loyalties. Yes, it's true—even despite all the evidence before me, I kept hoping my father actually loved me and would at some point put my needs and a desire to protect me above himself and his own safety.

Incoherent was simpler. Like caring for a pre-verbal infant. Harder than a baby because of his size, weight and strength, but the part where I didn't have to worry about him betraying me simply because he could was a relief.

I clenched my claws, deeper, going in where blood could be drawn and mixed with the soon-to-be-dead surface layers of skin. Coming away dry. My father's eyes went rounder, but there was otherwise no sign that he noticed what I was doing. Which made me wonder. Did temporary skins feel pain? Could blood actually flow through veins borrowing their life force from elsewhere? I didn't want to torture him to find out—hello, yet another reason I'd left the Agency—but this was one of those times it would have been so helpful to be able to check my morality at the door.

Instead I worked with what I *could* rationalize. Digging in my claws and pulling, just a bit. Not enough to injure, or even apparently cause pain, but enough that whatever I had a grip on…moved. Twisted. A parchment-thin scarf with pleats and folds that needed to be arranged just *so*.

Sam noticed it too. I was relieved to have a witness in all this. Things without sense made more normal with someone else to see. My father shuddered then started twitching. Blinking, rapid, then everything went rigid, his eyes wide and his body stiffening as the fingers attached to the wrist I was gouging splayed out in a starfish formation.

"Is he having a heart attack? Or a seizure?" My own heart thudded, heavy against my ribs; I retracted my claws and reverted to human again. Reaching out to feel the pulse beside his jaw. *Nothing.* My own breath quickening as I grabbed his arm to press my index and forefinger against the spot where I'd been claws-deep in moments earlier. Still nothing.

Did we kill my father? Inadvertently? *No.* He couldn't be dead. Not after everything.

He was still blinking. And breathing, the rise and fall of his chest validating that he still lived.

I remembered in that moment to breathe as well.

Sam put his hand on my shoulder and squeezed. I jumped, then relaxed. *Right.* I wasn't alone.

"Dad?" Whatever he'd planned, whatever he'd done, that pronoun still applied to him. Based on biology if nothing else. And still I didn't want him to die.

The blinking slowed and the expression behind them shifted. Crafty where before it had been befuddled.

"Well," said a silky voice decidedly not my father's. "What have we here?"

I dove for the furthest corner of the room. Sam mirrored my actions a beat later, except he went in the opposite direction. A strategic move. We had a better chance of taking someone down if we came at them from different sides.

Alina, wearing Ezra's face, seemed unconcerned. Really, by her standards, we were essentially fleas capable of annoying by ankle biting but were otherwise of no concern. Except for me, of course. And whatever those dots on my back and the blood in my veins could do.

She was peering at the books the way Sam had;

apparently the titles were funny because Alina was snickering. A strange sound shaped by the mouth of Ezra and yet not.

I knew better than to get drawn in. Her sense of humor included electro-shocks and pulling the wings off flies.

Alina drifted closer to the table where the portal maps were scattered. *Shit.*

My palms were sweaty and my fingers streaked moisture across the glass surface of my phone a few times without making technology-responsive contact. Not good. I pressed harder and this time the icons I wanted slid across the screen into place. Swipe, scroll, swipe and press. Hoping that what had worked in my truck would work again up here. Even though I had no idea what the connection was between music and changing the channel on whoever was inhabiting the skin.

There.

Guns N' Roses, cranked to 10. "Paradise City" wasn't exactly the death metal that had gotten rid of Ezra in flesh suit form the last time, but it was worth a shot. Alina flinched at the sound but otherwise continued her assessing stroll around the attic room. *Damn.*

I tried again.

"Run to the Hills" by Iron Maiden. Maybe?

Alina growled at the sound but kept on going, getting closer to that place we needed her not to be.

This would have worked by now with Ezra. Then again, he was all about the jazz and classical music. Maybe it had less to do with the skin itself and more with the temperament of whoever was wearing it?

Of course, I had no idea what Alina was—or wasn't—into musically. So I had to keep trying. Besides, it's not like she'd given any indication she either cared or noticed my playlist up to now. Nothing to lose.

This time I went punk: "Soup Is Good Food" from the Dead Kennedys. I'm not sure how she did it but Alina actually managed to dance to the beat.

Cycled through my playlist, genre by genre, trying and discarding each after a sample of about ten seconds when Alina didn't respond. I even tried Justin Bieber. She just started laughing.

Only one thing left to try.

I dug deep, and took a breath that was deeper.

The 1980s power ballad duet between Neil Diamond and Barbra Streisand: "You Don't Bring Me Flowers."

"Noooooooooo!" Alina's shriek knotted my nerves and threw darts at my eardrums. But if it meant Alina got gone, it was totally worth it. Except, despite having her hands over her ears, she was still here. *Damn it!*

I started humming along; a nervous tic. Alina flinched and drew back, away from the added sound that was me. *Interesting.* I hummed louder; she closed her eyes. OK. I could totally do this.

As Barbra's part kicked in, I added my voice to the mix, motioning Sam to do the same. He shook his head. I gave him Meaningful Look Part 2, hoping he got the urgency. It didn't have to be amazing. It just had to work.

And then Sam started singing.

I tried not to gape. Sam's baritone was rich and textured and *damn* but I wanted to roll the taste around on my tongue.

Instead we flowed the words back and forth. Torturing Alina in our own way as the music wove around and between us.

Not even noticing, as we neared those final chords, that Alina had vanished and the Ezra Gerbrecht she'd been wearing right along with it.

Staring at each other. Tears in my eyes. Over-identification much?

But I didn't want to tell Sam goodbye. Not now. Not ever.

"Hey," he said, stepping out from where he'd been crouched. Looking around; a single nod to confirm that Alina was gone. Coming to stand in front of me, brushing my tears away with a gentle thumb. "What's wrong?"

I sniffed and shook my head. Tried to swallow it back; instead the tears flowed harder. There may have been a sob or two. *Nice one, Dana. Way to be the weepy, needy female.* I may have been in distress, but I was hardly a damsel in need of rescuing.

Although some honesty from me for Sam was long overdue.

"That does it," Sam said, smiling a teasing kindness. "No more power ballads for you."

I sniffled harder. What was wrong with me? Turned away to cross the room for my shoulder bag; dug around inside until I found a few not-yet-disintegrated tissues to use.

"Dana?" Sam's voice was gentle, but he wasn't dropping it. "Talk to me."

"Fine." I crossed the room to drop into the yellow velveteen armchair not recently occupied by my father.

"Fine," Sam said, settling into the side of the couch closest to where I was.

"Well," I said. Trying to stall. "There's scary-ass Alina. She freaks me out."

Sam nodded, waving his hand for me to continue.

"There's that thing where my father, who is supposed to love me, made a deal with said scary-ass demon to save himself while tossing me under the metaphorical oncoming bus."

"Yeah," said Sam. "Was he always like that?"

I shook my head. "I don't remember him like this. But then he's been supposedly dead for years. Maybe he always was a self-serving prick and I didn't realize it."

"A father who tattoos an inter-dimensional portal map on his baby's back without telling the mother, his wife, while pretending he took the kid to the doctor?" Sam shook his head. "That's what I'd call a fine up-standing citizen. Strong moral and empathetic fiber there."

"Fine," I said. "So he might not have been the best father in the world even when he was officially alive."

"Is that all of it? Or is there more?"

I didn't answer, choosing instead to slump backwards into the cushiony upholstery enveloping me in its foam-separated-by-fabric hug.

"Dana?" Sam was willing to wait, but not without a gentle verbal nudge to get me going.

I nodded, stifling yet another sob that threatened to punch through before I could get the words out.

"You," I finally managed.

"What about me?"

"I miss you," I said. Whoa, look at that—I could breathe again too.

"I'm right here."

"Come on," I said, voice stronger. "You know what I mean."

"Look," Sam said. "We've been over this. I get that

you feel you need an exit strategy, and that emotionally unavailable is your thing. So those other guys? Perfect choices. But I'm more than that, and you know it.
I haven't left you behind for some job, I'm not sleeping
with someone who wants you dead, and I'm definitely
not trading you in to be demon bait." Mirthless laugh,
short and sharp. "No, you need me and here I am, like
a *schmuck*, even though I shouldn't be."

"Because Anshell told you to do it." I sniffled.

"Anshell didn't tell me shit," said Sam. "I came because I wanted to make sure you were safe and had
backup, just in case."

"In case you got lucky?"

"Dana, I'm lucky I met you," Sam said. "And if
you're being honest, you feel the same way. Sex is sex.
Yes, it's good with us—but I'm not here just to get laid.
Although I'm happy to oblige..." Sam waggled his eyebrows and flashed me that *drop-your-panties-and-get-
over-here-now* grin.

"Ha," I replied. "Funny."

"Life is fast," Sam said. "You've got to grab it by the
balls and ride it until you can't hold on anymore and
your fingers are tired and all you want to do is give up.
But you can't." He reached out, gently lifting my left
hand and sandwiching it between his. "We don't know
what's going to happen in a few hours, never mind some
vague future. Things happen, and fast, and I don't know
about you but I don't want any regrets."

"I don't regret you," I said. Soft, as though someone
else might hear and take Sam away from me again.
Never mind the part where it had been me doing it to
myself.

"Good." Sam turned my hand over and brushed his

lips against my palm. I felt it all the way to my toes. And elsewhere. Tightening, inside; a shiver raising goose bumps in a room that really wasn't so cold.

A blink and I had Sam's hand turned around, wrist exposed, the skin-on-skin contact pulling my shift from me where we touched. No longer a hand, my paw stroked the back of his with claws retracted, all rough pads and kitten-soft hair. I bent over and kissed the surface of his palm before catching the still-human skin between my two front teeth. I sucked, leaving a tiny bruised line of purple for later.

Sam's eyes fluttered. The rumble in his throat was a purr, but not one like Fluffy the Domesticated Indoor Cat might dole out for a behind-the-ears scratch. I'd never seen a lion wild on the Savannah, but I imagined that this was more the sound it might make. Rolling around on its back in the sun, rubbing dirt and grit into the itchy places it couldn't reach with a paw.

I let him go only to move closer, slinking out of my safe zone and into his. On all fours now. Human again, covered in pink skin and downy fuzz. I kneeled in front of him, shifting any residual fur back to flesh, and leaned forward to undo his belt, then his pants.

Sam opened his eyes then, reaching out his arms to grasp mine. My decision but he was there to help if I needed it.

"Come here," he said.

I ran my palms up the sides of his legs, along his hips, dipping my fingers in beneath the waistband of his jeans to find that soft spot. Then along his chest, across, my breasts dangling within reach of his mouth. Sam released my arms only to find the gap between top and bottom, under my shirt, sliding it up my back to my shoulders before pulling me down until our mouths found each other.

"You don't need this, do you?" Sam was already pushing the fabric up and over my head, not waiting for my response. What would I have said? Thought chasing behind sensation, trying to catch up but never quite making it. He got as far as my neck; I reached back and pulled the fabric off the rest of the way.

"Hey," I said, straddling him now. Kissing beside his mouth, beneath, to his cheeks and his eyelids then back to his lips once more.

"Hey yourself," Sam replied, mouth brushing against mine, gentle, before pressing in again. And then, lower, his tongue lapping against my nipple, all things harder now, as I gripped his shoulders and arched back, pulling him forward with me.

He laughed, my breast still in his mouth, and *oh!* everything clenching heat inside. I felt something change, under the surface, and then his tongue was cat scratch sandpaper rough, and I forgot how to breathe, and I was falling and flying before tumbling back to earth again and into Sam's waiting arms.

I realized his shoulders were bleeding, pin-pricked droplets in the shape of my claws. The cost of my distraction.

"Don't worry about it," he said as I started to pull back, and out. Sam held me, hands around my waist, pressed against me where our bodies would have been joined if not for all that clothing in the way. We needed to do something about that. Fur rolling over his shoulders to drop down along his arms to shape claws of his own before he retracted everything again. It took seconds but I couldn't stop looking, the human skin left behind was pristine and pure again. Or at least as much as it had been before, but this time without the blood.

I rolled to one side, away from Sam; not too far. The only way I could extricate myself from him and my clothing.

"You're still wearing too much," I said, peeling my remaining layers off. "See? It's easy." I held up my underwear in one hand and twirled the leg opening around one finger. Not exactly the white flag of peace. But it got me a grin as Sam's eyes tracked the spin of purple and black together, on his feet and out of his pants.

Supe speed had its advantages.

Sam was in front of me and my breath caught as he looked down. Cupping my jaw with one hand, the other light on my back but pulling me in as the sparse tangles of his chest hair tickled my breasts. His hardness, lower, leaving no question of intent.

This was different. Sam kissed the top of my head, tender, then down along the side of my face to my neck. Claws out, raising goose bumps even in the heat; retracting back to soft tips and blunt nails tracing a line to my tailbone and then down some more. I wrapped one leg around Sam's waist and pulled him towards me.

But still he waited. There was ready and then there was something else. His fingers going deeper, spreading and lifting, heat made hotter by his touch. Too close to the full moon; fur suddenly poking up from straining pores, smooth but not from skin, my yowl of need catching in my throat and turning into something that was *other*.

And then his fur flowed over him, claws retracted just in time. *Pull it back again.* A whisper in my ear, or was it in my head? Still I heard, I listened, and I touched that thing inside that was human. Pink skin and human flesh flowing from me to Sam, from Sam to me. Being and altering to shape something different. I'd felt this energy between Sam and me, touch against touch, but I had no idea that alternating forms while in contact with someone else could feel so damned good.

This time we were fully human, hands clasped, and a surge of *need* and *want* and *now* was between us and inside us and around and behind and *there* and *oh!* there again. I nudged Sam forward until his calves were touching the edge of the couch; another push and he was sitting on the edge. Just long enough to find that he'd replenished his wallet-condom-of-hope supply and slide it on while fingers were still fingers without claws. And then I was straddling him, sliding until Sam was within and my legs were wrapped around his hips. Looking into each other's eyes.

Something feral prowled behind that gold-and-green-flecked gaze. I inhaled his scent of baked apple and cinnamon tea, the power of *otherness* twitching just beneath the surface.

"Pull it back again," Sam said, voice rough like the tongue tasting between my lips. And then he did it, and I did it. Tightening my core as his energy burst inside me.

Chapter Twenty-Nine

"I don't get it," said Sam, pulling on his underwear. "How many of them are there in that skin, and how do they keep from killing each other?"

"As far as I can tell," I said, bending over to fasten my bra before readjusting and layering my tank on over it, "it's just the three of them. My father, Ezra and Alina."

"And it always looks like that guy you used to work for?"

"Ezra?" *My pants were around here somewhere, right?*

"So far, yeah. Although sometimes the edges go fuzzy, like one time in the attic, and I can see my father sort of superimposed on Ezra."

"What about this place?" Sam found his t-shirt and pulled it over his head as I located my shorts. They'd gotten wedged between the arm and the side cushion of the sofa. "With Alina here, it might not be safe to come back."

I hadn't thought about that. *Shit.* Looked around to see what I was leaving behind and what I could take with me.

"Maybe we should grab those maps," I said. "Just in case."

"What if this is one of the portal gateways?"

"Yeah," I replied. "I was wondering that too. Especially since my father has it keyed into my blood somehow."

"His too," Sam pointed out. "This wasn't the first time you've seen him here, right?"

"Right. So if we accept the hypothesis that he's stuck in an alternate dimension, and add in the bit where he keeps popping up here specifically, then logically this place must be more permeable somehow." I paused, re-ran what I'd just said in my head. "Does that make any sense?"

"Sure," said Sam. "Although it doesn't explain how anyone wearing that skin can get to you in your truck."

"One *doesn't-make-sense* riddle at a time." A smile to soften the snark. "Could there be more than one skin?"

"Have you seen more than one?"

"No," I replied. Pressed my lips together; an unconscious habit when trying to figure something out. Yeah, I'm a lousy poker player. And I couldn't believe what I was thinking now—*hello, princess, you really think the world revolves around you?* But my father had been a brilliant scientist. "What if *I'm* the key? We already know that Alina's goal is to skin me for whatever I've got on my back. And that thumbprint tattoo looks familiar—what if it matches my actual thumbprint somehow? We also know my blood is an amplifier and that my father did a little something extra to it, even if we don't have proof yet that Ezra was involved. So logically there has to be a connection."

"We don't actually know for sure what else Daddy Dearest did to your blood," Sam pointed out. "When did he write that cryptic letter you found? Before or after this mysterious lab 'accident' that we keep hearing about without any details?"

I grimaced. Sam wasn't wrong. We were basing theories on a man with his own agenda, who may or may not have been telling the truth.

"At least we're sure that now I can shift into a big cat."

"Which," as Sam pointed out with an *I-know-what-you-were-doing-fifteen-minutes-ago-because-it-was-with-me* grin, "does have its advantages."

"True." I suddenly wanted to taste that grin; licked my lips and realized I still could. "Either way, everyone seems to think I can help open and close portal gateways. Remember that last time on the beach?"

Sam nodded.

"Plus those maps do stuff when I touch them. Or someone says *Danyankeleh*, my father's nickname for me." Even now, in this room, I could hear them rustling when I said the word.

"Speaking of—we should take what we can and get out of here, before someone else comes back for a visit."

He wasn't wrong.

Anshell had the coffee ready when we got there.

"Let's go over what we do know," he said. So we did—the skins, the contracts, my father's connection with D'Lee and Ezra's Agency arm via Owain, even Alina turning up in the attic room that shouldn't exist. Where was a dining room dry erase board when you needed it?

"There's got to be a reason this is happening again," I said. Frustrated. "It's been quiet for months. Why now?"

"The temperatures? We've had a lot of days that cracked 30°C already this year." I knew Sam was talking but I was suddenly distracted by a vision of him covered in sweat. Because why yes, indeed, there had been a lot of hot days this year and he was still talking and oh *shit* I'd missed it all re-imagining the taste of his inner thigh. *Focus.* Right, the heat. And how everything could be connected to that.

Except it didn't feel right.

"It's hot lately," I said. "Climate change. Plus June. But it's been hot before and none of this happened."

"True," said Anshell. "Could it be the time of year rather than the temperatures themselves?"

"I wish I knew." I was thinking out loud. Bonus: it distracted me from thoughts of naked sweaty Sam. *Eyes forward, Dana. Come on. You can do it.*

"It was super cold the last time. February freeze. So it's not like we've got weather forecasts in common. Timing makes more sense."

"Agreed," said Sam.

"The last time Alina surfaced, her portal-swinging-door ritual thingy was timed to harness the power of the third night of the full moon. Where are we at with that?"

"That was last night," said Anshell. "Remember? We had a meet scheduled?"

Oh. Right. That would explain my residual urge to drag Sam onto the kitchen table right now, with or without Anshell's viewing pleasure. Then again, maybe that was just me with Sam at this point.

Hang on—something else happened this time of year in Toronto. Like, for the entire month and culminating in a big party because June in Toronto was more than just heat—the weeks-long celebration of LGBTQ2 Pride. The Trans March was tonight, the women came out on Saturday and the full-on, hours-long Gay Pride parade was on Sunday. The moon would be starting to wane by then.

Still. There was nothing to suggest a portal crossing needed a party to function. Right?

"What if there is no causal connection between the *when* and the *why*? We know my father wants his marbles back, and that they've been shaken loose by spending so much time in an alternate dimension. He thinks having some of Gus's genetic material will allow him to solve that problem for himself. But he also has a plan B, and that's using me to get Alina to open a portal herself and bring him back. My father is a smart guy. He's hedging his bets."

"Neither of those things have a moon-dependent element," Sam pointed out.

"Which could mean that everything with your father, the timing, has been a series of coincidences," said Anshell.

"Exactly." I was starting to think the same thing myself. "Boy, I really won the Daddy jackpot here, didn't I?"

Sam squeezed my hand; I nodded, grateful for the support. His presence bore witness to a reality nobody would have otherwise believed.

"We still don't know why Ezra arranged for me specifically to get the Gus contract though," I pointed out. "And of all the people to send it with, he picked Owain? My ex?"

"Would he have known of your involvement with this

man Owain?" Anshell rubbed his skull, as though smoothing imaginary loose hairs. An unconscious gesture.

"It wasn't exactly a secret," I said. "But the Agency didn't love co-workers cohabiting like that, so we didn't make a big deal of it either. It wasn't anybody's business."

"Right. I forgot you two lived together." Sam pulled his hand back, leaning away from me in his chair and crossing his arms.

"Yeah," I said. "For about a year. Domicile, domesticity—and then desertion when he got a better offer." I mirrored his body language with some defensive arm and torso positioning of my own. "It was years ago." Sam gave me a look. Reminding me without words that my craving for some kind of closure with Owain had cost me Sam, albeit temporarily. I shrugged and tried to force a smile. Yep, that was me: Scary Smiling Dana Spice. But it *was* true. If I hadn't realized it before, I knew it now. Owain was my past. Sam was my future.

Anshell cleared his throat, reminding us that we weren't alone in the room. Also that there were other matters to discuss than the past/present/future of my relationship with Sam.

"Right," I said. "Sorry."

"Sorry," echoed Sam.

Anshell took a sip of his coffee in the temporary absence of conversation that followed. Thinking. Because my father as the bad guy with Ezra as—well, not good exactly but not as bad as I'd thought either—required an unexpected alteration in my worldview.

"If Ezra isn't actively trying to harm me, then what the hell is going on?"

"Perhaps," said Anshell, "the time has come for you to ask him yourself."

* * *

I expected blaring sirens as I got off the elevator at his floor; certainly by the time I crossed the threshold of his department. My one-inch-thick Doc Marten rubber soles squelched against the polished stone floor as I walked. After everything, could it really be this simple? I could walk back in and nothing would happen to me?"

Sam hadn't been happy about my going alone. I didn't blame him. We were gambling on a theory that seemed implausible now under the fluorescent track lighting of my past. Our compromise was that he wouldn't go far, grabbing a drink in the Arbor Room of Hart House. If I didn't check in within thirty minutes, even by text, Sam would be coming to get me with claws blazing.

Bleach, floor wax, sweat and sawdust. Maybe they were renovating. So many memories reaching out their hands to play with my hair, pulling me backwards even as I propelled myself in the opposite direction. Away from this life and everything it had held. Even as I found myself here, with clearance and a signed contract, sucked back in again.

"Ezra," I said, standing in the doorway to his office. His assistant wasn't anywhere I could see, which was a good thing. Better chance of me staying conscious.

He looked up from his desk, eyes blank for milliseconds before narrowing their focus in on me. Delayed recognition. Maybe he'd been spending too much time inter-dimension-side too.

"Dana," he said, glancing around to check whether we were alone. "What can I do for you?"

Not quite the reception I was anticipating.

"The snatch-and-grab gig," I said. Business first. "That came from you, right?"

Ezra narrowed his eyes, evaluating, before giving me the nod.

"Why? Why me?"

"What," Ezra said, leaning back as he watched my face. Reading me without the words; a touch-free Braille for motivations. "You can't use the work?"

"Of course I can," I said. "*So* not the point. And why did you bring Owain in to deliver the offer?"

"You didn't want to see him again?" Amazing how Ezra could pull off innocent when I knew he was anything but.

"It wasn't keeping me up nights." Not anymore, anyway. "What's your end game?"

"Stop looking for what's not there," Ezra said. "Did you come here to play pin the question on the doddering professor's posterior, or are you prepared to talk about the job yet? Hmm?"

"Fine," I said. "First tell me what you want this guy for."

"No," said Ezra. "If you do the work then I owe you the fee. All the details you need to fulfill it successfully were in the file, which I assume you've read by now."

I nodded.

"So what more do you need? You do your job and I'll do mine."

I let that sit a moment. Then:

"What if I get you bio materials from the target instead of bringing in the target himself?" *C'mon Dana, you can do this. Blank face. Bunnies and kittens and ice cream.* "He's a big guy, and he's already tried to kill me at least once. Do you actually need him whole, and alive?"

"You mean could you bring me an ear and still get

paid?" Ezra's lips were twisted; I think he was trying not to laugh. "Bring me what you can."

"I'll still get paid?"

"Depends on what I get," said Ezra, the Man in Charge persona shutting down the humor in an eye blink.

I watched his face. For any sign of Crazy Ezra, Absent-Minded Ezra, or Ezra the Guy Working with Alina.

"Dana?" Ezra raised his hand, palm up, in the sign of *nu?*

"Is there anything else?"

I stared. The inside of his wrist was smooth, un-marked. No thumbprint-shaped tattoo.

"What?" Ezra looked from me to his wrist and back again. "Is there something else you want to renegotiate? Or are we done here?"

"Your wrist," I managed.

"What about it?"

"Didn't you have a tattoo before?"

"A what?" Ezra's laugh was short, and I saw the fo-cused man I recognized from before the casual cruelty of the last few months. "I'm too old to put decorative art on my wrinkled carcass." His eyes narrowed. "You've seen me with a tattoo? Where?"

"There," I said, pointing. "Your inner wrist."

"Really," he said. "And you're sure it was me."

"Stop fucking with me." I lost my patience with the circling-around-each-other game. "You had a tattoo on your inner wrist and you've been sharing space in there with my father and a demon named Alina."

Ezra stared at me. I stared back. He was really going

to try and sell this whole *I-have-no-idea-what-you're-talking-about* routine?

Then he threw his head back, the sound of his guffaws filling the space.

"Oh Dana," he said, tears in his eyes from laughing so hard. "You should see your face right now."

"The fuck, Ezra?" If I'd come here for answers, this was not helping. "What the fuck is going on?"

"Oh!" Sniffling, and not from sorrow. "And no need for all that profanity. You have to admit this is pretty amusing."

"What?" I put my hands on my hips—all the better to grab a weapon with, if needed. "I get that I'm missing the joke but…what? Tell me one true thing. Please."

"Your father is alive," said Ezra. "But you already knew that, yes?"

"Doesn't count. You knew I knew. Please tell me one true thing I *don't* know. Like how you're alive, even though I saw your head separated from your body a few months ago."

"Why should I?" Ezra peered up at me through brown and beige plastic weave, square-cut glasses with a mid-century modern aesthetic. "You've got to learn how to find answers yourself. I'm doing you no favors by handing over a shortcut."

Hang on. This entire experience was meant to be one long teachable moment?

"It's good that you're finally asking questions but they're not the right ones." Damn, Ezra could be obstructionist when he wanted. Or when he was trying to make a point.

So I did what he wanted, and thought about what I

was asking, and why. Where it all started, when, and with who.

The accident. The one that had supposedly killed my father.

"That lab thing. Where my father died. Only not," I amended. "You were there."

"Yes," said Ezra. "Go on."

"We all believed my father was dead because…you must have told us that's what happened." I was thinking out loud now. "Except it didn't. And you knew it. So what really took place that night in the lab?"

"You've come this far," Ezra said. "You tell me."

"I think that whatever happened to my father that night was because of you." Hopefully saying the words out loud wouldn't banish me to the same place. "I don't know how though." A quick glance at Ezra was no help; he'd be able to beat me and anyone else he went up against in poker no problem. "And you're not going to tell me."

Ezra shook his head.

"Can you at least let me know if I guess right or something?"

"I can do that," Ezra said. Who knows if he was telling the truth. "What do I get out of it?"

"A feeling of satisfaction at doing the right thing?" Yeah, I didn't buy it either. "What do you want?"

"You," he said. His goal all along. "Work for me again."

"Not going to happen," I said. Didn't even need a beat to consider. "But you knew that when you asked. Never lead with what you actually want—rule number one of negotiation. You taught me that."

"Good," he said, pride in his eyes. "You remember."

"I remember plenty," I said.

"What if you got a transfer?" Ezra leaned back in his chair, easing his left and then his right foot up on to the edge of his desk. Apparently we were being casual here. "Away from Covert Science. Research?"

I gave an involuntary shudder. I'd rather spend the day giving myself paper cuts.

"No matter. Assume we found a department able to meet your standards of intellectual stimulation and moral platitudes. Would you return to the fold then?"

Ezra wanted me back badly enough to let me choose my path? The role I'd play? I'd never heard of anyone getting an offer like this. Maybe he wanted me dead, or under Covert Science's observation. But if that was the case, there were easier ways to bring me in. A cloth hood and a paralytic, for instance.

Still, I wasn't looking to get married again so soon. Ezra wanted me back? We'd have to take things slow. Like glacier-at-the-end-of-an-ice-age slow.

Oh.

"The contract," I said. "That's what it was all about. You wanted me back—I still have no idea why—and you knew I'd be skittish." Ezra's smile managed smug and proud in equal parts. No idea how he did that. "So you make me an offer, not a permanent position but a little something something to tempt me. You throw in Owain, the guy you took from me, to sweeten it. How am I doing?"

"You're proving to me that my investment has not been a waste," Ezra replied. I'd swear *he* was the cat with a few canary feathers stuck out the side of his mouth if I didn't know better. Even without any supe blood in him.

"So what's your real bottom-line offer here?" The Ezra I remembered would have identified that minimum goal before he'd started any of the balls rolling in this game. And to him, the lucid Ezra, everything was one more angle to be played, one more set of odds to stare down and weigh out.

Lucid Ezra. Ezra the absent-minded professor. My tormentor. My mentor. Which one was real? Who was I negotiating this deal with, and was there any way to truly know?

"You fulfill this contract," said Ezra. "And just this once I will accept bio materials in lieu of making you haul in his big, blue demon carcass. No pro-rated fee for reduction. Take it as a sign of my committed reinvestment in this relationship. This should *not* be viewed as a precedent of any kind, and any future contracts are to be completed to spec. Understood?"

I nodded. Comprehension did not require acceptance. "That's it?" A girl can hope.

Ezra shook his head. Indulgence for the willful child.

"No," he replied. "You will also complete a minimum of four additional jobs for us over the next twelve months. You will be compensated," he added, as I opened my mouth to protest, "on an appropriate pay scale. The Agency may be many things, but we make sure our people are taken care of. As I'm sure you remember. If you don't, ask Owain how his bank accounts are doing these days."

"That's it?"

"That's it," Ezra confirmed. "For now."

"My turn then," I said. "Answers for questions— that's the deal, right?"

"With a caveat," said Ezra. "Knowledge comes with

a price, and yours is on the installment plan. Each job gets you paid, plus I'll answer five questions for you."

I shouldn't have been surprised. Of course Ezra would want insurance against my bailing before the terms of our verbal agreement were up. The only digital paper trail would be of me taking or declining an assigned job and then the payment. Knowledge for sweat was done off-book.

It was possible I'd figure things out for myself. Eventually. But a shortcut would certainly make things easier.

Then again, what was it they say about curiosity and cats?

Which reminded me—

"What about your good friend Alina and her death-inducing plans for me?"

Ezra shrugged on the absent-minded professor role he could play so well.

"Oh my," he said, a wheedling vacancy in his tone. "I don't know where that Dana girl could have gotten to. Last I heard she took one of those big metal flying machines—yes, that's right, a plane—very far away. Iqaluit. Or maybe it was Tel Aviv."

"You're saying you'd lie to protect me," I said.

"Assuming you make it worth my while," he replied, mind like the bear trap with flesh-piercing steel claws it was.

"And when I'm no longer useful to you?"

"Stay useful," he said. Not comforting. Then again, it wasn't meant to be. "I assume you plan to continue associating closely with members of the Moon with Seven Faces pack?"

"I do," I said. "That's not going to change under our

arrangement. I'm not going to quit my job at the Swan Song either. So if you were thinking that was happening, you can forget about it."

"You won't need the money," Ezra pointed out.

"You don't get to own me," I said by way of reply. "I live where I want, associate with whoever I want and take whatever jobs I choose—even if you don't like it. Agreed?"

"No conflict of interest gigs," Ezra warned. "And you already know about the non-disclosure guidelines."

"Fine," I said. Because Ezra wouldn't give anything away for free. Or even at a discount. "Case by case basis is probably best for both of us," I said, hedging. Once a commitment-phobe, apparently still a commitment-phobe.

"Agreed," Ezra said. "For now."

"And you'll keep Alina off my back?" I skipped the part where that could be literal.

"I will endeavor to keep our mutual *friend* away from both you and your back," he replied. "Although you realize that if she goes rogue, there's little I can do to stop her."

"I don't believe that," I said.

"Do we have a deal?"

Eyes on the bouncing information ball. I could do this. Right?

"Yes," I said. "We have a deal."

"Then ask."

"Are you responsible for my father being in another dimension?" I surprised myself with that one.

"Yes," Ezra replied. He didn't elaborate.

"Are you, my father and Alina all using some kind

of flesh suit to jump between dimensions, and does it have anything to do with me?"

"That's two questions," Ezra said. When I nodded: "As long as you're aware."

"I am."

"Then yes," he said, "and sort of yes."

"Does Alina need me dead?" At some point it had to be asked.

"No," said Ezra. "She's just being spiteful."

I opened my mouth to claim my last Ezra prize, but he held up his hand to stop me.

"Save it," he said, handing me his card. "By the time we see each other again, you'll need it."

Chapter Thirty

I was twenty minutes past the time I was supposed to have shown up at the Swan. There had been two texts from Sandor (so far) checking on whether or not I was actually going to show. I responded to the last one, finally: Sorry—running late. See u in 15. Hoping it would be enough.

Well, that and the part where I was apartmenting his brother.

The Swan was a sweaty tangle of arms and claws and fingers and feathers when I got there. Church Street had its Pride celebrations, and the fringe supe community grabbed its piece of the inclusivity coat of many colors to wrap itself in the flag as well. Table after table of slow smiles and lingering touches. The alcohol was flowing, but I had a feeling there was something extra-euphoric being passed around too.

Sandor was a big believer in safety first, so we'd spent the entire month making sure the wicker baskets filled with pretzels were paired with matching baskets of condoms. Public Health always had an abundant supply and they were willing to share, so Sandor made some kind of arrangement with them every year.

We also put out extra garbage bins. Because even though they couldn't be recycled, the last thing we needed in a packed bar was an exploded pipe from too many flushed condoms. Also—yuck.

Of course, I'd forgotten about all of this—albeit temporarily—wrapped as I was in my own drama. Just the kind of thing to endear a person to their co-workers.

Derek had that frantic twitch in his eye going when I showed up. Poor guy. He was good with pouring drinks, but I sensed that the seasonal energy was a bit much for his more reserved, fifth-generation Anglo-Canadian sensibilities. The big tough magic-wielder's shoulders were bunched to his ears, and the rapid rise/fall of his chest made me wonder if he was hyperventilating—or fighting it.

Janey threw me a glare before turning around to paste a smile back on her customer-facing self, confirming my *whoops* in the Team Player rulebook.

I stashed my stuff in back, slamming my locker shut hard to give the closest writhing bodies advance warning that someone was approaching. Not everyone cared, but at least the bashful ones got a heads up.

I grabbed an apron and fastened it while giving Derek the Nod. You know—the one that says *sorry I'm late*, and *I've got your back*, and *now would be a good time for you to go pee.* The look he flashed me was pure gratitude as he melted into the shadows, leaving me in charge.

Apparently, whatever tonight's patrons were on made them frisky, thirsty *and* hungry. The hands, claws and beaks they could keep to themselves. But the orders kept on coming. Gin Giblets—gin plus giblets marinated in a chili pepper/olive oil/port wine vinegar base—were a big hit. So were Flaming Hands—blood orange liqueur, candied lemon peels, grenadine and a shot of pomegranate syrup set on fire with those special order bloody finger happy birthday candles Sandor managed to get from who knows where. But the old Swan favorites were going strong too: Banana Banderos (banana liqueur, Banderos Demon ear juice, two millipedes and a chunk of fresh banana), Kahlúa Kangas (Kahlúa, sweetened condensed milk, fresh basil, Gnort balls and one glow worm served in a long-stemmed glass capable of conga line dancing with the right motivation) and more.

The food orders kept coming too. Cloven hooves battered in cornmeal and served deep-fried with melted shredded cheddar on top. Pig ear crisps made from a mixture of sawdust, wheat gluten and porcine hairs ground into a fine paste and baked at 375°C for forty-five minutes. I'm thinking the "pig" part of the dish's name came from those hairs. Nachos—of course—because the norms needed something too. Sandor had even added his version of a thin-crust pizza to the menu recently, with toppings ranging from black olives, mushrooms and onions to Zaldor heel scrapings, Snorflart Muckler dandruff flaked spice mix, and a jellyfish ink sauce option.

I felt a cool breeze on the back of my neck and the touch of fingers on my forearm, so familiar, with lips of chilled heat tasting of rose petals and musk and the faintest remnant of remembered death.

"Bloody Bloody Mary? Or will you be having the Rioja tonight?"

"Rioja," said Jon. "Whatever you have—as long as it's a good year."

I pulled the bottle out from beneath the countertop and peered at the orange texturized label.

"Last year wasn't bad for me," I said. "How 'bout you?"

And there it was. Wine from a time before my world had tilted sideways and to the left. Because of him. And the boyfriend he refused to leave behind.

I pulled out two glasses and poured some of the rich red liquid for each of us.

"Thanks," Jon said, sliding a twenty across the bar for his portion. "Keep the change."

I nodded. I'd more than earned that tip. Jon took a sip from his wine and waited. Such stillness. The frenzy of energy swirled around us but here, between him and me, there was a peace. Focus. And yet it was temporary because there were words needing to be said.

"Sorry about Claude," said Jon. "He gets jealous."

"He's a charmer all right. I didn't realize you were still seeing him like that."

Jon shrugged. "I know he did something he shouldn't have—"

"You mean scratching me and turning me into a shifter?" My life was more interesting now, and I'd discovered community as a result of that scratch, but it didn't make me any less pissed at Claude. Or disappointed with Jon for going back to him notwithstanding.

The silence stretched, and for once it was less companionable and more noisy with what it was long past time we said to each other. Finally, Jon did the honors. Even though I would have gotten there—eventually.

"We're done," Jon said. Not really a question; watching my face as the words passed his lips.

I nodded, the wine on my tongue turning acrid as it mixed with the taste of my tears.

"We are," I said. "Because—"

"Claude." Regret and understanding.

"Yeah," I said. "And Sam."

That got Jon's attention, but the smile stretching across his face—pleased?—surprised me.

"Sam is a good man," he said. "He accepted your apology this time?"

"Yeah."

"What did you do with Owain?" Jon was teasing, lightening the moment with the faintest wisp of a smile. He knew damned well what I'd almost done with Owain.

"Nothing," I said. "Owain and me, I think we're the way we are."

"Best of luck with that one," said Jon, gliding to standing.

"Thanks." And then, because I couldn't not ask: "Will I see you again?"

"If you need me, I'll come," he said. "We'll always be friends."

I nodded, swallowing the lump in my throat. "Good," I managed.

And then he was gone, melting into the throng.

No time to dwell on what could have been. Whatever lull Jon had wrapped around us, that single moment of peace, it crashed to an abrupt end as soon as he'd vanished from sight. Could the mayhem have been there all along and I'd somehow missed it?

At least the tips were good.

* * *

Sam showed up about an hour before closing. We were operating on Pride Standard Time—if a bar applied to the City for a special license, they could push last call to four in the morning from the usual *get-your-last-drink-orders-in-now* time of 2 AM.

Sam didn't make a production of his arrival, sliding into a seat at the end of the bar and checking out the room while he waited for me to find a spare moment for him. I made sure he had a bottle of the latest Junction microbrew we'd gotten in this week while he waited— a syrupy, dark ale called Zen Ghouled—and a bowl of fresh pretzels. Dating the bartender had to have *some* advantages, right?

You'd think once the kitchen closed the place would thin out. Most nights, patrons would either be stockpiling drinks before we cut them off, or they'd be chasing down their servers to settle tabs before the subways closed. It was either that or the Vomit Comet home—an all-night north/south bus rite of passage to be avoided if at all possible. Because vomit.

Not tonight. We'd be needing to do a sweep of all the Swan's nooks and crannies before we left, and cleanup would definitely require rubber gloves and construction-grade garbage bags.

Yuck.

I stared out over the bar, unfocusing my eyes, allowing the murmurs and pulsating techno-beats of dancers weaving through and up and around each other to flow through and around me as well. In my mind I was there with them, my heart pounding to the tempo of the song as sweat poured across my skin. Fabric gummy as it clung to my available surfaces.

Something wasn't right. A snarl caught in my throat and I clenched the counter, my fingers sprouting claws. Shivering. Even though the AC had been on all night, and the temperature hadn't changed at all. A quick glance at the thermometer gauge behind the pimento olive and lemon-slice trays confirmed it.

Sam was on his feet and scanning the room at my first growl. He'd sensed nothing other than me, but for him that was enough. Still human, but ready to change if needed.

I couldn't *see* anything. But I could feel it. A sensation unsafe to free if I was in feline form, not yet; I hid my paws until I could force them back to two sets of four fingers plus an opposable thumb on each side. Watching. Trying to identify this disjointed certainty that what I was seeing was not everything that was there.

Sandor's head popped out from the doorway of the Employees Only area. He'd probably been doing a preliminary count on tonight's take. Or maybe he'd been napping. Something had pulled him from that to bring him here; based on his perplexed nose-scratching, he didn't know what it was either.

Janey swung by with her tray and another round of drink orders. Her voice like tiny crab-apple fists bounding off a wall of rubber and foam, trying to get my attention; failing.

"Ah shit," she said, glancing over her shoulder, recognizing that look on my face. "Not again." Janey dropped her tray, clattering hard plastic against the harder Lucite, breaking through my fog and somehow getting Derek's attention while she did it. He'd left the drink management zone to get a start on the cleanup. I was betting wherever he lived was spotless and without clutter as well.

"OK, folks." Sandor's voice boomed over the scene, cutting through the music and the words. "We're getting ready to close up for the night. Let's settle those bills and have a great dawn."

Nothing happened.

Janey eased over to the soundboard and slid the master control audio level down to three from its previous seven or eight. Derek started turning the lights up; not full bright, not yet, but at least a couple of notches above the chocolate smoke of five minutes ago.

The dance floor was covered—vertically, horizontally and everything in between—with bodies, all very much alive and in motion. We stared. I wasn't exactly blushing with innocence—I don't think any of us were—but my cheeks actually flamed at the show.

And yet I couldn't look away.

There was a tentacle wrapped around a human man's leg, naked, and the strawberry-blond hairs covering him twinkled in the reflected glints of the disco ball above. A second and third tentacle worked their way up, suctioning on then off and then on again; the man's head was thrown back and his mouth parted in a silent screaming *O!* His hand gripped at a creature with five breasts, all of them purple—and not from the cold. She was facing him, licking her lips, but pushing her tail and ass back into the waiting face of I wasn't sure what but it involved claws and whiskers and both breasts—only two—plus a penis.

And so it went, with variations. No single group was like the other in any way—aside from the part where they were giving each other pleasure. There were the two women, one leaning against the wall while the other was on her knees in front of her, face buried between thighs that gripped back. A few feet over, another woman, another wall—this time the person in front of her was what I assumed was a human male until I saw the wingspan shift between his shoulder blades to flutter, teasing, across the woman's body. My breath caught.

"Whoa," said Sam. He'd glided up beside me without noticing. Can't imagine why I'd be distracted.

"Yeah," I managed. My heart was racing; the heat from Sam, even at two feet away, licked at my skin. Needed a taste. I angled towards him, reaching up and around the back of his neck to pull his lips to mine. Sam resisted at first. Unexpected. His eyes looking around, knowing himself now that something was not as it was meant to be; and yet, even so, he couldn't say no.

The kiss went places his lips were not touching, and I shivered against him. Sam's fingers in my hair, stroking, going lower. Fur under flesh, strands reaching out to touch, pushing at the surface, tickling in places we couldn't reach. The part where we weren't alone, surrounded by others who were feeling some version of that same energy, only made the moment hotter.

Need.

I didn't care that this was where I worked, that people I knew would be watching. Derek's eyes burning through my shirt, the clothes I still wore, wanting to see what was underneath. Janey stared too, but her lust for Derek and her jealousy of his attention on me in this moment was coarse salt on my tongue. With that small part of my brain still thinking beyond the haze, I was surprised by the force of her green-eyed passion. I had enough on my testosterone-laden plate without adding another player, especially one I had to see almost every day.

Sam didn't count. But I pulled away to look at him anyway.

And realized what was going on all around us.

Chapter Thirty-One

"Sam," I said, touching his forearm as he leaned in for another taste. I could stop anytime. Right? His lips on mine again, all other thoughts lost as his need pressed up against me. I slid my palm down against it, and he strained to reach me through the layers between us. Too many.

But. There were reasons to…not? Not what? Couldn't think beyond the now, heat sweating my skin, all things hard and soft and peaked and *fuck* I wanted him now, here, and who cares who sees us.

My breathing jagged, claws digging into his shoulders as I pushed Sam back to the bar. *Claws?* His hands on my hips as he lifted me up, setting me down on that same counter where I'd been cutting lemons minutes earlier. My ankles crossed behind his waist, pulling him in closer. His tongue sandpaper rough as he stroked along my neck; then, changing directions, as he slid up my shirt from below. My back to the larger room—some privacy at least. All I could do was follow the path of his tongue, wet friction, soaking through the thin veneer of my bra to what still lay hidden.

Sam's teeth fastened around the edge of lace and eased the scratchy material down, the bristle on his cheek flicking my nipple as it passed. *Oh.* His fingers doing the same, liberating my other breast to greet the blast of cold from the AC unit over his shoulder.

Grateful that I was facing away from anyone but Sam. Until I opened my eyes, fluttering, and realized I was facing the mirror behind and above the rows of bottles. Shielded from wider view by the muscle-tautened broadness of Sam—but not for much longer, as his kisses trailed down. Derek's stare fixated on my now-bare breasts and I thought about having him join us. Groaned and closed my eyes again as Sam found that spot, *there*, his hands refusing to be kept out by something as inconsequential as my underwear or anything I was wearing on top of it. My legs over his shoulders now.

In my head, Derek was leaning across the bar to play with my breasts, arms snaking around from behind. Rubbing my nipples between thumbs and forefingers, pressing together before releasing them again into Sam's waiting mouth. Teeth.

The neckline of Sam's t-shirt bunched in my hands as I used it to guide him upwards, his lips brushing across mine. My ankles hooked behind his neck; nowhere for him to get but closer. Sam chuckled. He didn't seem to mind, his eyes going dark and then golden as my hands found the tight slopes of his ass and dipped in further.

How far were we going to take this? With all these bodies around us not our own?

Wait. Thought. There was something I was trying to do, stop.

At the edge of what I could see, Janey had Derek against the shadows. On her knees, both of his hands buried in her hair, holding her in place.

Something not right.

I tried to follow that thought. I did. But then Sam remembered how to unbuckle his belt, and that my shorts were stretchy and easy to peel off, and there were condoms, and then it was too late. Sam was in, and I didn't care that Derek was watching or that the counter was wet or that whatever was going on didn't make sense. I arched my back and gave in, gave up, gave out as we reached that crest together.

And yet, and still, it wasn't enough.

That sense of something out of synch kept buzzing in my ears. I was still riding that wave, legs too rubbery to attempt walking or even standing yet, so instead I looked. And looked.

No longer could I make out individual shapes on the floors and tables and chairs that made up the central area of the Swan. Where before had been sex, now there was smoke and liquid and shadows twisting and turning into each other.

"Sam," I said, careful not to touch him this time. I raised my hips to pull my pants back up—they hadn't gone far anyway—maneuvering the cups of my bra back into place before pulling down my tank. "Look."

I motioned to the rest of the room, the players who weren't us. Sam nodded as he fixed his shirt, zipping up his pants while leaving his belt undone. Not focused. Glancing over but not registering what he was seeing.

I snapped my fingers in front of his nose; held up my index finger and moved it first to the right and then back to the left. Sam's eyes tracked me. *Good.* Now I had to get him to pay attention to something that wasn't me.

His own finger made contact, tracing a line along the

softer skin of my inner arm. Down to my wrist before sliding his hand into mine. Our fingers lacing together, palm against palm; I couldn't think past the taste-touch of his lips. Wanting more.

No.

I pulled away, twisting my body to one side so I was cross-legged. Not enough—I could still feel his heat. Blinked, and suddenly saw the energy in the room for what it was: gnarled threads of tonal vibrancy winding around and through an ever-expanding ball by something or someone at the other end of the room. Was it just me? I glanced around, checking for recognition in anyone else's eyes, but mine were the only pair not glazed over with need.

I concentrated, taking all of that craving reignited, rolling it between my palms into a sphere; visualizing purples and blues and oranges, kneading the air into a gooey mass until I could see turquoise blues and buttercup yellows and pastel pinks. Plucking at those threads to weave a cat's cradle string game of colored wax crayon air of unique strands. Tweezing them out, one and then another, before releasing the thread into nothingness. Hanging in the air before dissipating into the ether.

I looked up again and Sam's eyes were clear.

"What the...?"

"Look around," I said. "Something's not right."

"No," he replied, scanning the room. "It's not."

I glanced over at Janey and Derek. They'd changed positions; now Janey had her palms flat against the wall, skirt hiked over her hips and held there by Derek's hands as he plunged into her. The look she'd given me earlier cleared any doubts I had about whether this was something she really wanted. Even though I couldn't be sure that the haze hanging over all of us wasn't some kind of Rohipnol effect. *Damn.* Janey should get her moment with Derek, if that was what she wanted. The problem was that I couldn't be certain—and without her explicit, clear-minded consent, this entire scene took on an ick factor it was my responsibility to remedy. Whoever sees a problem has a responsibility to try and fix it, right?

So I came up behind Derek and tapped him on the shoulder. He ignored me.

"Fuck off," said Janey. Guess his rhythm must have faltered. "You had yours. I'm getting mine."

Derek's pace got faster, harder. Mashing Janey up against the wall as she arched her ass back to meet him. I was seeing more of both my co-workers than I wanted.

I glanced over at Sam, who shrugged. Yeah, I didn't have the answers either. So I took a deep breath and did what I could, holding out my hands and plucking at the jewel-toned threads.

Janey's were jagged emerald-cut greens, blasting siren reds, and underneath it all a magenta pink/purple out of synch with the others. A color-blind toddler elbows-deep in a basket of wool.

Derek's were different. Gunmetal grey, burning orange, reds that flowed darker and richer than Janey's. No wonder they hadn't gotten together before this.

I relaxed my eyelids and with them the muscles around my eyes. Pausing a moment; it *had* been a long night. No rest for the recently wicked, though. I dug my fingers in again, pulling at strands, breathing in the energy and releasing the driving pulsating force behind it. Focusing my eyes in again to see fluffy cotton candy pinks and blues, coffee cream off-whites and the freshly churned butter yellows. Maybe these two crazy kids had a chance after all.

They were still going at it, despite the lack of any compulsion at this point. So it really *was* their choice. Not my business, even with their business on full display; glass countertops with mirrors and all.

Which left me with the seething undulations of life forms on the dance floor. How the hell was I going to pull this off?

"How can I help?" Sam had come up beside me as I stood and stared. Trying not to let the sheer mass of carnally driven potential I needed to untangle scare me. Even though it did. I was only one person. Could I do this?

"I'm here," said Sam. Sliding his hand into mine, interlacing fingers which still held my scent.

"Do you feel that?" The strands of desire in front of us more amorphous than before. Janey and Derek had changed positions so that they faced each other now, with one of Janey's legs hooked over Derek's arm. Who knew she had such flexibility? At least with Derek's back to me he'd stopped staring.

"I didn't before," Sam replied, glancing down to where our hands joined then back at the former dance floor. He let me go, looked again. "Whoa."

"What?"

"I'm looking," he said. "There's dancing, there's fucking, there's some before and some after."

"OK…"

"But when I'm holding your hand," he said, actions matching his words, "I can't see individuals. It's this massive tangle of yarn that keeps moving." He turned to watch my face. "What's it like for you?"

"Yarn," I said. So whatever I was doing had nothing to do with my ability to shift. Otherwise Sam would be seeing it too.

I dropped Sam's hand to look again; the colors continued to writhe, but less vividly. Individuals less distinct. Slipped my hand back into his again and I could see that the blur of ashen smoke was specific and concrete, albeit in constant motion.

I wasn't sure why physical contact with Sam helped. Or why it didn't have me clawing at his clothes to get naked skin-on-skin time with him again.

"Try touching my shoulder instead," I suggested. An experiment. *Yes.* "That's good. As good as holding hands." At Sam's quizzical look, I clarified: "I need to leave my hands free to do this." He nodded his understanding, or at least as much as any of it made any sense.

"How about this?" Sam moved behind me, wrapping his arms loose around my waist. Pressing up, and against.

I shivered as I felt hardness, stirring. Opened eyes I'd shut in my temporary distraction. *Yes.* If I could keep from trying to climb onto Sam again while I did this, it could totally work. "Yeah," I managed, voice husky.

I closed my eyes, arms loose at my sides, breathing in the jumble of scents around me, winnowing through the murk to find that droplet of fresh, untainted air. Free of whatever had taken control of the Swan.

There.

I focused on that spot and inhaled, borrowing remnants of its purity, visualizing that drop becoming a smear I could expand into a puddle.

It was hard to breathe in air that felt like syrup. Hands slick with sweat, nails pressing so hard that the sulphur tickle of my own blood rushed to the surface, ready to spring free if the opportunity cut through. Shaking. I pressed my arms down to my sides, an attempt at control, but instead my teeth rattled as I banged at my thighs with closed fists.

Sam kissed the top of my head and squeezed me, his arms across my chest as the inhale/exhale rhythm of him against me reminded my body of what the tempo should be. I closed my eyes and counted down from sixty. Nothing else in that moment but Sam and me and the deepening of my shallow breaths until finally they synched up with his.

Opened my eyes. Almost shut them once more, resisting the need to run; Sam's warmth was still against my core and giving me roots where I stood. Alright then. Let's do this.

I held out my arms in front of me, loose, with palms upturned. Touching the chill of energy. Rotating my hands around each other, wrapping as I made contact with a force made malleable by touch. My touch. Around and around, a soccer ball or maybe a seven-month-old baby still in utero, balancing on the air in front of me. Arm hairs standing straight out, still human; a humming energy as my palms passed over each other without making contact. Intangible yet real.

It took a while. Tedious work. I might have gotten bored, pulling and sorting and releasing, if an *or else* certainty wasn't turning acid backwash backflips in my gut. The further into the core I got, the less it was an innocuous ball of yarn and the more it became a seething mass of M&M-colored worms. I dipped my fingers in and ran them through the clammy writhing wriggling bits.

Whatever was going on, the epicenter was the far end of the dance space where I could have sworn Sandor had been not so much earlier. More light would have helped, or maybe the addition of another sense would have been a distraction I couldn't afford.

Where had Sandor gone? He'd been there before Sam and I got lost in each other for a while. Right? I couldn't remember anymore. Maybe he'd found a hookup of his own? Now that was an image I *really* didn't want in my head. And yet, wanting didn't make it so and I had to pause what I was doing to clear my mind of the possibility of a green-assed Sandor going at it. *Ommm.* Sheep. The Cookie Monster. Coffee in bed with Sam on a cool Saturday morning after a night of heating up the room with our bodies. Not the cleanest of mental transitions, but it would have to do.

Emerald-green with jagged spikes of hematite-grey wrapped in ropey Johnny Walker velvet-bag purple and vein-slashed thorny red. This was the core. I could feel whatever it was sucking in the frenzied energy surrounding it, catching threads on its pinpricked points, snagging and swirling the bits I hadn't yet extricated from the birds' nest snarl.

It was fighting me now. Not with swords or guns or fists, but with a power that pushed back against my own. I was grateful for Sam's energy, ballasting and amplifying mine. And still I plucked and sorted, each collection of threads matching a sexual congress of some kind. Releasing the compulsion didn't have much effect on the floor though, with most of the players too far gone into their own pleasure to stop. There were a few dazed stragglers at the fringes, fumbling with straps and buttons. Nothing I could do to help them but hope they recovered from the experience—and got as far away from here as possible.

The dissolution was working its way inward now with the bubbling irregularity of paper held over a flame to fake that parchment effect. Uneven but persistent.

My muscles were aching, straining their limits without picking up so much as a sugar cube. I pressed again against that knot until it released tension in waves that made me sway, light-headed.

But now I recognized the source, even though I wished I hadn't.

Alina.

Chapter Thirty-Two

She sat on what used to be the floor, every bit the cross-legged Buddha in the lotus leaf patch. Her eyes were closed, with elbows bent and palms turned upwards so that her thumb and middle fingers touched. There was a yogic meditation pose name for it, I was sure of it, if only I could remember. Some other time, perhaps, when I was less likely to pee my pants in fear.

"Tell me you see her," I whispered, hoping Sam could hear me.

"Yes," he said, quiet in my ear.

If Alina knew we were there, she didn't care. A first. All around her the floor was dissolving to an inky blue—whether it was water, air, or something else, I had no idea. A demonic guru meditating on a magic carpet that never touched the ground because the ground was gone from underneath where she sat. The more she drew from the sexual energy of the room, the more the blue that was there without being there encroached on space recently solid.

I had to stop her. There was nobody else.

Closed my eyes and leaned back against Sam's bulk, the beat of his heart a pattern I could focus on. A constant. Warming the chill of fear in my chest, reminding me of why I had to survive this fight.

I opened my eyes and went back to work, pulling and plucking, working now to the pounding resonance of Sam behind me. Faster. Two hands now, shredding the lettuce leaves of Alina's exercise in sex-fueled love nesting. I wish I knew what else I could do but I had no idea what I was doing already, relying on instinct in lieu of training or knowledge.

Alina opened her eyes then, fathomless kaleidoscope swirls of color, and fixed them on me. My heart almost stopped and I tasted copper sulphur where I bit my cheek without wanting to do it.

"Stop that," she said.

I gulped down the bile that wanted to respond. Instead:

"No," I replied.

She flicked one set of fingers and I heard Sam gasp, his arms tightening around me.

"Don't...stop..." His whisper harsh, forced through the airways Alina was constricting for kicks.

I inhaled the energy of the room and did some finger flicking of my own, mimicking her motions. Each jerk releasing some of the power she was drawing on to open the sky at her feet and the air from Sam's lungs. Could I take it from her fast enough? She glared at me as I stared back. No more laughter. A flick from me and a gulp from her; a flick from her and a shudder from Sam. Hurting me by hurting him.

Yeah, she'd gotten that part right.

Even more reason for me to work, and go faster. Pushing the limits of a power I thought maybe I should explore further—assuming I survived this part.

The scary hole was shrinking, with more and more patrons shaking themselves free of their one-track mind and body fervor in its contracting wake. Could they see Alina? I thought maybe not since nobody was screaming. None of them stepped over the edge into the Great Beyond either though. Instinct?

No time to be sure, as Alina let out a nails-against-aluminum-siding shriek. Sam sagged, holding on to me to keep himself upright where before our needs had been reversed. But I wasn't complaining. Sam could breathe on his own again, and Alina was literally losing ground against me.

Suddenly I spotted the tusked green of Sandor's head as he pushed himself up from whatever he'd been up to in the midst of this carnal carnivale. I didn't know where his shirt had gone but I hoped he found it again soon. Those barbell-studded pieced nipples—all five of them—couldn't be unseen.

The pressure in the room dropped and I yawned to pop my ears. I wasn't the only one, as more and more bacchanalia participants were able to extricate themselves from Alina's lure.

"You good?" I had to speak louder than before; the decibel level of squawks and growls and other, less identifiable sounds, had risen.

"Yeah," Sam said. "I am now."

I nodded and went back to my *save-the-room-from-Alina* activities, tracking Sandor making his way towards me while keeping his distance from the epicenter. Poking my fingers into the balled energy Alina was sapping as fast as I was draining it. Texture and smell different now. Manure? *Fuck.*

I almost dropped the mass I was working with;

flicked my eyes over to Alina and saw her assessing her handiwork with narrowed eyes. *No.* It was an illusion. Not real. Muttering under my breath to reinforce the reality that must exist. It took almost sixty seconds for her to drop it, snarling. The gaping hole shrunk a few more feet in diameter.

"Here, let me help," said Sandor, grabbing one of my hands. I *so* didn't want to know where that had been a few minutes ago.

"Aw, Sandor, I didn't know you cared." Flashed him a grin I was trying to feel. The adrenaline of the moment was still there; I could keep going. Had to. Then realized that was Dana from two minutes ago. This new skin-on-skin contact with Sandor was a jolt like swapping out an almost drained battery for one with a full charge and then some. I blinked surprise. "Whoa," I managed.

"Yeah," said Sandor. "Kick her ass for me. For all of us," he amended, looking around the room.

I nodded. Except I needed both hands free, including that one Sandor was holding. We could be flexible, right? At my request, Sandor swapped positions so that his warted hand was under my shirt and lying palm-down flat on my stomach.

Sam growled then; neither one of us wanted me getting felt up by my boss. Even though I trusted Sandor. Mostly.

"Connects with her *chi*," Sandor said. "Sorry for the lack of decorum. It's only temporary. I hope," he added.

"It tickles," I said. My boss and my—what *was* Sam exactly now? Could I call him my boyfriend? That was weird. OK, well, whatever Sam was to me, both he and my troll-shaped boss were making skin-on-skin contact with me.

Nope. Not awkward at all.

But I couldn't deny the jolt of power singing through my veins and buzzing in my ears. Thank you, Sandor.

I straightened my spine and pushed back my shoulders, freeing the energy to move through me once more. Breathing it in as I drew on Sam's and Sandor's proffered strength. Sam's was similar to mine, fur and whiskers and heat. Also desire, but whether that was a strength or a weakness remained to be seen.

Sandor's was different. There was an icy core of cut crystals that glowed a paler shade of the ivy-dappled green skin he chose to share. Spiky and sparkling with ungrounded electricity. Not sure how Sandor managed usually, but there had to be some kind of physiological compensation involved.

This time, as I embraced the energy, I threw my arms open wide and pulled in as much as I could physically hold. Cradling a mass that I could only just get my arms around, wriggling jelly bean snakes that hissed and flicked their forked tongues at me before darting out to sink fang into my arms. So many pointed attacks, a staccato puncture beat of pain. Knowing it was another one of Alina's illusions didn't make it hurt any less.

I spared a moment to glance at what I was holding, what Alina wanted me to see: faceted jewel tones and primary colors with eyes that tracked me from thumbprint-flattened heads and rattled at me with intermittent shimmies from arrowhead-pointed tails. If I relied only on what I saw then self-doubt would tell me this couldn't be done. That there was no way to hold a passel of snakes in your arms when you don't even have the passel.

And yet, when I closed my eyes and looked with my

other senses, I was holding a giant ball of yarn, the kind
that wasn't a single solid color but rather one that faded
in and out from one spectrum extreme to another. There
were gnarls; I worried them free with fingers I could
no longer see. Somewhere there was an angry demon
who was fighting me. But she hadn't killed me yet so
small mercies. Maybe someone somewhere still needed
me alive. Lucky me.

"Almost there," said Sam, soft in my ear.

First there was a buzzing, the kind of sound that
made me think of cicadas in August. Then a pressure
popping against my ears. Painful; I yawned once more
to release it. A reflex. Pushing all exterior distractions
to that place in my head relegated to *I'll deal with it
later*. Getting closer to the center, that glowing spark
nudging at the gateway; a doorstop preventing me from
shutting off the path altogether.

And then it started: a familiar pain. Being gouged
with a thousand head-of-pin faery swords in my back.

I wanted this to be yet another Alina hallucination,
but I knew it wasn't. No—the dots tattooed on my back
were calling out to the gaping maw between this dimension and the next.

"What the…?" Sam loosened his grip on me as my
spots burned through what was left of my shirt to jump
across from me and onto his chest. *Fuck*. Sam let go of
me then to beat at the fire licking his shirt; my energy
pulse dropped by a third.

Alina cackled, enjoying the show now. Maybe I *was*
getting in her way. But I was inflicting pain on someone I cared about too, and that was popcorn with all
the fixings for Alina.

"Sam, you OK?"

He didn't answer right away, saving his focus for tamping the embers on his chest. Yeah, I didn't want him on fire either.

"I'm good," he said finally after one of the longest minutes of my life. "It's out." A brief pause. "Still need both hands free?"

"Yes."

Sam came around behind me again, careful not to touch my back this time. Slid his palms along the sides of my waist, away from the ink, as his fingers formed a loose vee in front. Any other time I'd be willing those fingers lower. Hell, I'd go for it right now—except for the part where I needed to seal a portal, get rid of a demon way more powerful than me, and oh yeah, my boss's scrabbly hand was just there above Sam's. A threesome not quite as enticing as you might think.

Plus there was that back-stabby thing where cleats were doing figure eights around my spine.

Pushed the pain to that *I'm ignoring you now* place, or as much as I could because *holy crap.* Tried to think.

Not easy through the humming of my blood and that buzzing in my ears. *So familiar.*

There were shadows around the floor, drapes of dark and folds of darker. I scanned the room for any sign of him. Until—*there.* Maybe six feet from Alina's back.

Our eyes met.

Of course. Why else would Alina pick this exact spot to open up a gaping inter-dimensional rift? Toronto was not a tiny city. Maybe it wasn't as big as New York or London or Shanghai, but that didn't mean we lacked land mass potential for portal openings. What did we have that they didn't? A bartender with the keys to a magical inter-dimensional map tattooed on her back.

Which meant Stuart Markovitz, a.k.a. Father of the Year, must have suggested it.

"Here kitty kitty kitty," Alina purred. "Yes," she said, "that's right. I know what you are, little girl. We have much to discuss."

"How?" Single words were the easiest.

"A jealous kitty told me," she said. Sam's grip tightened then, before loosening again. Someone from the Pack must have talked. Forgetting in the moment that my father was also a shifter. "Or maybe it was a frightened kitty. Y'all can be so twitchy."

She was trying to distract me. Pushing the boundaries of her dimensional puddle out again.

How *had* Alina been able to open a portal without needing the literal skin off my back? And why did she keep trying to do it? If I was extraneous to this process, what benefit did my father get from bringing Alina here so that her existence and mine could physically intersect?

My father's deal had been to deliver me—and here I was. Which meant *something* was supposed to have happened once she got that portal open. My guess? Phase two was the part I really wouldn't have liked.

I grabbed at the wriggling colored strings once more. Blocking out the pain. Blocking out Alina. I plucked at the power, the combined forces of myself and Sam and Sandor making my fingers nimble, then gasped as the searing pain on my back intensified. I had to get that portal closed.

Probably shouldn't let on that I didn't actually know how to do it, right?

Fortunately my body seemed to get what my mind

hadn't yet processed. All I needed to do was get out of my own way.

No stopping me now. No room for doubts, or pain, or fear. Alina was on her own, and she'd expended a lot of her strength to force this dimension crossing open here. Maybe riding the orgiastic surge made it easier for her to do what she wanted without passing out from the effort. Assuming demons like her could go unconscious.

I did wonder why she'd bothered. There were minions. There was maybe Ezra and definitely my father who were willing to do what she wanted in order to get what they wanted. Deals made and trust betrayed.

Sam adjusted his hands and my mental traction wavered. Radiant heat where he touched although this contact didn't hurt. There would be naked fun times if we survived this. *When.*

More pressure; a pulsating volleyball-sized orb that pushed against my palms. I squeezed and flexed, visualizing the mass shrinking even as I moved the space I couldn't see with hands that could.

Frost and fire, pulled together and amplified exponentially by our shared touch. Enough to make that last surge count as I flattened and released the rubber band ball, its remnants dissipating into the air.

"No!" Alina screeched her frustration, pushing herself off her magic carpet ride seconds before it was swallowed up. Curious—she'd opened a portal between dimensions, but didn't want to get stuck on the other side? She must still need something here, as much as or more than whatever she was trying to reach over there. At some point we were going to have to figure out what that was.

I hoped it had nothing to do with me.

And then she was launching herself at me, arms out-stretched, foregoing the metaphysical torture in favor of something more direct. Was she planning to choke me? Was I screwed?

Seconds moving in slow motion. My muscles like Jell-O, after the boiling water but before full solidification kicked in. I wanted to defend myself. Even moving out of her direct path would be good. It wasn't an enchantment planting roots that wrapped around my ankles this time though—it was exhaustion.

Sam pulled me to the side moments before impact. Realizing, I guess, that getting out of the way myself was more than I could manage.

There was a popping sound as Alina lunged towards me once more. And then she vanished, inches before making contact. It happened so fast that the sound of her voice still hung in lingering waves for several seconds past the point where I could see her.

Sandor moved his hand from my abdomen and stuck it in his pocket. So he *was* wearing pants.

"Good to know some of those wards actually work," he said.

"All of a sudden?" I wasn't convinced. "Without any help at all?"

"What, you think she's actually gone?" Sandor reached out to pat me on the head, with a *there there* and a *dear deluded girl*. I batted his head away before it made contact because come on. "She found this place—she found *you*. She'll be back."

"A fair assessment of the current situation."

The voice came from the shadows.

Chapter Thirty-Three

Ezra.

Where the hell had *he* come from? How much had he seen?

"Stuart," he said. "What do you think?"

My father melted out of the gloom to stand beside his friend. Apparently Dad hadn't followed Alina wherever it was that she'd gone. He kept glancing down at his hands, turning them over, then touching himself on the jaw and the top of his head. I'd be wondering if this was real too if I was inside his head.

Wait. My father *and* Ezra. Inhabiting the same space at the same time, each one looking like themselves. Neither wearing the transporto-skin, since they each were themselves. I recognized my father even though it had been so many years, even though I'd only seen him in shadow up to now, a film image superimposed on the form of his old friend Ezra.

He'd aged. But then, so had we all.

High road. I could find it there somewhere.

"Sandor, I'd like you to meet my father, Stuart Markovitz. Sam, I believe you two have already met."

They all nodded the tough-guy chin bob of cool

but didn't shake hands. Because let's be serious—this wasn't a hug it out, family reunion kind of moment here.

"Dad, Sandor and Sam." I didn't add the bit about them being my friends, or boyfriend and boss, or whatever. The less information my father and Ezra had about the relationships in my life, the better—what they didn't know couldn't be used against me later. "And of course this is Ezra Gerbrecht. I believe I've told you about him as well."

Another set of nods without physical contact all around. My, but weren't we being all civilized here.

It was almost as though there wasn't the (literal) tail end of an orgy going on in the same room as us.

"I believe you have something for me," said Ezra, once we had pleasantries in surrealism out of the way.

"Do you see a big, blue demon in here? Because I don't."

Ezra raised his eyebrows at my words, making a show of it.

"Exactly," I said. "We have a deal and I'm honoring it. I've just been a bit busy since we talked earlier." I paused and waved my hand across the mayhem that continued to consume the Swan. "As you can see."

"Excuses." Ezra made some kind of tutting noise.

"Whatever." He could be as pompous as he wanted; I was still the closest thing Ezra had to what he needed. For whatever reason. Speaking of reasons…my father had been working to get the same demon droppings as Ezra. The key to my father's ability to come back to this dimension and be here rather than there, or so he'd said.

So how did he come to be here now? Didn't my father make a deal with Alina to hand me over to save himself? What had their plan been for me once that portal was opened? Suddenly grateful that I was here, and even my father was here, but Alina was not.

"She does not let me go," said my father, voice querulous; I could barely make out what he was saying over the moans. Distracting. Except now, beyond the thrall, I was actually feeling my inner prude and wishing everyone would just finish up, clean themselves off and leave. "If I am here and not there, it is at her pleasure and not mine. She will find a way to take it all from me again when it suits her best."

"What you're saying," and I couldn't believe *I* was saying this, "is that she never needed me to free you? That you gave me up for, what, a chance to stand close to the flame and hope it didn't burn you?" Sam squeezed my shoulder, firm, reminding me that he was still there for me. Even if my father was a dick.

"I needed her." Simple. Words unadorned. "*Need* her. She could never want the way I do; my flesh is ultimately mortal, and more life-endingly permeable than hers. But we both suffer from dimensional dementia to varying degrees. Me, more than her. That's why you have to get me the biogenetic materials I seek. Why I hired the Cephalorite Order to encourage your assistance."

"Because threats are so much more effective than, you know, asking." I wasn't bitter. Nope. I turned towards Ezra. "And what about you? I'm guessing you've been working with my father on this Alina deal all along, right?"

"Not exactly," said Ezra. Touching my father's shoulder; Ezra's eyes rolling back in his head from contact with one half of my genetic precursive material. I wondered if everyone got a one-step-removed contact rush from Alina or whether Ezra and my dad were special.

Ezra shook it off first.

"I am curious about my old friend Stuart's research outcomes, of course. Being able to cure inter-dimensional dementia, finding a way to prevent it from happening—that would be invaluable from a mission perspective."

What wasn't I seeing? It had to be something bigger than fixing portal-jumping damage. Something obvious, that Ezra could point to once I figured it out and say *see?* A teachable moment. Attainable by deductive logic. Which meant that somewhere I already had the answer—or a sizeable piece of it.

OK. What had my father and Ezra been working on in the lab before the accident that may or may not have been accidental? Something about DNA. *Right.* Identifying the differences and overlapping similarities between the DNA of shifters relative to norms. But it had been at least twenty years since then. Ezra could have continued the research on his own. Who knows what he'd found out by now? Or which branches of inquiry he may have pursued?

Both my father and Ezra were watching me. Waiting for me to figure it out.

"So what's going on here? Ya'll gonna introduce us to your friends?" Janey and Derek had wandered over, hand in hand, while we'd all been paying attention to anything but them. At least all their clothing bits were back where I remembered them being before forays into interactions I couldn't un-see.

High road. I could go high.

"Janey, Derek—these are Ezra and Stuart." No reason either Janey or Derek needed to know who these men were to me. And vice versa. First names only.

Janey nodded, and there were more chin bobs all around. I was starting to wonder if Chin Bobs 101 came standard in the testosterone starter kit. There were several long moments of awkward before Sandor stepped in and smoothed the way.

"Why don't you see what you can do about clearing the place out," Sandor said, nudging their attention towards the stragglers still refusing to give up on the dance floor partner pleasure principle. "It's been fun, folks," Sandor said, louder and aiming his voice towards the ones still left. "But time to wrap things up. Take it outside, call it a night—dealer's choice. Just get yourself out of my bar for a bit so we can clean up and get ready to serve you again in a few hours. Thank you for your continued patronage," he added, in case anyone was feeling his delivery was less than properly polite. After all, this *was* Canada.

Sandor looked over at me, then Sam. "You two got this?"

"Yeah." I nodded for emphasis. "Thanks."

"Mistress could be back for me at any moment." My father interrupted the moment without moving. "Deliver the genetic materials to your Cephalopod faction contact. Whatever format you and my old friend Ezra agree on is fine with me." The image of my *pater famiglia* went static grey at the edges before dissipating into a series of stacked lines—baby pinks and cornflower blues and ripe banana yellows—warping and dancing into an ever-diminishing dot before winking out, taking him with it.

A flash, light flickering, and I saw the place where

I'd seen my father before. Where he'd been for the last however many years. And something new—a flat-screen monitor, maybe five by five feet, hoisted high against the flat surface I assumed was a wall. It took me a moment to focus my eyes in on what I was seeing. There were moans, not unlike what I'd been hearing around me maybe half an hour ago. Lights strobing as the camera panned across the floor to the bar, then along it. Wait. Was that—?

I recognized that look, the expression of intensity as Sam stared directly into the lens a moment without realizing he was doing it. A theory confirmed by his growl beside me. Sam's hands were hidden from view, but I remembered where they'd been. And then, as I arched back before curling in towards him again. It was a braless moment, my back on full display to anyone who might be looking. An attempt at modesty that I now realized was planned.

I have no idea who was filming—maybe Sam would remember?—but whoever it was got that money shot: a close up of my back, well lit, with the scattershot of my tattooed dots on full display. Alina's toe-curling laughter that even now stilled my breath and made places darker and lower clench in response.

And then the scene, along with both my father and Alina, were gone.

Don't ask me to examine my feelings too closely on that one.

"Stay in touch," Ezra said. Either he hadn't noticed that Alina now had access to an image of the map on my back, or he didn't care enough to comment. "I expect to see you by tomorrow with the package contents we agreed upon. I don't need to threaten you with what happens if you don't show up, correct?"

I nodded.

"If I guess right on what you're up to, will you tell me?"

Ezra shook his head with a smile, not answering, and managed to stroll out the front door without touching any of the now-flaccid limbs entangled on the floor.

Chapter Thirty-Four

The sun was peeking up over the horizon and the gulls were making their hunger *screes* known by the time we were able to leave the Swan. Cleanup was hell, and I suspected a lot of the bio-matter we'd disposed of would be going to an incinerator somewhere instead of the landfill.

"Your place or mine?" I meant it as a joke, but it might have come out sharper than I'd intended because holy crap was I tired.

"Let's get what you need from Gustav before he takes off again." Sam leaned back against my truck, watching my face. Mentally noting the dark smudges underneath my eyes, the flakes on my lips, the way my makeup had wandered into the smile lines beside my eyes making the shadows more pronounced. The sway in my legs as I took my hand off the door handle for just a moment. "You sure you're up to driving?"

"No," I said shortly. "But I'll manage. You'll follow me?"

Sam nodded.

"Let's do this."

Amazingly, Gus was back on my couch and snoring in a power-drill staccato of congested sinuses. Maybe he

suffered from allergies. The good news was that he was
wearing sweats and a hoodie again, so there was no risk
of me seeing his chaps-(sort of)-covered ass this time.

Small mercies.

Sam went to the kitchen to put on coffee while I settled into the armchair opposite Gus Who Could Sleep
Through Anything. *Almost* anything, I self-corrected,
as I saw his nostrils flare and his right cheek start to
twitch.

His snoring stopped, abrupt.

"Girl," Gus said, without even cracking an eyelid.
"There's a hot shower with your name on it right over
there. Nothing you want to say to me could possibly be
more important than that. Trust."

I did an experimental pit sniff and grimaced. He
wasn't wrong.

"What happened to your friend?" I was genuinely
curious.

"He has work later," said Gus. "One of those glass
towers way downtown. Timmy, or Tommy, or whatever
his name really was—"

"Troy?"

"Yeah. He's some kind of senior-level muckity muck."

"You're telling me that guy works at a bank?"

"Senior VP of Investments or something like that,"
Gus said, daring me to judge.

I shrugged and let it drop. Everyone needs to have
fun sometimes, and I guess for Troy, this past week-
end's fun was Gus.

"Here." Sam plunked three mugs of coffee down
on the table, then went back to grab sugar, spoons and
rice milk.

"Your friend there is comfortable in your kitchen."

Gus watched Sam with a smirk, his head angled so that all three of his eyes could get a better posterior view of the shifter. "Getting all chummy with your coffee and sweeteners and such. Something you want to share with the group?"

"No." My voice was clipped. Embarrassed? "Not yet."

"Not yet what?" Sam was back, and apparently had caught the last bit of our conversation. He looked from me to Gus and then back again, waiting to be filled in.

"Gus thinks we're a thing because you know where I keep my coffee," I blurted. Smooth, Dana. Really smooth.

"I see," said Sam. Like we were discussing the weather. "Did you tell him what you negotiated on his behalf?"

Right. Because my relationship status with Sam was really none of Gus's business.

"Didn't have a chance yet. Apparently my body odor was distracting him."

Sam wrinkled his nose. "I think that's both of us," he acknowledged. Then, to Gus: "You'll stick around while we get clean?"

"Depends on the deal." Gus narrowed all three of his eyes, wary now. "I'll pretend you two don't stink of all kinds of bodily and interspecies…*intermingling*…if you stop with the dramatic suspense and tell me who wants what from me. Also why they want it, if you have that information—knowing the *whys* helps with future planning, avoiding imminent death, that kind of thing."

"Neither contract requires you to go anywhere—as long as you're willing to give me some of your own bio-matter that I can put in specimen bags and deliver to the interested parties."

"Meaning?" Gus wasn't going willingly along with anything before he had as many details as he could get.

"Both my father and Ezra—the Agency—want samples of your genetic material for them to test. Experiment on."

"So you think you know what all the older men in your life are up to, then." Gus pushed himself to sitting cross-legged in the middle of the couch. I wasn't the only one overdue for a shower. And, oh yeah, that particular piece of furniture was future curb fodder for sure. Steam cleaning could only do so much. "You're taking their words as gospel truths?"

"Hardly. But I've bought us both some time regardless." I bent over to pull the specimen kits out of my bag. "My father wants to use you to cure himself of inter-dimensional dementia. If he gets extra ambitious, he'll come up with a cure for everyone else, or even a vaccine. But I'm not holding my breath on that last part."

"I wouldn't," Sam muttered into his coffee.

"And once it goes to market," I continued, "those octo-squidly pains in both our butts will get a cut. So that's their motivation."

"What about Ezra Gerbrecht?" Gus went in hard on the consonants. "I'm all aflutter to find out what the Great Man has envisioned for my future well-being."

"He wasn't specific," I admitted.

Gus snorted. "Not surprised," he said.

"My guess?" Because of course I had one. "I think he's taking whatever he and my father were working on way back when and branching it in a different direction. Not just studying, but actually figuring out how to create hybrid supes in the lab. My gut says the Ezra skin with the tattoo that probably matches my thumb-print is part of it."

"You got all that from your conversation with Ger-brecht yesterday?" Sam was right to be concerned. *I* was concerned.

"I'm guessing," I said. "But it's a theory that feels right. I think my father noticed that Gus wasn't affected by inter-dimensional travel, and he probably mentioned it to Ezra in passing during one of his visits. So now they're both curious to get a taste of the Gus Got It Going On Special."

"I'm sorry," said Sam. "But why do we want to help them at all? The less they know about all of us, the better."

"They're not coming after you for your stuff, buddy." Gus was rubbing his I-just-ate-two-whole-chickens-for-dinner belly. "It's all me."

"Fair enough," said Sam. I didn't disagree. This was the Agency, Ezra and now my father.

"If it buys us time," I said, "let's give them what they want. *Ish.*"

Gus raised all three of his eyebrows at me.

"Here's what I'm thinking…"

Sam sat with Gus while I washed away the last twenty-four hours, then I returned the favor. I didn't ask Gus to get any cleaner himself; considering everywhere he'd been and everyone he'd been with, I didn't want to make it too easy.

"C'mon, sneeze for me." I held out a four-by-four plastic sheet in front of Gus, who kept his mouth shut and his lips pressed together in two blue sausages of not-gonna-happen. "What? We agreed."

"I'd much rather bend over and have you wipe my ass with it."

"Thanks, but no." I stifled the imagery that might go along with fulfilling his preference. "What are you willing to part with?"

Gus had obviously been thinking about it because he didn't hesitate.

"Daddy Dearest—yours, not mine—gets three snot diamonds, some nail clippings, a swab or two of ear wax, and a pinch of that crap I dig out of my belly button." Mmm, yummy. *Not.* "The Agency gets the same plus two hairs and a throat swab. Seeing as you're making some bank off that arrangement."

"So you're doing it for me, then." Sure he was. I could believe that. Except for the part where I didn't.

"I don't like your father; don't want to help him too much." I let the silence stretch until finally Gus filled it with something more closely resembling truth. "Fine. Ezra is a dick too, but he carries a bigger stick than your father does. And I want them *both* off my scaly-ass back." I pretty much felt the same way. Apparently blood isn't always thicker than water after all.

Chapter Thirty-Five

It seemed to be enough.

I delivered my father's samples to Squid D'Lee at the Swan, and dropped the rest off at Ezra's office during my break. I still didn't know how screwed we were now that Alina had a picture of my back tats to hang on her wall or whatever, but that was going to have to be a problem for another day.

I ended things officially with Owain. Not that anything had started really. But if I was going to try this thing with Sam for real, I had to be honest with all the other guys in my life first. Jon had done the honors for me the other night; it was my turn to do the same with Owain.

We met for coffee. A small place on a side street between Ossington and Christie, maybe a five-minute walk from my place.

"It's been great seeing you again," I started.

"I'm heading out," Owain interrupted, before I had the chance to make my speech. Beating me to it once more. "I leave tomorrow morning, first thing."

Of course he was. Because clearly *Unavailable Bad Boy* was my type. Or had been.

Before Sam.

"An early flight out of town?" I nodded through my smile, and if my eyes were a touch too shiny, well, it was just the sunlight and blinking was so very helpful with that. "Nope, not clichéd at all."

"What, you were hoping I'd be staying?"

"I didn't expect anything, Owain," I said. "We're good. You planning to come back?"

"Undecided." From the way Owain cocked his head to the side and hesitated, looking for more words or maybe just the right ones, I got the sense I'd surprised him somehow. "You have my number now. You need anything, you contact me, OK?"

We parted with a hug that lasted a few seconds past platonic, did the European *kiss kiss* on both cheeks, said our goodbyes.

And then there was one.

I arrived at the house on Roxborough not long after that with lattes and two pinwheel croissant pastries that tasted of cinnamon and vanilla and air. Realizing belatedly, as I knocked, that if anyone other than Sam was home I was being incredibly rude not bringing enough to share.

I guess Sam had just gotten out of the shower because his hair was still damp and his t-shirt clung to his chest in moistened bits. Great chest. And the bits weren't so bad either.

"Hey," he said. I held up my offerings and his smile stretched wider. "C'mon in."

"Can we talk?" Might as well get it all up front and out there. Before I took off my shoes and got too comfortable.

"Sure." Sam headed in a different direction than usual, through the fancy room, the one that in previous times would have been reserved for company—plastic-covered upholstery, grand piano and all. We were going formal now? But then he continued through and past it to a set of French doors I'd never noticed before, leading to a stacked flagstone veranda overlooking a section of lushly tended English-style garden. Pretty sure there were yellow roses too.

He settled into a mesh chair and I sank into the one opposite him. Passed him his coffee, and a pastry, trying to remember that there were words and I knew somehow somewhere I could speak them. Then, finally:

"I'm done with Jon. And I never really started with Owain, despite what you thought." Sam didn't say anything, waiting for me to go on. "You wanted me on my own, no sharing? Well, you've got me."

Sam opened his mouth to say something but I barreled on. "You know I suck at this, right? Relationships? I need lots of space, I'm twitchy at the best of times, and I don't even know if this is going to work. But I'm willing to try. If you are."

Sam leaned back in his chair with a smile that drifted across his lips. I wanted to take a taste. Didn't, because it was his turn to speak now. Make a move, any kind of move.

"Cool," he said. And when I stared, wanting more, he said, "Come closer. You're too far away."

I stood up and Sam touched my fingertips with his before interlacing them, palm to palm, pulling me towards him and into his lap.

"Let's stay like this for a while," he said, kissing my neck and wrapping his arms around me.

I tensed, then relaxed into him.

I could do this, right?

* * * * *

Acknowledgments

Second books are *hard.* As many people as it took to get that first book published, that next one is you and the inside of your brain and you're mostly on your own—only this time with a deadline.

There is no way this book could have come together as coherently and as quickly as it did without the above-and-beyond support, encouragement, talents and insight of my Carina Press editor, Stephanie Doig. I owe her a huge debt of gratitude. If you ever get the chance to work with her in the future, take it—she is phenomenal.

Thank you to my agent, Rena Bunder Rossner, the adviser and cheerleader (minus the literal pom-poms) in my virtual corner. All the coffee, chocolate and bourbon for you.

Thank you to Patrick Dixon for late-night wordplay consultations, as well as for Toronto Pride and LGBTQ community reality checks. Any mistakes are my own.

Love and gratitude to my "core group"—Judy Silver, Linda Silver Dranoff and Jack Marmer—for your enduring support and love. A lifetime with you at my back makes where I am now possible.

So much love for Zak Dranoff-Caspi. For helping me find the door in every plot wall I hit, for late-night brainstorming sessions, and for your consistent encouragement and support for my words and my stories.

And finally to Opher Caspi—my best friend and partner—for always believing I could do this thing (even when I wasn't so sure) and for supporting me no matter what. You've inspired some of the best qualities of the heroes I write about.

About the Author

Beth Dranoff lives somewhere in the vicinity of the Greater Toronto Area, Canada, with her family, her dog and more books than she can count. Is it before noon? Then there's probably a mug of coffee nearby, too.

Find Beth Dranoff online at:

Facebook—www.Facebook.com/BethDranoff
Twitter—www.Twitter.com/RandomlyBibi
Web—www.BethDranoff.com
Instagram—www.Instagram.com/RandomlyBibi